shrill a two got loose

...she was wearing at the back of her neck, and it fell across my face. She gave me a passionate bear hug. She was a strong woman with good back muscles and she was using every one she had.

I couldn't afford to be as impetuous as she was. "Take it easy," I muttered. She paid no attention. She was carried away by the audience.

She gave me a kiss smack on the mouth, a direct frontal kiss that forced my lips against my teeth rather painfully. It was a hard, sex-starved kiss from a passionate lady who hadn't seen her husband for one long week and who had been telling everyone how much she loved him.

I muttered again, "Hey, take it easy!"

"I can't," she hissed. "I told everyone how much I missed you."

So I kissed her back. It started out as a supporting role for my Academy Award friend, but after two seconds it got out of control. I realized the lady was serious. She was pressing her breasts against me. She was wearing a thin nylon blouse of an apricot color, and a thin nylon bra underneath. I was wearing a thin cotton jacket on top of a thin drip-dry blue shirt, and I could feel her nipples bulging into my chest as hard as cherry candy.

I finally pulled away. The small of her back was soaked with sweat.

I let her take my attaché case and I followed her out to the car. I didn't like her carrying it. And that shows you how stupid I was. I thought somehow she'd be less involved if she wouldn't have touched it. As if she wasn't in it already like someone caught in quicksand...

SOME OTHER HARD CASE CRIME BOOKS
YOU WILL ENJOY:

LUCKY AT CARDS by *Lawrence Block*
ROBBIE'S WIFE by *Russell Hill*
THE VENGEFUL VIRGIN by *Gil Brewer*
THE WOUNDED AND THE SLAIN by *David Goodis*
BLACKMAILER by *George Axelrod*
SONGS OF INNOCENCE by *Richard Aleas*
FRIGHT by *Cornell Woolrich*
KILL NOW, PAY LATER by *Robert Terrall*
SLIDE by *Ken Bruen and Jason Starr*
DEAD STREET by *Mickey Spillane*
DEADLY BELOVED by *Max Allan Collins*
A DIET OF TREACLE by *Lawrence Block*
MONEY SHOT by *Christa Faust*
ZERO COOL by *John Lange*
SHOOTING STAR/SPIDERWEB by *Robert Bloch*

The MURDERER Vine

by **Shepard Rifkin**

A HARD CASE CRIME NOVEL

A HARD CASE CRIME BOOK
(HCC-043)
May 2008

Published by

Dorchester Publishing Co., Inc.
200 Madison Avenue
New York, NY 10016

in collaboration with Winterfall LLC

If you purchased this book without a cover, you should know that it is stolen property. It was reported as "unsold and destroyed" to the publisher, and neither the author nor the publisher has received any payment for this "stripped book."

Copyright © 1970 by Shepard Rifkin

Cover painting copyright © 2008 by Ken Laager

All rights reserved. No part of this book may be reproduced or transmitted in any form or by any electronic or mechanical means, including photocopying, recording or by any information storage and retrieval system, without the written permission of the publisher, except where permitted by law.

This book is a work of fiction. Names, characters, places, and incidents either are the products of the author's imagination or are used fictitiously, and any resemblance to actual events or persons, living or dead, is entirely coincidental.

ISBN 0-8439-5961-4
ISBN-13 978-0-8439-5961-1

Cover design by Cooley Design Lab

Typeset by Swordsmith Productions

The name "Hard Case Crime" and the Hard Case Crime logo are trademarks of Winterfall LLC. Hard Case Crime books are selected and edited by Charles Ardai.

Printed in the United States of America

Visit us on the web at www.HardCaseCrime.com

*With many thanks
to Joseph Barrett and Evelyn Farrell*
SHEPARD RIFKIN

In the vast jungles of the Amazon Basin the silent war among the plants never stops. They continually strive to penetrate the leaf canopy and attain sunlight—one hundred and fifty feet above the perpetual twilight of the forest floor.

Here there grows a certain vine.

In order to reach the light it so desperately needs, it clings for support to the nearest tree.

Year by year it climbs higher and higher. As it grows, it sends out two armlike tentacles every few feet around the trunk of its host. Thus, securely anchored, it climbs a few more feet. The vine finally reaches the roof of the forest and greedily spreads out its leaves in the sunlight for which it had been searching ever since it sprouted.

But as the host grows, it slowly becomes strangled by the ever-thickening arms of the vine. Eventually, the green-growing layer of the tree is severed.

The tree dies.

And when the day comes in which a powerful windstorm arrives, the tree crashes to the earth, bringing the vine with it.

Since the vine can no longer reach the light, it also dies.

In South America, the vine is called

La Liana Matador
or
The Murderer Vine

1

Here we sit in Puerto Lagarto—Port Lizard. It's on the old Mosquito Coast. Lizard and Mosquito, the two specialties down here. We're far below Yucatán. Compared to this dump Yucatán is civilization. You put on a fresh shirt and thirty seconds later it's sopping wet. No paved streets and only one place with ice. That's the local cantina, La Amargura de Amor. The Bitterness of Love. Narcisco Ramirez owns it. He owns the only refrigerator. He packs it full of beer every morning. I sit in the Bitterness and drink my way from the front to the back of the refrigerator and look at the bay.

I've been here two years now. I haven't seen a single person from outside all that time except you. You're the first. People paddle down in their canoes from the interior. They bring alligator and boa constrictor skins. Once in a while jaguar. They call it *tigre* here. They sell the skins to Narcisco and go back up the river with salt and cartridges and cans of peaches. No one else visits. No tourists. No ruins to look at, no hotels, no airports. If someone came here by mistake, he wouldn't like the food or the damp heat or the hammocks or the people. I don't like them either. But there's one big advantage living here. They don't extradite.

Narcisco is also the *jefe de policía*. His cousin Alejandro works up in the capital in the Guardia Nacional, the combination army-police force of the country. Alejandro is a major and he reads and speaks English pretty good. It's his job to censor all the cables and letters and to interview all the English-speaking travelers who look interesting.

All police business in English goes through him. He also grants the entry permits. You want to visit this country, you see Alejandro. Yes, he's the man you saw on Calle Bolívar, in that office overlooking the patio filled with bougainvillea and palms.

I made a deal with Alejandro and Narciso. They each get fifty bucks a month from me. That's a lot of money down here. They don't get it directly either. That would give them the idea they could lay their hands on the cash all at once. They'd figure they could persuade me to talk and tell them where the little metal box is with all the gringo pesos. If I'd have it in a local bank it would take a little more time.

I order my bank in Geneva—yes, Father, I have one of those numbered accounts—I order my bank to mail them each a check on the first of the month. And on Christmas they each get a thousand bucks to show how much I like them. If something happens to me—no more checks.

I told them that maybe someday someone might be down here looking for me. Maybe a private citizen, maybe a couple detectives with a State Department request. Maybe there might be a cable making preliminary inquiries. Someone might offer five thousand bucks for information—or ten. "That's a lot of money," I told them. "But you each get sixteen hundred a year from me. In ten years that's sixteen thousand. In fifteen years that's twenty-four thousand. And so on."

They looked at me thoughtfully. So now Alejandro watches at the capital and Narciso, who owns three fishing boats, keeps a very good eye out for me along the coast. He's sort of my personal Coast Guard.

You ought to see Narciso when I want to go swimming and there's sharks around. He also worries about my diet. He won't let a woman come near me unless she's been carefully checked out by the doctor. He's spread word around that anyone who messes around with me will be very, very sorry.

How do you put a price tag on that?

2

You know why I tell you all this, Father. How can you repeat it? And the idea of an American in a clerical collar chasing butterflies with a net because that's his idea of a vacation—well, when I saw you plunging into the swamp next to the landing, you gave me the best laugh I've had in months.

Father, that's Yucateca you're drinking. The best beer in the Western Hemisphere. It comes out of Mexico, and the best beer in Mexico comes from Yucatán, and the best beer in Yucatán is Yucateca.

I drink it a lot. I sit and put my hands around the cold, sweating glass. Then I rub my hands across my face. It's the closest I can come to winter in New York. Did you ever drive through Central Park after it had snowed all night? And be the first one? And see how all the branches were bending with the weight of the snow? I miss that. I think about those days. I would rather not.

I used to be on the cops in New York. Detectives. Then I quit and became a private detective. My own outfit. I did pretty good for a few years. Then this thing.

Narcisco once let me go out on one of his boats when I first came here—the *Dolores*. I laid in four cases of Yucateca. We threw the empties overboard and shot at them with Narcisco's rusty Winchester. My nose turned red in the sun. My skin had salt spray all over it. I felt bone-tired. I slept ten hours in a row. Ten hours! I haven't slept three hours straight since it happened. Next week I went out again. But there was no flavor in it. So I didn't do it anymore.

You're not going to sleep much tonight, Father. It's too hot. The only air conditioning we get down here comes with the hurricane season. But we're months away from that. So it's going to be bad, with the heat and the mosquitoes. And it'll take you too long to get used to sleeping in a hammock. So have another beer. I'll start from the beginning. If you don't mind, I'll take rum.

3

It all began in Haskell. You ever been in Haskell? It's an hour's train ride northeast of Grand Central Station. The streets are named Powder Flask Road and Deborah Pond's Pike. Very colonial, no? But they put in those streets about fifteen years ago. All the houses are very rigidly colonial, with those zigzag split-rail fences and a wagon wheel on each side of the driveway. The houses are in the $75,000–$150,000 range. The big TV network people live there, the admen, and maybe a writer or so if he wipes his feet before he crosses their doorsteps.

The way I wound up there, up at Haskell, one day some big shot wholesaler in heroin thought it would be a good idea to move in on all that easy allowance money. So he sent a pusher to hang around the drive-ins where the kids with the hot rods hang out. He hung around the luncheonette near the high school. He had an attaché case with compartments. Speed balls, goof balls, pot, you name it. And heroin.

And it was home free. The fix was in. They had gotten

to the state, county, and local law. So when a kid shows up in school looking nervous and jumpy and sleepy, and wearing a pair of dark glasses to protect the enlarged pupils from too much light—one of the effects of pot—the kids' parents had seen enough movies on their own networks to realize what the score was. And then one of the mothers walks in one evening into her fifteen-year-old daughter's room to find the kid mainlining horse into her thigh. Horse, that's heroin.

The parents went to the cops. No good. Dropped for lack of evidence. All right, they're not stupid. They hire a private detective, some clown from Bridgeport. He managed to dig up some more evidence. It was presented to the D.A.'s office with cries of triumph. Then the file gets stolen from the D.A.'s office. Naturally.

One of the parents was a guy named Harry Gilbert. He was a fifth, maybe sixth assistant vice-president on one of the big TV networks.

When he was wondering what his next step was, he happened to be down the block from my office. He had just taken a client to one of those expensive French restaurants nearby. The client had hailed a cab and then offered Gilbert a lift, but just then he noticed my little sign painted on the second-floor window: *Confidential Security. Discreet Inquiries*. That's a great word, discreet. It brings in a lot of business.

Gilbert told me about the drug scene in Haskell. He asked me what I could do. I said, "Nothing."

"What do you mean by that?"

Here I have to give a supposedly intelligent guy a lecture when I have a report to write. So it bugged me a little. I restrained myself.

"If the fix is in, there's nothing I can do."

He looked unsatisfied.

I crossed the t's.

"When I get evidence," I said, "what do I do with it? I

take it to the authorities. They run it up the flagpole and salute it, as you guys say."

He stared at me.

"The only way we operate," I went on, "is strictly within the law. The law stinks, that's your tough luck."

"Do you have any kids?"

I shook my head.

"Try to imagine you have a fifteen-year-old daughter," he began. "Your wife meets you at the station and tells you she went into the girl's room. She found a hypodermic needle."

I stopped listening; for a while he went on. He was using the most basic emotional appeal—children.

I remembered the old game of blindman's buff I used to play when I was a kid. I'd be blindfolded, someone would spin me around till I had lost all sense of direction. Then I'd be shoved violently into the center of the room. I never liked the feeling of being handled and directed—then or now.

Once when I was on undercover duty I sat with a dealer in his Park Avenue apartment. I was playing a big buyer from Utica. The doorbell rang. The dealer got up and let in an attractive, well-dressed woman about thirty-five. She gave me a nervous smile. She was sweating and fumbling with her gloves, her pocketbook, patting her hair into place, adjusting her earrings. I recognized the first stages of withdrawal syndrome. He told her I was okay. He took out a deck of heroin and decided to show off. He held it up.

"Wanna see what I trained her to do?" he asked. I didn't want to see, but I said sure, I'd like to see.

He turned and said, "All right, baby, go into your act." She sank to her knees. She bent forward and licked his shoes.

After she had left, he said he used to be a shoeshine boy. "I used to polish the shoes of rich people like she is," he said. When the time came, I took a lot of pleasure in nailing him.

"I don't need the hard sell," I told Gilbert.

He flushed. "Yet you tell me there's nothing you can do."

"Yep."

"How about a ride around the block?"

If he was going to enter upon a conspiracy, he didn't want anyone listening. There was something I could do and both of us knew it. But I couldn't do it and keep my license. He started the car and began. "I—"

I asked him to let me think a while. I thought. Something should be done out in Haskell. The cops weren't doing it. It would get worse and worse. More kids would get hooked. I lit a cigarette. He drove four times around the block and I shushed him twice. The cop on the beat began to get interested, but he saw me and relaxed.

I could not only get my Private Detective license lifted. I'd also lose my gun license because I would have a poor moral character. And I'd go to jail. But for a good cause. Hurray.

Because vigilantes are always a good thing—wherever law breaks down or doesn't exist. But judges don't take that viewpoint. And they're right. The trouble with all vigilante groups is simple. They find power exhilarating. After they run out the bums, they look around and realize they never liked the way the guy down the road keeps old tires on his front lawn instead of keeping it mowed neatly like everyone else on the block. And that guy there, he lets his kids grow long hair and he doesn't go to church. Why not give him a little night visit?

Gilbert was talking. I listened this time.

"I want plenty," I said.

"We're prepared for that," he said. "One thousand."

After I looked at him for a few seconds, I said, "Five."

"Are you serious?"

"Let me out, please."

I got out. I leaned in the window and kept my voice down. "You don't have to meet my price," I said. "All you have to do is go to Stillman's gym and pick yourself a punch-drunk fighter. You give him ten bucks in advance. No more. He'll drink it up. Then you hope he'll make it up there in the train and remember to get off at the right place. But the chances are that he'll get lost somewhere. So he gets up to Haskell, looking like a beached whale and about as unobtrusive. You hope he'll find the right guy. Then you hope he'll get to him before the locals start to break it up. Then you hope he'll keep his trap shut if he winds up in the local jail—where they'll give him a good going-over because he tried to dump one of their boys. If he gets away after doing the job, you hope he won't start bragging in some bar somewhere along the Avenue how he made an easy C-note or two. Some bar where word will get to the top that you're the guy who started the whole thing."

Gilbert was looking uncomfortable.

"And a week or so later," I went on, "you get in your car and press the starter button and you and the car wind up scattered all over the east end of Fairfield County. See you around."

I got five feet away before he called me back.

"All right. Five."

I'm good on the hard sell myself.

4

I went back to the office. Kirby was typing. She had an upper-class Southern accent. She was taking diction lessons trying to lose it. I would be sorry when that would happen. She had a fast, eager, faintly amused way of looking at me whenever I talked to her. She probably found working for a private detective exciting. I'm sure she had memorized the various types that came to the office. And me. I'm sure she had memorized me. I would catch her staring at me from time to time. She probably did me for her actor friends.

I made a phone call.

Mel answered. He was very sleepy. He was an old contact I used once in a while. Only once in a while. You push your contacts too much and they resent it. Mel knew the drug scene inside out. I didn't push him. He knew the chemistry of the sedatives, the analgesics, the barbiturates —anything that would give you a high—or cool you—as well as any chemist in the Police Laboratory. He could have made a brilliant career in any field. But he lived in a filthy furnished room in Spanish Harlem. He didn't want to be further away than two minutes from heroin. He had been a pusher for twenty years. Yet once he had been so naïve, he told me, that he thought heroin was a misspelled bird.

I asked him who was pushing the stuff in Haskell.

"Huh?"

"You just wake up?"

"Yeah. Mr. Dunne, I been up all night."

Up all night. Sell five decks and earn one for yourself. He was a mainliner. Mel had once told me that he didn't go for the slow glow when the needle went into some general flesh. He mainlined because the feeling of a mainline shot right into a vein is like the greatest orgasm indefinitely prolonged. He almost had me wanting to try it.

"Who's working Haskell?" I repeated patiently. "It's a few miles north of Westport."

"You wanna call me back in ten minutes?"

I hung up. I looked down at the street. I walked out and drank some water. Kirby looked at me out of the corner of her eye. I was nervous and I didn't know it. I picked up an old copy of *Security Magazine* and read about the newest locks. For the thousandth time I wondered why someone didn't invent a fingerprint lock. I opened my desk drawer and threw out all pencils under five inches. The phone rang.

Kirby started to pick it up. I said sharply, "All right, I've got it!" She looked at me surprised. I mumbled that I was sorry. She frowned and hung up.

"Mr. Dunne?"

"Yeah. Go ahead."

"He hits there about two-thirty every day. He waits around for the high school crowd, you know?"

"What's he carry?"

"Horse and pot. The horse comes straight from the other side, you know? It runs between two twenty-seven and two thirty-four."

The higher the melting point of heroin, the better it is. Our friend was selling very good stuff to the rich kids. Another advantage in picking rich parents.

"Does he like it up there?"

"Oh, man, you know, he's only been goin' there a month, and already he's selling a load each afternoon, you know?"

A load is twenty-five decks. A deck is five grains.

"He charges fifteen bucks a deck, more'n he gets down here. No competition. The fix is in. An' he gets all that fresh air for free, you know? He figures in a month he'll be sellin' a bundle a day."

A bundle is three to five loads.

"How about pot?"

"Pot is for kids. There's not enough money in it. You know?"

I couldn't stand his habit of saying "you know" after every sentence.

"Besides, it's too easy for anyone to pick it up in

Mexico and it drives the price down. And it's got too much bulk. Now, how's an amateur gonna get hold of horse? Right? You move in and the big boys carry you out in a box."

"What's he look like?"

"He's good. He looks like a college kid. He lives on One Hundred and Third Street. He wears a cashmere sweater and dirty white sneakers. He drives a Chevy Impala, New York 3D–6754. Remember, he's got nasty friends."

"Thanks."

"Hey, Mr. Dunne, how much? I mean, how much for me?"

"It's not a hijack operation, friend."

"Yeah, but I asked around. Sumpin happen, they come lookin' for me with an army."

"Don't worry. I'll keep you clear."

" 'Don't worry,' he says. I worry about *everything*."

So the guy risked something. When I was a cop, I could have sent him up once from seven to ten, but I let him go in exchange for an occasional phone call. In eight years I had phoned him three times. This was the fourth call.

"You're still ahead."

He started to whine. I shut him up fast. "You could still be in prison right now and you wouldn't have to deal with me at all if you didn't want to. You made your choice eight years ago."

"Jeeze, you're some kind of a—"

"Yeah. I am. And I'll tell you how much your opinion of me grieves me. As soon as you hang up, I'm going to eat a big steak with French fries and then I'm going to do some dealing. Then I'm going to go home and sleep. That's how much it worries me. But I'll give you fifty. You be at the southeast corner of Eighty-ninth and First Avenue in twenty minutes." I hung up.

I told Kirby I'd be out for the afternoon. She kept her eyes on the typewriter. She was still angry because I had snapped at her.

I got my car and drove up to Eighty-ninth and First. It was no area for action for pushers, so it was safe. Mel was standing on the corner nodding and yawning. Pushers should not use the stuff they sell. But then pushers should not do a lot of things. He leaned on the window. I gave him the fifty. He wanted to chat, but I brushed him.

I took the East River Drive to the end, cut across the north end of the Triboro Bridge into Bruckner Boulevard, and then onto the New England Thruway. I got off at Westport and took a leafy road northward along the Saugatuck River for a few miles. It wound around groves of oaks and willows, past farms and estates and little lakes edged with cattails and tiger lilies. I passed thoroughbred horses up to their hocks in the rich grass. I turned off on a little dirt road and stopped on the crest of a ridge where I could see anyone coming from either direction.

I changed the plates for a set of phony Connecticut plates that a very good metal worker had made for me earlier in the year.

Then I drove out again to the main road. Four miles further brought me to Haskell. It had big white houses with lilac bushes in the center of town. The new high school was on the edge of town, and the houses there were planted with magnolias and English yew. I parked near Haskell High and wished I could have gone to a school with a pond in the front of it and big trees scattered over its green lawn. I sat down in the luncheonette and ordered a cup of coffee. It was terrible. I sipped it as slowly as possible. Halfway through, a red Chevrolet Impala parked across the street. NY 3D-6754. The driver got out and walked into the comfort station in the park next to the high school grounds.

Then he came out and sauntered toward the luncheonette. I had paid and was out on the street before he had set foot on the sidewalk on my side.

I entered the comfort station. I looked under the radiator. There it was. A plastic bag. One deck. Not much imagination for hiding places. Every pusher's idea of a good place.

I walked back.

The pusher was talking to some kid who looked about seventeen. He was wearing the usual uniform of his group, the khaki pants, the brown loafers, and the button-down Brooks Brothers shirt. He was nervous. He looked at me, but I was reading a newspaper. He turned back and gave my friend a twenty-dollar bill. He listened carefully to the instructions and left. I folded the paper neatly, got up, and walked over to the booth. I was wearing a different jacket and a loud tie and a hat. I never wear hats. Loud ties make people concentrate on that instead of your face. I keep a couple of ties in my glove compartment at all times. A tie and a hat—better disguises than all the false whiskers ever invented.

I showed him my private detective badge. I put it away after a second. I was counting on the hope that my man didn't know Connecticut's detective badges. And if you work on the cool assumption that your man is sure you're a cop, he'll frequently believe that the badge is a police badge.

"Nilsson," I said. "State police. May I see your identification?"

He smiled. "Have a seat, Nilsson," he said. I put on the proper, stiff look that a state trooper would get when called by his last name. I repeated my request very politely, but with some annoyance in my tone. He shrugged. He had nothing on him, and there wasn't a damn thing I could prove. His attaché case was in his car, and most likely he had a hidden compartment for it that no hick cop would ever find. He pulled out his driver's license.

"Montecalvo, Montecalvo," I said thoughtfully. I gave it back to him.

"Mr. Montecalvo," I said, "you don't seem to have visible means of support."

"You can't book me," he said. He took out a wallet. It was about an inch thick with green stuff. He was taking it all very calmly. The fix must really be in, but solid. He sighed. He decided that I was looking for a contribution for my own charitable foundation. On my own. Beyond the normal payoff.

"Look," he said, "would you like a new hat?"

The old phrase made me grin. He relaxed.

"You know how it is," I said.

He took his wallet out. I shook my head.

"Yeah, sure," he said. "Look," he said, leaning close. "I could drop a C-note on the floor. I could look out the window. And not see what happens—you know? I couldn't testify then. Never. Right, Captain?"

He opened the wallet. The green stuff was tens and twenties.

"I'm very sorry, sir," I said regretfully, giving him the sort of polite handling he wasn't used to in New York. "It's the Lieutenant who wants to talk to you. I'm only a trooper. And what the Lieutenant wants, he gets."

"Yeah. He gets. And *gets*."

He stood up. He was feeling sour. His mind was as transparent as his plastic bags. The local bite, he was thinking, was going to get bigger. He was thinking that it was my job to give him this little speech on how expenses were getting higher and could he get up a little more? He was getting mad. He had been told the fix was in, and here he was, being arrested or being dragged in, it was all the same, and maybe the fix *was* in, and my lieutenant was getting greedy on his own. So he would make a phone call to the mob's local lawyer and he'd get out, but that would kill the afternoon.

I held the door open for him like a well-bred cop on the take. He got in. I had tossed a copy of *Law and Order,* the police professional magazine, onto the front seat. He picked it up idly. I liked the magazine lying there, it was a nice touch.

"Mind if I look at it?"

"It's a free country."

"Ha-ha."

When we drove by police headquarters, he jerked his head up.

"Hey, man, we ain't stoppin'?"

"I'm a state trooper," I reminded him. "We're going to the state trooper barracks at Redfield."

"Redfield! That's twenty-four miles, for crissakes!"

"There's no way I can bring it closer, sir." State police always say "sir."

"You're new, aincha?"

"Yes, sir."

That explained it. It hadn't been made clear to me that the fix was in.

"You better stop and lemme make a phone call, Jack. You're makin' a big mistake and you'll get your ass in a jam."

"Sorry, sir. My orders are to bring you in. No stops for anything, the Lieutenant said." I was getting closer to my abandoned dirt road where I had changed my plates.

That clinched it. No stops meant we were really going to shake him down for a little extra before we released him. We were going to try and scare him. He looked at me with the contempt I deserved.

"You'd better go back. I don't feel like goin' forty-eight miles round trip, even if you're a new guy. I got important appointments."

I was getting more and more sick of this snotty pusher with his influential friends.

"I'm sorry, sir. I do what I'm told."

He was beginning to steam. I turned onto the dirt road.

"*Now* where the hell are you goin'?"

"Short cut to Redfield, sir. This way it's only eighteen miles. A bit rough, but we'll save fifteen minutes."

He wasn't grateful. He took out a little notebook.

"What's your shield number?"

I gave him the last four numbers of his license plate. He looked thoughtful. They had struck some buried recollection, but he couldn't figure it out. Most people don't know their own license numbers.

He wanted my full name. Oh, boy, he was going to go all the way up with his squeal. I told him I was Sigurd Nilsson. He had a lot of trouble with the spelling and he was still repeating the two s's of my last name when the bouncing of the car down the rutted little road brought his eyes off the page.

I got out. He stared at me.

"What—" he began. I took out my gun and held it on him.

"Out," I said.

"Listen, you—"

"Out!"

I had never hit anyone in my life except in self-defense, and then only just enough to overcome opposition.

I had never been one of those cops who take out their fears and tensions beating up some helpless kid.

But when I thought of the plastic envelope in my pocket, I did get some satisfaction in what I was doing. Not pleasure. Satisfaction. There was a difference. If this was the only way this slow murderer could be blocked, then it had to be done. It took about a minute. Most of it with the barrel. I didn't want my knuckles damaged. And the barrel is very effective. I carry permanent proof of its efficacy at the bridge of my nose. Some guy shot off his bullets at me but he missed. He had better aim with the barrel.

When I finished with him, I bent down.

"Listen to me, boy," I said. "Listen careful. You hear me?"

He said nothing. I lifted the gun.

"I hear ya," he mumbled. His front teeth were broken and he was spitting blood.

"You come back again to Haskell, and you don't get off this easy."

"You're crazy, cop," he said. So he still thought I was after money.

I took out the plastic envelope.

"I don't want to see this, or you, or your attaché case, or any of your friends. The fix is in. But that isn't going to do any good. Because we'll get you on the road or back on One Hundred and Third Street."

That little piece of Mel's information was effective. He didn't like the fact that I knew his home address.

"You ain't no cop."

"Pass the word, friend."

I pulled out his shirt and wiped the barrel. I took the attaché case. A mile away I found another little road. I pulled in and changed the plates back to New York. I buried the attaché case deep in the leaf-mold. I buried the Connecticut plates and my loud dollar tie under a bush. They'd never be useful anymore. His boss would have a long memory, and I wouldn't want to make it easy for him. I got into the car and got out just in time. I vomited. That sure was a surprise.

I got in again and drove slowly down the beautiful, lush summer lanes. I kept thinking about the German occupation of Poland in World War II. The Polish underground set up a secret court to try traitors. A real lawyer was chosen as judge, another one was the prosecuting attorney, and a third was defense attorney. The problem was that the accused never could learn that he was on trial. The defense attorney's duty was to provide as good reasons as he could that his absent client should not be found guilty. But when the verdict was guilty, an executioner was chosen. He would study his victim's movements, and then, in an isolated place, he would brace him, say, "I execute you in the name of the Polish Republic," and then carry out his orders. The interesting thing about this process was that these devoted members of the underground, who had not wanted to kill but accepted it as a duty, found themselves liking it. It was finally decided that a man would only be permitted to kill three times. No more. He had begun to like it.

Well, I hadn't liked my little session one single bit. That was a comforting sign.

5

Next morning I was sitting at my desk drinking some terrible coffee from a container. I had drunk too much the night before and I felt lousy. I was looking at the mail. Two pieces of junk mail and the light bill. The phone rang. It was Gilbert. "Thanks for the shipment," he said.

I said nothing.

"Would you like payment?"

A stupid question.

"Yes."

"How about us having lunch together?"

"No."

I was feeling monosyllabic. There was an unhappy silence. I ran my tongue along the back of my teeth. Everything felt like sandpaper.

"You don't want lunch?"

He wanted to be loved.

"I don't eat business lunches."

He probably had two-hour business lunches with ulcer appetizers.

"Would you like payment?"

"Yes. Now."

He came up half an hour later. He gave me a thick manila envelope. "I thought you'd like it in small bills," he said. "It's in twenties. I hear from the hospital they spent four hours patching up some guy from out of town who claims he was jumped by three muggers."

"Policing remote areas is a problem."

"I suppose so. I see you awarded yourself a bonus."

I looked at him.

"He says he was rolled."

"Any objection?"

"Out of curiosity, how much did you get?"

"Five hundred eighty-five."

He looked at me in a funny way and stood up.

"It takes all kinds, I suppose," he said. He stared at me as if I was the guy in the sideshow who bit the heads off live chickens. I was just in the mood to be affronted.

"Now you listen to me," I said. "You needed a dirty job done. I did it. He didn't get that five eighty-five being nice to your kids. I hurt him bad in the body and I hurt him bad in the wallet. He won't be back."

"It's nice to feel virtuous when you rob somebody, isn't it?"

Gilbert and I were co-conspirators. It wouldn't be smart for me to dump him, although the fact that there wouldn't be any witnesses was tempting.

I looked at him for a couple of seconds.

"Honest to God," I said, "I don't understand guys like you, I really don't. You want to sell a window cleaner on your network, you show a car without a windshield to prove how really, really clean your product cleans. You sell a cigarette, so you say your filter traps one point four milligrams more tar, or whatever the hell it is, than your biggest competitor, and all the time you have the laboratory report in front of you telling you that your variation is meaningless in lung cancer incidence. You take some lousy white bread jammed full of chemicals so it looks fresher, and it doesn't have any butter in it, and the eggs are the worst grade on the market, and it smells like wall plaster, and you say it develops strong muscles umpteen ways, and *you* wouldn't permit it in your house because you eat freshly baked Italian bread. I beat up this guy for money, and he deserved it. I did it because he had to be kept away from your kids. I took his money because you might, you just *might*, talk a little too much, and the big bad people might hear I was responsible, and they might come looking for me. I need that edge the five eighty-five gives me. Now why don't you get the hell out?"

He got the hell out.

6

Well, that's the background. One rainy afternoon about a week later a man named Parrish came into my office. He was carrying a big black umbrella. I watched him idly through the open door. I was lying back in my chair with my hands laced behind my neck, trying to figure out whether to go to Antigua or Acapulco, for a vacation. Antigua was cheaper, but I had never been to Acapulco. In those days I thought that was a big problem.

Parrish looked like a rich guy with a problem. He was a big tanned man, and watching him shake out the umbrella in the hallway, I had him figured for a banker with a nice

Bahama tan and a wandering wife who may have been necking with the mate of his chartered fishing boat. He looked as if he wanted me to make sure.

Or maybe he had dropped a bundle playing cards and he thought he was being cheated. Or maybe he had unknowingly posed for some interesting pictures.

He came in and stood next to my desk.

"Yes?" I said.

He leaned forward and spoke quietly. As you can see, I was wrong on all counts.

He said, "I want you to kill five people."

7

"You're in the wrong place, mister."

"I understand the fee will be large."

All right. You get them from time to time.

"Sorry, I'm busy." He didn't move.

"If you'll just leave, please." Sometimes the nose deep in the documents works. I buried the nose deep in the documents. I looked at the reports I had to write. There weren't many. Some ladies had been bad and had jumped into other people's beds for solace or amusement, or revenge, or all three. I kept an eye on him in case he turned violent.

A chain of bookstores was being shoplifted into bankruptcy by their own employees. A rich young married woman was being blackmailed by a lesbian. None of them were people I would care to have for friends. To be specific, they were disgusting.

"A lot of money, Mr. Dunne. A lot." He didn't look crazy.

"Does my name mean anything to you?"

"Nope."

He grinned. "Parrish Enterprises."

That did. P.E. built dams and bridges all over the world.

Parrish took out a pigskin cigar case and offered me one. I shook my head. "Save it for later," he said, and put one on the desk. He selected one for himself and cut off the end with a sterling silver cigar cutter. "I rolled my own long enough," he observed. "I deserve this." He lit it carefully and waited for me to talk.

I shoved the reports aside. Crazy he was not.

He indicated Kirby with his raised eyebrows.

"She doesn't kneel at keyholes."

"Nevertheless, Mr. Dunne."

All right. I got up and opened the door. She wasn't kneeling at the keyhole. She had just finished typing up a report on some obscene photographs I had commissioned for some correctly suspicious husband. My typing was erratic four-finger, and clients somehow wanted a neat typing job for their report reading. It wouldn't matter to me whether important material was printed in crayon, but it's variety that livens up this dull business.

She was reading a book while she waited for me to hand her another of my slightly blown-up reports. She had put her legs up on the desk. For the first time I noticed how long they were. She was holding the book above eye level, and her head was tilted backward. Her long yellow hair was swinging free. She was smiling at the book and tugging at her earlobe. I suppose that was the first time I noticed her.

"Miss Jamison."

She whipped her legs off the desk and blushed. "Yes, suh."

"Go away for a while."

It was an order she was used to with some of my clients.

"It's rainin' fierce," she said, standing up.

"Buy stamps," I said. "Stamps are useful. Several six-cent ones. Maybe we should splurge and buy four airmail stamps."

As soon as the door closed behind her, Parrish said, "I suggest you phone Harry Gilbert."

I phoned Gilbert. I hadn't spoken to him since the time I had ordered him out of my office a week before.

He said, "Gilbert here."

I never liked that style of answering a phone.

I content myself with saying, "Dunne."

"What can I do for you?" His voice was cautious.

I was about to tell him but I restrained myself.

"A Mr. Parrish suggested I phone you."

"Yes, yes! He's a neighbor. Last night I was talking to him, and I told him about the way you had fulfilled our contract—"

A partner for life, I told myself, that's what you got. It serves you right, Dunne, for being stupid and greedy.

"—and he liked the way you handled it."

"How about taking a full-page ad?"

"You object to a reference?"

"I kept my part of the agreement. You keep yours, goddam you!"

I slammed down the receiver.

Parrish was grinning. "He'll keep quiet from now on."

"Yeah? An advertising man?"

"May I have the phone?"

I gave it to him. He dialed and asked for Gilbert. While he was waiting, he said, "Through my firms and the interlocking directorates, I control about five million bucks' worth of advertising a year. He gets it. He loves it. Harry. This is Parrish. Harry—yes, thanks, I'm seeing him now. Harry, I wonder if you'd do me a little favor."

I could hear Gilbert's minimized electronic voice crawling and wagging its tail and promising anything.

"Harry, from now on, don't mention your contract

with our friend to anyone. From now on. Not at a party, or when you're drunk, or even to recommend him to someone who had the same problem. I mean *never*. You understand. Yes, all right. And to make sure you do, Harry, if I ever hear in any way that you haven't kept your word, I'll instruct my lawyers to break my contract with you. So will you do that little thing? As a personal favor to me? You will? Thanks." He hung up and looked at me.

"How's that?"

I awarded him back his cigar.

8

We looked each other over. He was four inches taller than me and twenty pounds heavier. He drew on his cigar.

"You don't look anything special," he observed. He was right.

I'm five eight, and the bridge of my nose got pushed to one side once.

I was five pounds overweight, which is what happens when I sit a lot and have nothing much on my mind.

My hair is black and close-cropped. A few gray hairs are scattered through it. I had a neat part on the right side. I have gray eyes and crow's-feet at the corners from scrunching them a lot in the sun from fishing a lot in the summertime.

My hands aren't too big. I couldn't even span an octave when my mother made me take piano lessons when I was a kid. My shoulders are wider across than my rear end. I swim once a week in a gym. I do it for the same reason I keep my short-barreled detective special oiled: my body is a tool and I don't want it breaking down when I might need it very bad. But all in all, nothing special.

"What did you expect?" I asked.

"Someone sophisticated yet brutal. And you know what you look like?"

"Sure. A broken-down professional football player ten years after his last game, working as a used-car salesman."

He grinned. "You surprise me with your frankness."

"I surprise myself sometimes. But I know exactly what I look like. I have to know. For instance, you'd never take me for a private detective. Right?"

"Right."

"I look like I could be a treasurer of a local in the Teamsters' Union? I look like the guy who comes up to your place to put in a new phone? Someone grubby, sincere, and honest, like a reliable mechanic?"

He knocked the ash off his cigar and waited.

"Suppose you saw me down at Paradise Beach down in the Bahamas. I'll tell you what. You'd sit in your private beach cabana and think, here's this guy been saving up for five years, not going anywhere, and now he's having an all-out vacation with the rich folks and to hell with the cost. And his tie is wrong and so are his shoes, the poor schmuck."

"Well, maybe I'd leave out the word schmuck, but I'll buy the rest of it."

"But there's one thing that could never enter your mind. That I'd be a private detective."

"You know," he said, "I think we'll get along. Shall I begin?"

I nodded.

9

"My son is in his third year at Harvard. He was supposed to spend his summer vacation this year with my wife and me on our yacht. Instead, he chose to pass it doing voter registration in the Deep South. I objected. I've built roads and bridges down there and I know what those people are like. He made the usual statement denouncing me and my generation. He went off with two pairs of blue jeans, two shirts, and ten bucks.

"I liked his stubbornness. But I wouldn't let him see it. I was real pleased that he had his own mind. But I told him he was a stupid kid and I made him promise he would write or phone his mother every night. Collect. He said he would. Good enough. David always kept his promises. I asked him if he needed money. He said he thought he could make it without Pop's money, just like the other two boys he was going down with. I liked that. I remembered when I was a kid, I picked up a chrysalis and kept it in a jar until the butterfly started to come out. So I broke open the cocoon to make it easier for the butterfly. When it finally came out, I noticed that it flew sort of feebly. And then it died. Then I found out that it's the struggle the butterfly makes trying to break through the cocoon that makes its wings strong.

"For three weeks he wrote a card every day. Or he phoned his mother. The Voter Registration people gave him enough money for razor blades and Cokes. For food and lodging they were dependent upon the Negro families where they worked."

"I gather he wasn't alone."

"No. He worked with a team. The others were Negroes—I mean blacks. Both were college boys. One was a friend of his from Harvard. The other was from Columbia."

"Go on."

"Three weeks ago the phone calls stopped. So did the cards."

"And the other boys?"

"I called their families. Same thing. No letters, no calls." He reached in a pocket. "Here's his last card."

It said: "Dear Mother and Dad: They are very good to us here. They give us the best they have, which usually isn't much. Tonight we're going fishing for catfish. They fix it real good, with cornbread. Love, Dave."

I turned it over. It was a cheap colored card showing the state capitol building. It was dated August 16, Okalusa.

"What do the Voter Registration people say?"

"They contacted the local police."

"Well?"

He looked at me with a cynical smile. "They said they couldn't be bothered with a couple of beatniks."

"All right. You could bring heavy pressure. Did you?"

"I didn't waste my time. I told my Atlanta branch office to hire a good local private detective. I figured a local boy would do better there than anyone I could send down."

"And?"

"He checked out all the doctors, private hospitals, police stations. Nothing."

I had my doubts as to how carefully a Southern detective agency would check out a delicate problem like this one. I said nothing, but he caught my expression.

"You don't think it was any use?"

"Not much. Did you notify the FBI?"

"What would you expect of an ex-CPA or lawyer who has to go around with a folded handkerchief in his breast pocket and ask people 'Have you seen this man?'"

He was right. The FBI won't share their information

with cops, so the local police are reluctant to work with them. And when you add to that the hostility of Southern cops to any Federal outfit trying to enforce Negro voters' rights—forget it.

"How do you know five are involved?"

"I had that Atlanta detective work on it."

"What's the name of the firm?"

"Georgia Security."

Georgia Security was good. If Daniels, who ran Georgia Security, felt he couldn't give you a good job, or if he felt he couldn't put a suitable man on the job, he'd refuse the assignment.

"What did he find out?"

"He said the local gossip had five men present at the killings. The sheriff, a bus driver, and three others who work at part-time jobs—a little trucking, a little fishing, some railroad work, a little farming. Then I went to the Voter Registration people. They have an office in Harlem. They were very sympathetic and said their information, mostly from Negro sources in Milliken County, was that five men were involved. The sheriff, a bus driver, and three others."

He looked at his cigar. He took it and turned it slowly in his big hands.

"I know they're dead. I don't know what your political views are and I don't care. But I think you know what justice is. If it doesn't exist, then you make it. I want my boy's body. And I want justice."

"You mean revenge."

"I don't make any distinction. Shall we talk business?"

I nodded.

"For finding the bodies, twenty-five thousand. For proving who the killers are—proof that will stand up in court—fifty thousand. For the execution of each killer—one hundred thousand."

"Wait a minute. You ask for proof that will stand up

in court, then you ask for the execution of each one. It doesn't make sense."

"*I'm* the court."

We stared at each other carefully.

"The money will be deposited to your account anywhere in the world. In cash. In any denomination you want. As soon as you give me proof."

I felt very tired and very old. I stood up and looked out the window. There was Kirby with her nose pressed against an expensive window across the street, looking at a five-hundred-dollar dress. She was idly twirling her umbrella.

"Suppose there turns out to be more than five? Or less?"

"Deduct or add one hundred thousand, whichever the case might be."

"Expenses?"

"I'll bear them."

"The chances of failure are very high."

"Yes."

"A guy could get killed down there."

"Why do you think you're getting a hundred thousand apiece?"

He had something there.

"I have a Yankee accent. That will ruin it."

"You're an intelligent man, Mr. Dunne. You thrive on opposition."

"Sure. But a man can choke on too much of it."

"Mr. Dunne, we don't seem to be getting anywhere." He took out a card and wrote Fairfield 3–1767. "I'll give orders that your call will be put through any time you call. How about twenty-four hours to think it over before I start looking elsewhere?"

"Fair enough," I said. We shook hands. I watched him walk out. There was a guy who could put me on easy street for the rest of my life. He could set me up very nicely with a numbered Swiss bank account. He could just put it in for me. I wouldn't even have to fly to Geneva with all that suspicious cash. His people would simply stick it in the bank. All they needed was my signature. He could take that on the back of one of his cards. I could also stick a thumbprint on the back of it. His man would take it to Geneva and a day or so later I would call him and he would just say the name of the bank and the number. Then I would lock up the office with no regrets whatsoever. I would pull down twenty-five thousand a year interest on my new capital. He could help me live somewhere on an island like Bora Bora. I could sip daiquiris and go fishing on the reef and go to parties with wealthy people who might tolerate me and my poverty. Who might just. If I handled it right.

10

I called Kirby in. She sat down, crossed her long legs, and muttered a soft curse. A run had started in her stocking. She sighed, flipped open her notebook and said, "Shoot."

She closed her eyes. Her eyelids were painted a pale blue. I watched as she ran an index finger over the left one and her thumb over the other. They were the color of an early morning sky in summer.

"Headache?"

"Hangover," she said briefly, with hatred. "It went away this morning but it's come back to h'ant me." I felt a strange emotion. It was only much later that I realized that I was experiencing jealousy for the man who had helped her achieve her headache. "Also debts. Debts give me migraine."

I opened a drawer and shook out two aspirins from the

company bottle. Four months ago I had bought a big bottle with hundreds of tablets. The large economy size. I unscrewed the cap. She wrinkled her nose at the reek of vinegar.

"They're no good," she said.

"What do you mean, no good?"

"No good means no good," she said with asperity.

Her headache was making her insolent. It didn't annoy me at all.

"I grew up with five brothers and two sisters," she said. "You bought too many and aspirin grows old. You bought a good buy if you would be runnin' U.S. Steel, but you ain't. You are runnin' me an' all I have is one lil ol' side-splitter here that needs action."

Whenever she was mad, her Southern accent took over completely.

"With your permission, suh." She got up and put on her raincoat, went downstairs, and walked into the drugstore at the corner. I watched her emerge a moment later, and instead of walking back promptly to her waiting employer, she dawdled at the window of the expensive dress shop a few doors down. Finally she turned. I could almost hear her sigh of regret at not being able to buy that pale green five-hundred-dollar job. It looked all right, but why anyone should pay that much money for a couple yards of material has always escaped me.

She came back up, shook out her umbrella, sat down, remembered something, opened her pocketbook, and took out several stamps. She took out a petty cash voucher and began to fill it in. I was thinking hard about Parrish and I suppose when I think hard my face must look like a police court judge's. She misunderstood it completely. She flushed. "I spent seventy sayints," she said curtly, "an' I c'n prove it."

I held up my hand quickly. "I believe you," I said. "For Christ sake, take the chip off your shoulder!"

She growled an apology. I had forgotten why I had called her in. I just took pleasure in watching the play of moods that swept over her face like clouds across the sun. It amused me and touched me.

When I said nothing, she thought I had not accepted her words of apology. She explained.

"Mah diction teacher is mad at me because I haven't paid the old bag for the last four lessons. An' I haven't paid her for reasons you very well know, Mr. Dunne."

The well-known reasons were that there were a few clients who had been slow about paying.

"So who can I get mad at?" she demanded.

"Me. Try me."

"I don't want to get mad, Mr. Dunne. Because I will lose control and insult you and then you'll fire me an' I do find the job interestin'. So I thought I'd solve everything and treat myself to a headache."

I liked the way her accent flared up and died down, depending on her mood.

"How much are the diction lessons?"

"Six dollars apiece."

I had twenty-nine in my wallet. I was going to buy a good drip-dry shirt for eight dollars, then go through my little black book when I got home and see who'd be willing to share my bed after being rendered amiable by a good dinner. I sighed and gave her twenty-four of man's best friends. I never saw anyone's eyebrows go up so fast and so high. She stood there and stared at the money.

"Take it fast before I regret the whole thing," I said.

She grabbed it. Good reaction in an emergency. She opened a desk drawer, took out one of my expensive bond envelopes with raised lettering—I'm one for the big front—crossed out the expensive return address, wrote hers in its place—105 Charles Street—that would be the west side of Greenwich Village. Then she wrote down her teacher's address, 247 West 56th Street. That would be in that nest of voice teachers, singing coaches, and ballet schools back of Carnegie Hall. She took out one of my stamps from the petty cash box, licked and banged it triumphantly into place. I opened my mouth, but she cut me short as she rolled her fist back and forth over the stamp.

"Every secretary does that. I just do it in front of your back."

The front of my back would be my front.

"I accept that," I said.

There went my shirt, a good meal, and a happy horizontal evening in bed. And she had the effrontery to steal my stamp right in front of me. And that way she defused me.

I said, "Miss Jamison."

"Sir?" she said, tucking the letter in her purse.

"I'm going to close up for two or three weeks."

"Oh, I see. You're looking for an excuse to fire me?"

"No, sorry. Business."

"Yes."

"You'll miss me?" I asked dryly.

"Miss you hell. It's the ninety bucks I'll miss."

"I'm sorry. But there isn't enough work to keep you on. Besides, you can collect unemployment insurance."

"How? I need twenty-six weeks during the last fiscal year to collect that—I'm an expert on the subject—and I've only been here three months." She spun the ashtray on her desk absentmindedly and sighed. "Your loss will benefit Macy's. God, I hate selling! Where are you going, if I may ask?"

I saw no reason not to tell her.

"Down South."

"In Dixie Land where I was born!" She perked up at once. "What part?"

"Mississippi."

"Mah favorite cousin's state. Jackson?"

"No. A small town."

She stopped spinning the ashtray. "You," she said, "*You* are going to dig up some information in a *small* town in *Mississippi?*"

Three stresses in one sentence was really pushing it. But when you fire a girl, you have to be patient.

"Yep."

"You are not going to get any. No sirree bob, you are not."

I had a feeling she was right.

"You never know."

"I know. I was born and bred in Dixie, remember? You ain't going to get off home plate."

"Ah'll git me a Southren accent, ma'am."

She chortled with amusement. "God, are you corny!"

"It sounded pretty good to me," I said, a bit irritated.

"It don't signify what it sounds like to you. What signifies is what it sounds lahk to Mississippi ears, and, brother, you better stay home."

"I think I can make out."

"You have as much chance of persuadin' anyone down there that you're a Southerner as daylight has of gettin' past a rooster."

I recognized expert advice and shut up.

"Best thing would be if y'all were in a wheelchair an' I was pushin' it as your ever-lovin'. Tellin' everyone you had laryngitis and was totally paralyzed besides from tryin' to argue with me an' losin'. Evvabody feel sorry for you and poh lil ole faithful Mrs. Dunne and they'd bring me okra gumbo and yams because I has a genuwine flair to make Southern folk open up real soft. But you, Mr. Dunne, they play rough an' dirty once you get out of the cities an' bigger towns. They'll kill you all right and force a pint of whisky down your throat before the sheriff gets there. Or maybe it'll be the sheriff himself doin' all that."

I bought that.

"I do not, repeat do *not* want to work for Macy's for my bed and board. Ever, ever again. I am now applying to your personnel department, Dixie division, for a job."

I was real stupid at times. "Job?" I asked.

"As camouflage."

"Camouflage?"

"I can rent you," she said crisply, "a very good, only in slight disrepair, upper middle-class Georgia accent. Guaranteed to make all status-conscious Southern listeners just *know* great-grandpappy had a plantation along the best bottom lands of the Tombigbee, with one hundred and seventy top field hands, forty-seven house servants, rhododendrons thirty feet high along the piazza, a piano brought over special from England, and we lost a right smart piece of it because he went up North to Saratoga Springs in the hot spell and he lost considerable to them Yankee gamblers, and the War of the Rebellion finished off the rest."

"Is that all true?"

"Well, yes, 'tis. You blue bellies following Sherman broke up our boxwood hedge for firewood and you stabled your horses in our drawing room, and our faithful, honest, and devoted slaves just up and told you where Massa kept his hand-rolled Havana seegars, the smoked hams, and the family silver. And you took it. Boy, did you ever take it!"

She was getting indignant at the old affront.

I was shaking my head trying to say no as nicely as I could when there suddenly flashed into my old, dim-witted skull the thought that here were several pieces for my jigsaw puzzle being neatly placed into my hands. Why was I throwing them away? Because she wasn't a professional? She was fast and clever, and, from the imitation of me I had seen her give once to a delivery boy when she thought I had left for the day, probably a very good actress. The wheelchair bit was purposely ridiculous, and was meant to be, but that and her half-joking offer to serve as camouflage had given me an idea.

She started to say something, but I held up my hand impatiently. "Hold it a second," I said. The hazy idea that was beginning to take shape like a vague cloud was quickly getting some sharp outlines.

Suppose I would have a damn good reason for being down there?

Suppose this idea accounted for my Northern accent?

Suppose my reason had nothing to do with voter registration or civil liberties?

She was placing her books on her desk. When times were slow, she kept a few textbooks on speech in one of the drawers. The top one was titled *American Regional Dialects for Performers*.

And my idea suddenly became sharp and clear. I had it. I had something that might work out very well, and with her help I thought I knew just how to pull it off.

"I think you've got yourself a job," I said.

"Great! When do I start?"

"Let's get a few things straight."

"The spy lecture! I'm ready."

No, she wasn't. Not when she called it the spy lecture.

"You've gotten your ideas about this line of work from movies or from TV. Forget it all. This is about the dullest job in the world, and it requires a very good memory at the same time. That's the hard part. You're going to fake emotions. You're going to make friends of people you really hate. And you might have to make friends with someone you like—and then you'll have to do him dirty. But there's one consolation—it pays well. And afterwards, it'll make you the life of the party."

"How much?"

So she hadn't listened. It would be her headache. But she was in. She wanted to know how much. When I would be all finished with this project—what an innocent word, "project"—she'd be out of a job. And no unemployment insurance. And having to pay rent and take her diction lessons and I suppose her acting lessons as well. I was going to make enough money to be able to afford a generous gesture as a goodbye present for a loyal lieutenant. I calculated: if she were to get Unemployment she'd get the maximum, twenty-six weeks at fifty bucks a week, that would come to fifteen hundred bucks.

"I'll need you for three weeks. How about five hundred a week?"

"Holy mackerel," she said softly. "Holy cats."

Her eyes fell upon the twenty-four-dollar envelope.

"I won't need any diction lessons for a while. Right?"

"Yes. Improving your diction would ruin your usefulness."

"Then here you are, sir," she said. She tore open the envelope and gave me back the contents. I put it back in my wallet and watched her tear off the stamp and carefully put it back in the petty cash box.

"Take the afternoon off," I said.

"What about the Burger report?"

"The what?"

"You know, the guy who embezzled his corporation. They didn't want anyone to know, so you went out and found him."

"Oh, that," I said. "To hell with Burger."

"With pleasure, sir." She put on her coat and sailed out. I watched her twirl her furled umbrella like a Guards officer in civvies as she crossed Madison Avenue. She marched up to the same expensive window that had been attracting her off and on all day. She turned, walked away firmly, just as firmly stopped, wheeled, returned, turned away again, and then suddenly and decisively plunged into the shop.

There went a big chunk of that fifteen hundred bucks.

11

But I wasn't sure whether to go ahead. There were a lot of things I would need. A name. A passport. A new driver's license. Birth certificate. Other things. But I knew people who would help me get them.

I took a pad of yellow legal paper and wrote down a list of illegal things I needed, illegal things I needed done. I wrote down several names of illegal people and connected them with pencil lines to my list. I doodled. Crossed out. Reinserted. Crossed out again. I must have changed my mind as many times as Kirby had when she was looking in that window across the street.

Next I wrote down my plot. I wrote it out briefly as if I were a writer writing a screen treatment for a cynical film producer who had a superb sense of film construction. I wrote it as if a very critical film reviewer were to look at it when it became a movie. But there would be a big difference. There was a big difference between a lousy review and winding up dead somewhere on a lonely country road in northern Mississippi. So I picked my cast of characters very carefully. I rewrote my plot. I crossed out scenes and rewrote them. I went over it again and again for obvious flaws. I went over it for the flaws that would develop under stress. There was the big problem. I would have to play a great deal by hunches. There was no way out of it.

When I finished, I realized with a start that four hours had passed since Kirby had left. I was so involved I hadn't even turned on the lights. My desk picked up the street lights outside when they went on, and I had worked closer to the paper. I laughed. I certainly wanted that half a million more than I had ever wanted anything. I had never worked out a cover story with such intensity. My back and shoulders and fingers were cramped. What I needed was a brief break so that I could give my idea a fresh look.

I jammed the yellow pages into a pocket, locked up, and went downstairs to the nice little ladies' restaurant on the corner.

I very seldom saw any men there. A few decorators and hair stylists came in from the fashionable salons, but they were discreet enough. I liked it because it was quiet, had a rug on the floor, and no one ever yelled or talked loudly. I liked the soft-spoken Irish heifers who were imported in herds and obviously pastured in some inaccessible meadow where male hands could not come near them. They blushed whenever they took my order. I chewed carefully and swallowed thoughtfully. My mother would have been proud of my table manners if she were still alive. That was another reason why I was going ahead with Parrish: there was no one to take the rap, no one to be interviewed, no one to feel any bitterness. A man responsible only to himself works in a fine atmosphere where few variables exist. It makes serious decisions easy. Well, not easy. But fast.

When I came out into the street, I realized that I had not the faintest idea what I had eaten. Easy, Joe, I said to myself, easy. Take it slow. You get this excited, you're bound to make a boo-boo.

I went back to the office. I took out the notes. I had been away half an hour. That was enough time to get a good, clear new look at things, wasn't it? So I reread the notes. I tried to pick them apart. And there was nothing wrong. Nothing. I burned them and then dialed Fairfield 3–1767.

When Parrish answered, I said, "I'm in."

I heard him sigh.

"I just want to ask one question. Where did they spend the last night?"

"I don't know. You could ask the Voter Registration people."

"I could. But if I'm seen anywhere near them, there goes my cover story, blam."

"I didn't think of that."

I thought of it. I thought of it because only a careful old alley cat like me can survive this kind of living.

"I wish I could help, but—wait a minute. I remember something." He sounded apologetic. "It might not mean anything."

"Yes?"

"On his last phone call my boy told his mother something about way down in Egypt land with Moses. She says she thought it was some kind of an in-joke, because she heard the other boys laughing at the phrase."

" 'Way down in Egypt land with Moses'—that right?"

"Yes."

I filed the information away in the Dunne filing cabinet. The cabinet consists of several billion drawers. It's my brain, and usually it's a pretty good information retrieval center, especially when there's a half-a-million-dollar bone dangling in front of its nose.

After that call I phoned Montreal. Montreal had a hangover but would see me next day.

I had Kirby's diction money and twelve hours before my plane. The third call I made was willing to spend them with me.

12

Parrish's messenger met me at Kennedy with a manila envelope. Once we were airborne, I opened it in the lavatory. As requested, it had fifty one-hundred-dollar bills. Operating expenses. A little typewritten note had been slipped under the big paper clip that was holding them together. It said, "More when you want it." No signature.

Three minutes after the plane landed, I had Moran on the phone. He was curt, as usual.

"You at the airport?"

"Yes."

"Grab a taxi and meet me at the Whore Lodge."

That's what it sounded like, anyway.

"The what?"

"L. Apostrophe. H. O. R. L. O. G. E. You wanna know what it means?"

I had spent two years in Paris on the GI Bill after I had graduated alive from Korea. He didn't have to define *l'horloge* for me.

"No," I said.

"It's frog for clock."

"Oh, Jesus."

"It's where a lot of good-looking and expensive tail hangs out. The Whore Lodge. See?" He paused for my laugh. When it didn't come, he added, "What do you mean, 'Oh, Jesus'?"

Sometimes you'd only get through to Moran after a six-second gap, like on all-night talk programs on radio.

In twenty seconds he made a lousy pun, tells me to take a cab instead of the cheaper airport bus which passed by the restaurant anyway and stopped a block away, makes a lunch date at Montreal's most expensive restaurant, insults Canada's largest minority group, gives me a definition I don't need after I had told him I didn't need it, and then feels insulted. All in twenty seconds.

"Oh, Jesus, I'll meet you there," I said, and hung up. I went out of the booth, disobeyed orders, and got in the airport bus.

Moran had been a lawyer, been disbarred, used some pull, and got a private detective's license, got too greedy, and had the license lifted. As a result, he got a lot of work. This seeming paradox came about because legitimate private detectives wouldn't dare touch a lot of things because their license would be lifted. This he didn't have to worry about any more.

The situation was made to order for Moran. No one liked him, no one trusted him, but he would do dirty things. And he produced. The problem with Moran was that he drank too much. He talked too much. You had to get him at just the right time, for the former, and threaten him gently so that he wouldn't do the latter.

It was a lot like landing a big sailfish. You had to drop the bait in the right place, just when he was hungry enough to take it, and when he took it, you had to keep enough strain on the line so that he wouldn't break it in a sudden lunge. You had to pray that he wouldn't wrap the line several times around a big coral head and have the boat's momentum rip the rod from your hands.

I always liked the challenge of doing business with him. But I would prefer rolling in an easy swell, say somewhere off Grand Cayman, drinking ice-cold orange juice laced with that gold Martinique rum—I would prefer that to doing business with challenging people like Moran. I was getting too old for the fast stepping required in my business. I put those thoughts aside when I came into L'Horloge.

He was on his second highball. He didn't waste time on useless formalities like saying hello.

"You're paying for it, right? I told them you were."

"Yeah. They know you here."

"My reputation is lousy, that's what you mean?"

"Order steak." I saw he had been looking at things like flounder and London broil.

He forgot the insult while he ate. I wasn't hungry enough to eat more than a sandwich, and Moran had a strict rule about not talking business while he ate. It was the only attractive ethical part of the whole range of his personality, and I respected it. He ate like he had a contract to keep two rectums working full-time. I watched.

"You eat like a slob," I said.

"When I get to eat steak, I don't want to waste time trying to win a merit badge," he said, unruffled. While he ate, he looked over the women. There were two single girls near us, sitting at the bar with that unmistakable look of expensive call girls on the make in an expensive bar. They had eyes as coldly appraising as a pawnbroker's scale, and every single male who came in was weighed and assayed for gold content. They had looked us over, decided I was not interested, looked at Moran, but he had started in on the cole slaw the waiter had placed in front of him while he went to give the order to the chef. Moran at the cole slaw was quite a sight. It stuck out at the corners of his mouth, and the dressing dribbled down on his chin.

"For crissakes," I said, "wipe yourself."

"Later," he said, his mouth full of slaw, "later." The two girls had caught sight of that spectacle, and they had decided against any of that. Moran told me their fee was fifty for an hour, or one hundred and fifty all night. The two together could be rented for seventy-five an hour, or two hundred and twenty-five all night.

"You hungry?"

"Haven't eaten for two days."

"Broke?"

"Drinking, drinking. Should eat. That way you avoid the d.t.'s. You know the d.t.'s is a diet deficiency disease?"

I hadn't come for a lecture on food, but it was useless to talk to Moran about business until he had finished stuffing. It might as well be diet as anything else. After he told me all about how he never drank more than three days straight, because then the lack of vitamins would begin to tell on him, he shifted to more interesting matters.

"After the Fair this town is dead. D. E. A. D."

Moran liked to spell out words.

He pushed the wreckage away and wiped his greasy face on his napkin. "Am I clean enough for you now?" he asked.

"I could go for you myself."

He made a couple of jokes about faggots while he ate his Peach Melba. I listened patiently. When I went fishing once down in the Carribbean, off Margarita, one of those little islands off the Venezuelan coast, I learned, once and for all, to accept the fact that certain things, like ship sailings, came to take place when they took place. In other words, don't push things that cannot be pushed. I drifted with Moran's filthy conversation.

He ate the dessert like a pig. Then he ordered coffee. By his rules coffee was not part of a meal, and business could be discussed over coffee.

"Okay?"

"Yeah, Dunne. Okay. Shoot."

I shot. When I finished with my list, he grunted.

"That's a lot you're after. A lot."

"Come on, Jack. Quit trying to force the price up."

He grinned. "Ought not to be too hard. I'll need some money to break the ice here and there. To get in some record files. Some payoff money. Then I'll have to scout around for a careful, old-fashioned burglar. They're not around much anymore. Then I'll need a good shoplifter. And then the car."

I listened patiently. I knew all that; those were some of the things I had written out the night before. But I never cut short an expert when he talks about his specialty.

"It'll run you—let's see—how's three thousand strike you?"

"It strikes me as crazy."

"What do you like?"

"I like two."

"Two! For what you want? I'm gonna ask some guy to risk a five-to-ten. You gotta pay a guy plenty. In advance. If he gets caught, he won't squeal. That's not cheap. And the car? And all those little extras?"

"I don't want a Lincoln, Jack. I want a five-, six-year-old heap that's been well maintained. That won't run over seven hundred. Don't make it so heartrending."

"Who's your cheap client?" he asked, with a sneer.

That was fine. I was glad he asked. Jack was clever. He probably thought that I might get a bit mad and tell him off with my important client. He would file this information away carefully. It might be useful someday.

"My cheap client, Jack, my cheap client comes from Sicily. He lives in New York. He's going to bring in a couple friends from Sicily he trusts, and they're coming back over the border and they're going to live in Montreal. From time to time they'll drive down to Philadelphia or Baltimore or Charleston to see their friends who might be dropping in with some good cooking from the old country. They'll—"

Jack held up both hands. "All right, all right, Joe. That's enough. I don't want to know any more."

Just the hint of the Mafia was enough for Jack. When he was still a lawyer, he arranged some corporation papers for a front for a Mafia man, and they didn't like a little extra billing he slipped in. It wasn't worth a hit, but it was worth a swift, efficient beating in an alley.

"So how about three days?"

"Three days. Yeah, three days will do it. Look for me in three days down at your office."

I gave him fifteen hundred. It was a calculated risk. It was enough for him to go on a splendid bat, but the thought of my client plus the thought of the balance ought to hold him in check and make him mind his manners.

As I was paying the check, I saw him eyeing one of the tastier bits. She eyed him coldly and turned the other way.

"Oh, wait till I get you in bed, baby," he muttered, just loud enough for me to hear.

"Control it for three days," I said. "Be a pal for three days."

"Yeah," he said, his voice thick with lust. He stopped at her table. He pretended not to notice her. He took out his wallet and counted the fifteen crisp new one-hundred-dollar bills I had just handed him.

"Aren't they pretty!" he said.

"Very," I said. Her eyes were like two ice-cold blue marbles. She couldn't look away.

"Today is Tuesday, Mr. Onassis," he said. "I'll meet you here for dinner on Friday. Say at eight. And if you can't make it, I'd hate to eat alone. I surely would hate it."

I went along with him. "I don't think I can make it," I said.

He pretended to notice her for the first time. "Why, hello there!" he said. Her face arranged itself in a smile. As we left, she wiggled her fingers at us.

"I wonder how I can explain my sudden magnetism," he said as we waited for a cab.

"It's your charm," I said. "It is well known that all Canadians are loaded with it. In the meantime, did you notice the way her eyes were glued to your wallet? They burned a hole right through your jacket after you put it in your pocket."

"Don't worry about me, Yank," he said. "When I step out with that broad on Friday, all of it except one hundred and fifty is going to be in my safe-deposit box."

"Next to the cobwebs."

He liked that.

It's a pleasure to deal with smart operators.

13

After the cab had gone a few blocks, I told the driver to pull over. He was annoyed at losing the long haul to the airport, but he had better manners than a New York hackie would in a similar situation. I waited till he had disappeared. Then I took another cab to McGill University. I have never been there. Moran's excellent nervousness about the Mafia would suffer a serious setback if he ever found out that I had gone personally to look over McGill.

I got out. I spent two hours walking slowly around the campus, looking at the buildings, memorizing their names and position on the campus. I ambled in and out of the stores that supplied the students.

In a bookstore I bought several books on my new specialty. I made sure they were all secondhand. Then I bought three of the most recent ones. That hurt because the subject was somewhat obscure, and in my field's postgraduate level that meant fifteen to twenty bucks apiece. But what the hell, it was a business expense, and I grinned as I realized I was automatically thinking of the income tax deductions.

I went by the medical school with my new purchases

under my arm. I really looked like a member of McGill, and several students nodded to me, on the principle that it paid to be courteous to any professor. I went up the steps, looking for authentic bits of local color, the kind that could be casually sprinkled in conversation. The kind that would automatically clinch a position. Imagine that you've only been in New York for two hours. You wind up walking through Washington Square Park. You stop for a moment and watch the chess games going on at the inlaid tables at the southwest corner of the park. Years later someone asks you if you know New York. You respond with, "Sure. Remember those chess games they used to play on those inlaid tables at the southwest corner of Washington Square Park?" You've got it made.

I wandered over to the side streets and found an old bar named Delehanty's. It must have been popular ever since McGill was founded, judging from the way the wood tables in the back were carved up with initials and years.

I went to the men's room. Not only did I go there for the usual reason, but because men's rooms near universities usually have some good remarks lettered above the urinals. As long as you're there, you might as well write. This urinal was a six-foot-tall porcelain giant, with a huge cake of ice at the bottom into which everyone there earlier had been trying to drill holes. A huge brass handle flushed it with a roar afterwards. There were two good graffiti I decided to memorize. One said: *Tomorrow will be canceled because of technical difficulties. GOD.* The other one said simply, *The whole white race is queer.* Noted for possible use in Mississippi.

The bartender would be a good source of local color. I ordered a beer. There was no one else around. He was a disgruntled man of sixty or so, with lantern jaw and gold-rimmed spectacles. He was polishing glasses and looking off into space.

"Nice day," I offered.

He looked at me with loathing. He was not Rheingold's image of your friendly neighborhood bartender.

I amended my remark to "It *was* nice till I came in."

Nothing.

"Does it snow here in the winter, mister?" I asked, beginning to get annoyed.

He spoke. He said, "You think if you buy one lousy beer you can file a homestead claim on me for the afternoon?"

He had something there.

"Well, no," I said, trying reason, "but a friendly hello from a stranger is worth a friendly—"

He reached under the bar and placed a friendly hickory club on the counter.

I could have stayed and escalated our little talk to prove to him and to myself that his manners were bad. But then I would wind up in police court and some bored reporter might give it some play. This was not a good idea if I wanted to make half a million bucks. Some shrewd Southern private detective might be drifting up here someday and, as a lawyer tells clients planning a Nevada divorce and that six-week stay, "Leave a trail of indicia behind you." I didn't want to leave any indicia. Discretion —and cash—is the better part of valor.

"That's the most amazing thing I've ever seen in my life," I said. I paused. Since you can't be in Canada five minutes without finding out what steams up a good, solid, non-French Canadian, I had my exit line. I moved toward the door, turned and said, "I leave you with this thought for the day: *Vive Québec Libre!*"

I felt better all the way to the airport.

14

When I got into the office next morning at nine-thirty, Kirby was already there. She demanded to know how soon she could be a spy.

"Soon, soon," I said. "Type up the Burger report." Three hundred and fifty bucks could come in handy, and that embezzler's firm might pay immediately if I attached a little note saying I needed cash right away. Because I'd never see it if things worked out all right with the Parrish deal.

"Yes, sir," she said. Her spirits seemed dampened.

"And start forgetting all those diction lessons," I said. "Let's have that cornpone and fried-chicken routine."

"Yassuh," she said glumly, inserting carbons between the blank pages. "Oh, but yassuh."

I closed the door and phoned Bryan. He said to come on over. I hung up and was there in ten minutes. Bryan was probably the best still photographer alive. He had been a combat photographer in Korea. We met when I was firing a machine gun with serious intent to maim and I suddenly became aware that this little creature, whom I had seen only once before when our captain told us he had been assigned to our outfit, was prone on his belly and looking for a good composition. He wanted to get both me and the North Chinese coming up the hill at me. He had a very expensive Leica with a lens as long as my middle finger and another one for color.

"Hold it!" he said.

I didn't hold it. Instead I said, "Take that baby Brownie and shove it up your ass!" We've been friends ever since.

After Korea he went to Paris on the GI Bill, where he studied art. He got a job with the Paris edition of *Vogue* while he was there and built himself a reputation. From there he went to M.I.T. and studied the physics of light. From then on all he had to do was name his price. From time to time he would go somewhere and take pictures. They were made into books. No gimmicks, no tricks. He could take any camera made and put it together in the dark.

Yet he was the most unnoticeable little man I ever saw. He was five feet four, with an ordinary face and ordinary hair. He was so completely ordinary that he would make the perfect tail. I mean, he could follow some guy for hours who would be suspicious to start with. The guy would turn around and see Bryan three steps behind him staring at him. He'd pay no attention and look for someone else. Ten minutes later he'd turn around, say in an elevator with only the two of them in it, and Bryan would be six inches behind him. "No," the guy would mutter to himself. "No. This can't possibly be following me."

But he was the most talented photographer in the world.

He had a studio and loft combined off Fifth Avenue at 19th Street. It wasn't a fashionable area, but he didn't lose any sleep over it. I walked up the creaking, sagging wooden steps three flights to his door.

Outside two private cops were sitting on kitchen chairs.

When I approached, one of them said very politely, "May I help you, sir?"

I was puzzled. "I don't think so," I said. "My business is with Mr. Farr." I started to pass him, but he stood up and blocked me.

I began to get annoyed. "May I have your name, sir?" he asked. I told him.

He opened the door and called inside, "A Mr. Dunne to see you, sir."

I heard Bryan's voice yelling, "The international jewel thief! Send him in." The guard didn't think that was funny, and I failed to see the point of it myself until I entered.

The studio always looked to me a mile long. There was a big skylight at the far end. There was nothing in the place except Bryan and a naked girl.

"Is she that much in demand?" I asked, jerking a thumb toward the two cops.

"No, but her necklace is," Bryan said.

The girl was very slender, with sharp little breasts. She had a cold, remote, untouchable, and very expensive aura. She would only be photographed stepping out of a Rolls, or wearing a cashmere sweater and patting a thoroughbred race horse. With hollow cheeks, high cheekbones, sharp little muzzle, and with her yellow-green eyes that were giving me a polar stare, she looked like a bitch-wolf.

I tore my gaze away finally from her private goodies and looked at the necklace.

"It's got twenty-eight diamonds on it," Bryan said, "each the size of an almond. It used to belong to ze Grand Duchess Olga of ze Russian imperial family."

"She give it to you?"

"You really think I look like a gigolo?" he asked, flattered.

"No."

"Well, nevertheless, the neck—"

"Hurry up, will you, Mr. Farr," she said. "This goddam necklace weighs a ton, honest."

She tugged it up with one aristocratic slender hand while the other set of long exquisite fingers rubbed the back of her neck.

"Hold on," he said. "It'll be over soon."

While he was adjusting a muslin sheet under the skylight, he spoke. "It belongs to Will Howell. He just bought it. I'm taking the shot to illustrate the full-page ad he's going to run in *Fortune*. It'll just show Elisa here backing up the necklace and at the bottom it'll read, spelled out, no figures, seven hundred and fifty thousand. Plus tax. At the upper left-hand corner it'll say, small, lowercase, *Will Howell*. And at the lower right hand it'll say, awful small, *Bryan Farr*."

"You've come far, Bryan."

Elisa burst out into laughter. "That's funny!" she cried. "That's really awfully funny." I thought she was kidding, but I realized she was serious. She was holding the necklace up in the air and the strain on her shoulder made that perfect little cone stick out all by itself.

"Throw the necklace out the window," I said. "The valuable item is underneath it."

I walked over and held the necklace up so that I took the weight off her neck. I thought she was kidding a little about the weight but this girl was serious about everything. It *was* heavy.

"Hey," she said to Bryan, twisting around to look up at me, "I like your friend."

"All right, Joe. You can help. Hold up the necklace. I got to get this light just right." He was using natural light plus a purple spot to bring out the highlights in the diamonds. He prowled around, trying the spot at different heights.

"Boy," she said, "you don't know what a relief it is to get that thing off my boobs. They're sensitive to pressure, you know."

"So I hear."

She had round little nipples the size and color of ripe raspberries.

"You like me?"

"Bryan," I said, "go to the movies."

"Not when she gets seventy-five bucks an hour. Control yourself."

"I can tell you're not a fag," she said. "This business is

just loaded with them. Oh, not Mr. Farr! He said I'm not his style. He said I'm too skinny. He said when I pulled out my permanent back molars to get this great high cheekbone effect, he said, Lisa, you have the brains of a cockroach. He said, Lisa, if brains were beans, he said, you don't have enough to make a mosquito fart."

She giggled.

I began to reconsider our romance.

"Yes," she said, "he really did say that." She repeated it in case I might have missed it the first time. "Listen," she said, "I really like you. Even though you're old, and got some gray hair. Why don't you ask me for a date?"

I didn't want to ask her for a date anymore. But who knows, if I kept her mouth filled with food and liquor she might stop talking.

"How about tonight?"

"Great!"

"Shall I pick you up at eight?"

"Sure. But you'll have to bring me home by nine-thirty. I go to bed by ten."

"And that's exactly right, Joe."

"Yes," Lisa said primly. "I sleep ten hours every night. Except Saturday night. Saturday night I can stay up till midnight. You know why?"

"Because then you turn into a pumpkin?"

"No, you're silly! But that's funny! A pumpkin!"

There was something appealing about a girl who liked all my jokes. One could get attached to her. I began to rethink my sour attitude.

"I stay up till midnight on Saturday," she continued, "because unless I get ten hours a night, it shows around my eyes. They get all baggy. On Saturday night it doesn't matter so much because on Sunday I go to bed at seven to make up for the time I lost on Saturday. Those three hours extra—"

"I get it," I said kindly.

"Those three hours extra," she went on, "they make up for going to bed late on Saturday. You know why I need so much sleep? Because," she said impressively, "because the camera *does not lie*."

"That's a very impressive statement," I said. "Please repeat it so I won't forget it."

"Oh, for God's sake," Bryan said.

She repeated it.

"I must remember that," I said.

"Joe," Bryan said, "as a matter of fact, why don't you go and stand in the hallway for a few minutes? I don't think I can stand this much more."

I went out and stood next to the cops. They eyed me and kept their hands near their gun butts. I told them to relax.

"That's a very valuable piece in there," one of them said importantly.

"I don't know about that," I said. "Chemically, she's only worth about eighty-three cents."

He clammed up. I leaned on the dusty banister and smoked. Five minutes later Bryan called us in. The cops put the necklace in a small velvet-lined box. "How do you know that's not a paste substitute you just put in there?" I asked.

They went out worried, still with their hands on their butts. I held the door and watched them go down the stairs. They kept looking up at me, and one of them tripped on the bottom step. I closed the door.

Bryan said, "You made their day. Why pick on a couple jerks doing their duty?"

"I don't like nervous guys around guns," I said. "Some poor kid'll ask them for a match and they'll each put five slugs in his belly."

Bryan was at the window. "Look, look!" he chortled. "They don't know whether we've got the real necklace up here or not, after that crack of yours."

I went over and looked down. They were arguing outside the armored truck. We were still grinning when Lisa appeared. "Goodbye, Mr. Farr," she said. She thrust a piece of paper at me with her phone number on it. She giggled and went out. When the door closed, I crumpled it and tossed it in the wastebasket.

"You're better off, believe me," Bryan said. He reversed the film in his Leica. "All right. When you wouldn't tell me over the phone, I knew it was serious."

"Here's the situation. I know enough to take flash at night and get those action shots which mean so much to us. You taught me how to get that kind of stuff, how to get it in good focus, suitable for eight-by-ten blowups. But this time it's going to be a lot more complicated. I need a camera that will take extreme close-ups."

"Close-ups of what?"

"Teeth."

He stared at me.

"For dental identification."

"That's not hard. You get a good lens, a tripod, take your exposure correctly, and then—"

"You're assuming good light conditions."

"Yes."

"I can't assume that. Assume light will be lousy. And no flash."

"You don't want to attract attention?"

I nodded.

"Extreme close-up," he mused. "Depth of field important, especially on teeth. Bad light. You don't want much, do you?"

"Can do?"

"You'll need a damn good lens. To grab all the available light. You might need a time exposure. You'll need a good light meter. A fifty millimeter lens, let's see—" He began to write down what I would need. "—and a tripod," he finished.

"A *tripod?*"

"You might think you have steady hands, but at half or a fifth of a second you'll wobble that lens like a drunken sailor. And you want a very sharp image which has to be blown up. This isn't one of your hundredth-of-a-second jobs with flash showing two naked people sitting up in bed, Joe baby. This has got to be real careful and professional. I take it you can't go back if the first try doesn't work out."

"Not likely."

"Take this list and take it to Sam Belliss, down on Chambers Street. Have Sam put the lens into this model Leica box. Just mention my name. It'll help a lot. He'll take off twenty percent. The whole deal should run you about three fifty."

"Okay. Whatever you say." He gave me the list.

"And get yourself a depth-of-field scale and study it."

"A what?"

"You mean you don't know what a depth-of-field scale is?"

"Nope."

He held his head.

"Joe. I was supposed to get these prints out to Will Howell by seven tonight. The *New Yorker* goes to press in two days, and they want to make this issue. I wish I never met you. Take a cab to Sam's, get that stuff, and shoot back here. I'll give you a careful lecture. Why, oh, why did the Signal Corps stick me in your unit?"

15

The next day I showed all the symptoms of a man going crazy. I got up, shaved, went downstairs, ate breakfast, read the paper, walked around the block three times with my hands in my pockets, went upstairs, drank two cups of coffee, read a month-old magazine, and finally decided to do something intelligent.

I took out my combat Magnum, police undercover agent special. The last time I had used it was four months ago when a hijack mob stealing bolts of raw silk fired at me. I got one of them in the hip.

This job was a little beauty. She was .357 caliber. Two-and-a-half-inch barrel, and the stock was checked walnut. It was, as one of my police friends fondly said, "round as little sister's ass, and the rest of her was sweet as taffy candy." I decided it was time to scrub little sister.

Everything looked kosher, but you never know. The hammer was clean and moved nice and easy in its slot. The firing pin tip was hemispherical; if it gets too sharp, it pierces the primer and then the cylinder would freeze up on me when I would wish it wouldn't. I pulled the trigger. The pin went right through the face of the standing breech. Okay. I took a Q-tip from the medicine chest and cleaned out some un-burned powder grains and assorted pieces of gook—lint, tobacco fragments. They came from under the extractor star—and that's another thing that could happen—and they might jam the cylinder.

The ejector rod had loosened up. That could get serious. I mean, if it got worse, it could bend against the forward locking lug and then the cylinder wouldn't rotate. That means I wouldn't be able to fire little sister. I tightened it. I began whistling. The timing was all right. The blueing was a little worn off the fore sight, but nothing serious. If I had to use it, I didn't think I'd be using a fore sight, anyway. I'd probably be pointing it like a nozzle on a hose.

Okay. There she was, ready to roll. I had taken fifteen minutes to check her out and scrub her for the road. I carefully put her away in the Bucheimer holster. I liked that holster. I could stick the Magnum in it and turn it upside-down and shake it. Little sister would stay inside and wouldn't come out. It had an adjustable screw tension post that held her snug. It also had a nice hammer shroud that I liked, ever since last time I had to get her in a hurry and I found out that the hammer caught in my jacket lining and ripped it. The holster cost plenty, but it was worth it. I sat and stared fondly at the both of them. And then I said to myself, Stupid. Boy, you are stupid.

Because I couldn't take her with me. Why? Because I had to assume suspicion on their part down there. Sooner or later someone might just take a peek at my luggage. Plenty of people pack handguns down there, but who packs a .38 detective special that would set them back a hundred and twenty bucks? No good. It was the traditional police detective weapon.

If I wanted to, I could pick up a cheap handgun down there and keep it in my glove compartment like everyone else, but then, why would a nice peaceful Canadian Ph.D. candidate from the ivy-clad walls of McGill go around toting a gun?

No. A gun like little sister would have to stay home.

I would eventually need a gun, and I would have to make damn sure no one ever caught sight of it until they had to look at it, but by then it wouldn't matter. And it would have to be some spectacular arrangement of a weapon. Something really special. In the meantime, I had wasted fifteen minutes polishing and whistling. It would be better for me to get out of the house before I cut my throat. I was getting more and more nervous. It wasn't like me at all. But then I never had had a chance at half a million before. I guess it was excusable.

I shaved again without realizing I had already done so. I put on a clean shirt, tied a knot carefully in the tie, and walked west one block and up five to the Metropolitan Museum. I went up the steps three at a time to get rid of some of that energy, arrived at the top without puffing—those once weekly swimming sessions pay off, eh, Dunne?—and went by the usual giggling group of school kids clustered around the big naked statue of some Roman emperor. Their teacher was telling them about the glories of Ancient Rome with her eyes grimly fixed on the emperor's toes. I grinned and walked through Ancient Greece and looked at a vase with a javelin thrower poised to really give it a good heave.

Damn it, that made me think of my problem again.

Suppose I arrived at the critical moment. I knew who my five people were. What would I do, stalk them one by one? Let's say I pick off the first. Maybe I get away with it. How about the second? Maybe I can pull that off too. But by then everyone else will be alerted. It would be about impossible to get close to them. They'd stay up all night with shotguns. And a man can't go around all night in a small town and escape observation. No. No good.

I found myself in front of the Japanese weapon collection. A staff member had some people arranged in front of him in a semicircle. I stopped to listen.

"Never before or since the eleventh century," he was saying, "has anyone, anywhere, improved upon the steel in the eleventh-century Japanese sword. The man who made it had priestly status. Women were not allowed nearby while he was working on the sword. It was drawn several times, folded over, drawn again, and so forth. A blade was tested by cutting through twenty copper coins arranged in a stack. If the blade became nicked, it was rejected. The samurai were permitted to try out the blade on prisoners condemned to death. The usual stroke entered the body at the left shoulder blade and made its exit at—"

So long. The first part was interesting. The details I preferred to skip. I slid around the group and looked in the restaurant by the pool. It looked inviting and not crowded. I took a cup of coffee, found a table next to the water, and listened to the splashing from the bronze figures scattered about the pool.

I tested out some more ideas. Good names for me and Kirby. Moran would be bringing down two blank Canadian driving licenses, neatly stamped and issued. He knew someone who would remove the real names and data chemically, and Kirby and I would have two nicely worn proofs we really existed.

"Is this table taken?"

"I beg your pardon?"

"This is a table for four, young man, and you're sitting all alone. Are you or are you *not* waiting for your friends?"

The restaurant had filled up while I was daydreaming.

"No, ma'am." I pulled my legs under my chair, brought my elbows close to my body, and dragged the ashtray in front of me. I had been sprawled all over.

"You had your legs stretched out," she began, in a piercing whine. She removed her bread pudding and salad with Russian dressing. She banged down her empty tray at my elbow and sat down. She picked up her spoon and added, "All I can say is, some people are very inconsiderate."

"I beg your pardon." I pulled my legs even more tightly under my chair.

She hadn't finished.

Oh, the women I'd been meeting! The first was my date on Kirby's diction money. Alice was all right, and adequate in bed, a cheese sandwich when you're hungry. It stops the hunger, but its anticipation and consumption and after-image and desire to repeat are at zero degrees.

Then those two call girls at L'Horloge, the ones with arctic eyes. No point in thinking further about them.

Then Lisa. Good instincts, but the brain capacity of early Neanderthal woman.

And now this stupid bag who'd gotten the world's hook in her mouth—by her looks, at an early age—complained about it feverishly, and would die in ten minutes, like a fish out of water, if it were suddenly removed.

"I'm really very sorry. I had no idea I was obstructing—"

You have to admit I was trying.

"The trouble with New York, young man—" she began, but I took last honors there.

"Is *you* madam," I said, and got up.

I wandered out and wound up somehow in the American Wing. I liked the simple looks of colonial furniture. I stopped at the dining room of a rich Charlestown merchant, 1745. There was a full-size mannequin of the lady of the house, standing near the fireplace and smiling at me, as if she was welcoming me to her house.

"Hello, baby," I said.

She kept smiling. I suddenly found myself thinking of Kirby. She could be standing there in front of the fireplace, in one of those long, low-cut gowns, with a white powdered wig, a black heart-shaped beauty mark just at the swell of the left breast. I bet she'd look great, with her long legs and firm bust, and with that shrewd little sparkle in her eyes that came whenever she was excited and interested in what was going on.

There wouldn't be any herbivorous calm or icy calculation or stupidity or a perpetual whine about her. I began to think I was very lucky at having her for an assistant—no, it was her idea to use her accent as camouflage. Let's call her an associate in this joint venture. I felt suddenly much better about the whole thing. I'd always operated alone; it felt damn good to work for a change with someone bright and funny. Thinking of her was a good omen, and, ten minutes later, when I was in the antique gun collection looking at a sixteenth-century pistol with six barrels, each having its own trigger, I had an idea that would solve my last problem.

I went right to the museum entrance, got into a phone booth, and called George Foglia.

16

George never talked on phones. You said, "Hi, George, how's things?" He knew that meant you wanted to discuss serious matters. If he said, "Fine, how's yourself?" it meant he was open for a meeting.

George answered the phone. "Hi, George," I said. "Joe Dunne. How's things?"

"Fine. How's yourself?"

"Fine, just fine, George."

"Where you hangin' out these days?"

"The Metropolitan Museum."

"You're kiddin'."

When I convinced him I was really there, he said, "You know, I never made a sale there yet."

"There's always the first time."

"Well, why not? I'll be over right away."

We met in the bookshop off the main entrance. I was killing time by looking through a book on Etruscan art. He came in and peeked at it over my shoulder.

"Hey," he said, "ain't that one the forgery we sold the Museum? That guy with the sword?"

It was. George swelled with pride.

"You gotta admit it," he said, "we wops are great at forgeries. Catch some wop museum buyin' a forgery! It'll never happen. Right?"

"Right." I steered him into the cafeteria while he was boasting of Michelangelo's and Cellini's expertise at fakes and how they fooled everybody by burying a statue and letting someone dig it up.

When we had our coffee in front of us, he leaned close and said, "Okay."

I told him what I wanted. He put three heaping teaspoons of sugar in his cup and stirred it slowly.

"Makin' a movie?"

"Call it that."

"You the star?"

He looked at me and said, "Sorry, Mr. Dunne. You know me and my jokes. I got no taste. Right?"

"Right."

"You wanna get down to business?"

I looked at him.

"Yeah. Well, the army just developed a cutie for Vietnam. It's for them Green Berets, it's for troops operatin' behind enemy lines. You know, hit hard, beat it, go on, hit hard, and zoom! beat it again. You need somethin' light, that won't rust or jam, and you need it quiet. The M-14 ain't so good. They're all right for regular combat, when you don't give a damn if the enemy knows you're there, but for these boys they're no good, they make a hell of a racket. So the army goes and makes this here machine gun down at Aberdeen Provin' Grounds. It's made of some new tough plastic that floats. You drop it in the water and it floats, honest to God. They got some wild steel-magnesium-aluminum alloy for all the metal parts, so it don't weigh hardly nothin'. All that weighs are the cartridges. And they don't weigh hardly anythin' either. Ask me why."

"Why?"

"Because they're twenty-twos."

"Twenty-twos? What good are twenty-twos?"

"Twenty-twos is damn good. They got this low powder charge, see? A twenty-two with a big powder load would go *zing!* right through you and leave a tiny hole. So this one goes real slow, you might say it loafs along, but don't worry, it can move faster than you can run, and the riflin' in the barrel is designed to give it wobble when it comes out. Man, they make a *big* hole. You wouldn't use it for any target over twenty-five yards away, the cartridge would be spinnin' like a merry-go-round and be off maybe six inches to a foot. But for very close-range jungle fightin', you can't beat it. And if you want to play real dirty, you can cut a little cross at the end of each cartridge."

I made a face.

"You gonna tell me dum-dums are against international law? I got news for you. I got a kid brother with the Marines out there. If a dum-dum saves his life, God bless him for makin' one. He's got a Comanche buddy from Oklahoma. Know what this crazy Indian does? He takes scalps. And that ain't all. Hold onto your seat belt for this one. He sends the scalps home and his folks jump up and down all around them and pound them old family drums. They hold scalp dances, for Christ's sakes. Dum-dum, scalp-schmalp, whoever comes out alive wins." He drank some coffee. "Excuse the speech. Let me tell you the convincer about this new job. It's got a silencer. A *plastic* silencer."

"Jesus."

"Empty, the whole unit weighs four pounds—count 'em—four. A drum of sixty cartridges weighs three pounds more. Add 'em—you got yourself somethin' real interestin' there that weighs seven pounds."

Seven pounds. And my cute little Magnum weighs thirty-one ounces. Almost two pounds. Empty. That's an awful lot of weight balanced against operating conditions and effect.

"How much?"

"Take it easy! They only got five or six out there at Aberdeen. That's all there is in the whole world. You want one, it's gonna cost."

"Well?"

"Lemme figure. I got a good guy in Baltimore, he knows practically everybody at Aberdeen. He contacts one of 'em an' makes the pitch. The guy is gonna want plenty. You see why. An' then you just don't walk out with it. It ain't like walkin' out of Abercrombie and Fitch."

George didn't make sales talks. If he really faced problems, he faced them.

"This guy, he's gonna have to take it out a piece at a time. An' if they catch him, it's his ass. I mean, he's had it. It'll cost you a grand."

You didn't bargain with George. He made a price and he stuck to it like a barnacle.

"Okay. How soon?"

"I'll give you a call day after tomorrow. Okay?"

"Okay."

We shook hands. We stood up and strolled out. We walked through the Roman section. George stopped in front of the naked Roman emperor. He stared up, bursting with pride.

"Hey, paesan!" he said, bunching his fingers and thumb together and shaking them.

He turned to me. "I got a cousin in Palermo," he said. "He went to art school in Rome. He's got a lousy job teachin' art to schoolkids. I'll write him to cook up somethin' for the Met. Let's take 'em! Who's the boss here?"

"So long, George," I said. "You're on your own."

17

Kirby opened the door next morning. I was sitting at my desk with my chin supported on a palm, drawing cubes and shading them carefully.

"There's someone to see you, Mr. Dunne," she said. I could tell by her icy formality that she didn't like the someone.

"Is his name Moran?"

"So he says."

"Send him in."

Moran came in bleary-eyed and needing a shave. He was yawning. His clothes smelled of Moran. The collar of his shirt was dirty, and so was his tie.

"Yeah, I know," he said wearily, holding up a hand. "I slept in the car to save a few bucks." He displayed his hands. They were filthy. "I had a flat."

"Wash up," I said. I gave him a towel and a bar of soap and the key to the washroom down the hall. I stood by Kirby's desk and watched her look at him. Then she looked at me with her mouth pursed in distaste.

"Don't be so harsh," I said. "That's the guy who's helping you make fifteen hundred bucks."

Moran came back looking a little better. He had used the towel rather than the soap, but then I didn't have to live with him. Kirby was now looking at him with bright, speculative glances. He misunderstood. He swelled with pleasure.

When I closed the door to my office, he rolled his eyes and licked his lips. "Mmm," he said, "that is some dish. It's these quiet-looking ones turn out to be tigers in the sheets."

"Let's see what you have."

"Business, business, business. That's you, Joe. Business, business."

"And if you want your money, money, money, Moran, produce."

"I'll produce all right."

He put down two driver's licenses, all stamped and legal. "I had some guy remove the personal data with some chemical. How's it look?"

It looked perfect. "All right," I said.

"All right, hell! That's perfect. All you have to do is fill in and you've got it made."

He put down a Xerox copy of the registration card of a graduate student in the School of English Studies—one Harold Wilson.

"Here's a copy of the records at McGill on this guy. His whole school career. Said Wilson has pretty near all the specifications you asked for—five eight, a hundred and eighty, black hair, gray eyes, born nineteen twenty-eight in Dunsmuir, Saskatchewan— Hey, that fits you like a glove!"

The son of a bitch was sharp, all right. I thought that this might happen, and I wasn't a good enough actor to get past this spot easily.

"Fancy the amazing coincidence," I said sarcastically, and then, as if the whole subject wasn't interesting enough to talk about, I said, "What else you got?"

He gave me a slow, half-lidded look. Oh, the son of a bitch.

"Well, the guy lives in a little apartment a few blocks from McGill. I had my friend go through it. I told him to steal anything that wasn't nailed down, as if a crazy junkie had been in the place. So he grabs a twelve-dollar radio and a three-fifty alarm clock and a fifteen-dollar electric razor. He made it look like this hophead was going frantic in there looking for diamonds or cash hidden in the bureau or under the rug. He really turned it upside-down."

"Was it worth it?"

"He found some letters from the guy's mother, a whole stack. He took three. They probably wouldn't even be missed." Moran handed them to me. He grinned. "My friend was very humiliated. He said no respectable burglar would spend four seconds in a place like that."

"What did he do with the stuff?"

"What do you think?"

"Dumped it in the river?"

Moran chuckled and nodded. I looked at the letters.

"Dear Hal: I'm glad your studies are going so well. This is all we can spare. Business has been bad in the hardware line because of the drought. Mrs. Garrison broke her hip in a fall down the back stairs and I'm taking care of her—"

Nice family letters. Nice to take along and keep in a bureau drawer for someone to read over some night in case I'd be away—someone who might feel cynical about me. I was sorry to clip Harold, but maybe when it was all over I'd mail him an anonymous hundred bucks. It would give him something to brood about forever.

"Okay. What else?"

He took out two small manila envelopes. He opened one and shook it. Several clothing labels cascaded onto the desk. "From a good medium-priced department store, as requested." He put them back inside. The envelope was marked *W*. The other envelope was marked *M*. One was for women's clothes, the other for men's.

"This took some doing," he remarked. "I got a good shoplifter and told her not to shoplift. She thought I was kidding, but she went to work with a razor blade."

He put down two charge plates from the same department store. One was stamped *Mr. Harold Wilson;* the other, *Mrs. Harold Wilson*.

"Here is the registration for your '62 Chevy sedan, in decent mechanical condition." He put that down on the desk. He dropped the car keys into my hand. "She's parked half a block down. In front of a fire hydrant. The spare is flat. The jack works."

"Why park it at the hydrant, for Christ's sake?"

"I drove three hundred and fifty miles with a hangover, I got no sleep last night, I had a hell of a time latching on to some babe in the university record office. She cost me a lot of drinks and plenty cash besides. Not to mention looking for a good, smart burglar. Don't go nagging me about a lousy fifteen-dollar ticket."

He was right. I apologized. He was mollified.

"One thing more," I said. "Got any Canadian money? Small change?"

He grinned. "It wasn't in the deal, but you can have what I got." He pulled out three pennies, three nickels, two dimes and three quarters.

"I guess that's it," I said. I paid him the balance. He counted it again himself.

"All there?" I said dryly.

"You don't mind my checking up on you, do you, Joe? It's an evil world." He finished and put the money away carefully.

I walked him to the door. He kept staring at Kirby all through the office. His glance roamed from her breasts to her ankles and up again. She turned pink but wouldn't drop her eyes. She gave him stare for stare.

At the door he turned and whispered, "Joe, can you fix me up?"

"Not a chance."

"You laying her yourself, right?"

It was a fair question, sincerely intended and all it needed was a calm yes or no. Instead I wanted to punch him through the glass door. My face must have shown it, for he stepped outside quickly.

"Well, I'll be leaving."

"So long, Moran."

He looked at Kirby and looked at me. "Yeah. Well, so long, Mr. and Mrs. Wilson." He closed the door quickly. I would gain nothing by denying it. If I dropped the whole thing, he might figure I didn't consider that parting shot important. Parting shot was right. I felt like I'd been hooked right in the guts.

I turned and looked at Kirby.

"What did he say to you?"

"He said, 'Goodbye, Mr. and Mrs. Wilson.'"

"No, before."

"I forget."

"Your face became all cold, as if you wanted to kill him."

"He complained I had short-changed him."

"Oh. Well, good riddance." She bent over her work. Watching the long line of her neck and the way her hair fell, covering the side of her face, I realized that Moran had sensed my feeling toward Kirby pretty closely. Better than I had myself. In a way I was grateful to him for the warning. It would never work out for an employer to become involved with an employee. Never.

"Kirby. Come in."

She stood up and brushed the hair away with the back of her hand with an impatient gesture. I wanted to tell her if she ever cut her hair, I would kill her.

She came in and sat down.

"As you heard our departed friend say, we are now Mr. and Mrs. Harold Wilson."

"I don't like that name."

"I don't either. But you can pick yourself a first name."

"I like Kirby."

I liked it too. But it would be better to take another one. "How about 'Mary Lou'?" I said. "When I was in Korea there was a guy in the squad from Alabama. He had a big *Mary Lou* tattooed all across his chest. I said suppose you and Mary Lou have a falling-out? He gave me this big smile and said, 'We did. But it don't matter, because every third girl in the South is named Mary Lou.'"

"I want Kirby."

So I yielded on that one.

Somehow I liked the fact that I could still call her Kirby.

"Here is your driver's license. Fill it in and sign it 'Mrs. Kirby Wilson.' It'll be useful to cash checks with." I watched her fill it in. June 12, 1944. I'd send her something nice for her birthday next year from wherever I would be.

I gave her the clothing labels and told her to remove the old labels and sew them in as quickly as possible. I gave her the charge plate and the Canadian coins.

"Keep them in your change purse," I said. "As if you left in a hurry and didn't have time to use them all up. And here are the keys to our new car."

"A Caddy?"

"No, it is more fitting my lowly station in the university pecking order to own a five-year-old Chevy."

"I'll survive."

She was all set to go. "When do we start?"

I told her we'd have to wait a couple days more.

"Why not now?"

I couldn't very well tell her I had to buy a machine gun to kill five people with.

So I said I needed a good tape recorder and a good camera first.

"And then we'll drive down?" I nodded. She began chewing her thumbnail. I knew this was a sign of deep concentration. Then she said, "As a new spy, am I permitted to have ideas?"

I said yes.

"I think it would be better if I went down first," she said. "They'd be a little suspicious if we came down together, maybe a little cold. But if I went down alone, I could spread myself over town. I'd rent a furnished apartment, a cheap one, but not too cheap. Then I'd buy new drapes an' shelf paper. Then I would scrub like mad to get it real clean, lahk mah hubby's comin' down an' I want to get us a real nice snug lil place? I'll open a charge account at the gas station an' the grocery store an' the butcher's an' deposit a few hundred dollars in our joint account at the bank. Evvabody in town is goin' to be real curious about nice Mrs. Wilson, working so hard to make it homelike, an' she is goin' to tell 'em all about us, believe you me. They're goin' to find out all about the years you spent slavin' for your M.A. and tendin' furnace at night an' waitin' on table an' all. An' I met you an' it was love at first sight, even though I could have had the hand of the banker's son an' had a hundred-an'-fifty-thousand-dollar home out by the country club, with a swimmin' pool an' all. I'm goin'—"

"Hold it, hold it." She was getting carried away with the script.

"Then I'll tell all the nosy busybodies who keep pokin' their noses in the door an' offerin' to help that mah poor hard-workin' husband is at McGill, finishin' up some last-minute term papers, because he's an instructor in Freshman English, an' he *hates* it, he purely hates it. An' when he gets his Ph.D. thesis all done—an' that's why he's down here with me, on a grant—when it gets done, he's gonna get hisself a Ph.D. degree an' then he can be a professor an' then—he doesn't know it yet, but I do—I'm gonna make him move to the University of Georgia wheah our lil one"—and here she patted her stomach—"is goin' to be born an' raised, among his cousins an' uncles an' all his kin."

I liked it. I liked it very much.

"Then when you come down, clear sailing."

"All right. You win."

"What's the thesis going to be on?"

"The Relation of Deep South Rural English to Elizabethan English."

"Zowie!"

"I'll be getting all my notes ready, and spending our last few pennies buying a good tape recorder."

"Shall I take notes myself on our romance?"

"You'd better. Don't trip me up with some little anecdote I've never heard about. When I finish up marking the papers, I'll get all my notes together, pick up this good tape recorder which will use up about all our last few dollars, and then I'll take the bus down because it's cheaper."

"And I'll meet you at the bus station?"

"Yes."

"I'll put on a welcome scene that will get me the Academy Award."

"Just practice that Southern accent," I said. "You keep slipping into Northern speech habits."

"I declare! I keep tryin', but I don' know, it jus' keeps slippin' mah mind."

She stood up. I gave her a hundred for expenses on the way down. I gave her five hundred to start a joint account at the local bank. I told her that when she found a place she should write me a note general delivery, Jackson. I'd phone her when I knew what bus I'd be coming to Okalusa in.

"What'll I do with the labels for your clothes?"

"As soon as I get down there, I'll spend the evening watching you sew them on like a dutiful faculty wife."

"I'll do it if you read to me aloud from Chaucer."

I promised. One more thing. It was important.

"When you get a place," I said, "make sure it has two bedrooms. Or a living room with a sofa in it."

"Sure. But won't they get curious?"

"Tell 'em I need one for my office. I work nights and I don't want to disturb you."

"Sure."

Boy, the both of us were calm. We had everything under control.

"Good luck," I said. I put out my hand and she extended hers. She shook firmly. Then she stood there. I looked at her. She had a quizzical look that I couldn't figure out. We stared at each other. Then a little smile appeared at the corner of her mouth.

"Sir, may I make a suggestion?"

"Of course."

"The car."

The car. The brilliant thought struck me that she didn't know where it was. I calmly showed it to her from the window.

"It's the one at the hydrant?"

"Yes."

"Did he park it there?"

"Yes."

"Naturally."

After the door closed, I watched her walk up to the car. There was a green ticket under the windshield wiper. She slid the ticket out, got into the car, started it and, pulling out, moved expertly into the traffic stream. She was caught by a red light at the corner under the window. Just as the light changed, her hand came out, opened, and a shower of green confetti fluttered down. I grinned.

Mrs. Wilson had style.

18

I went home, made some scrambled eggs, ate them absentmindedly, phoned Bryan, asked for Lisa's number, dialed it, hung up, drank two cans of beer, and watched a terrible movie on TV. Kirby should be sleeping somewhere in central Virginia. I hoped she was staying at a good motel with a good mattress and not in some fleabag she fell into out of sheer exhaustion. I watched the late late show. A better sleeping pill could not be found.

Next morning I went to the office and checked out my sound-recording equipment. I had possession of several units designed by cynical people.

I had a miniature tape recorder that would fit inside

my inner jacket pocket and record for four hours. The mike was a wristwatch, and the mike wire ran up my arm and into my armpit and out again into the recorder. No good for hot climates where everyone went around in shirt sleeves.

All right. How about my more sophisticated unit? This job is a transmitter. It fits inside a pack of cigarettes and still leaves half a pack empty. Take out ten cigarettes, no, take them all out. Put the transmitter in, shove it over to the side under the still unbroken top, feed in the ten cigarettes and you're ready for business. Only what do you do with the ten left over? I know what I'd think if I visited some guy who would leave a half-opened pack of cigarettes on the table with ten cigarettes stuffed into an ashtray. I'd think he was a lousy detective, that's what I'd think. Leave it lying casually on the table. Only you're not quite ready. You need a portable FM receiver in the neighborhood. And that's still not enough if you're looking for proof worth a half a million bucks. But let's be calm about it. The receiver has a recording jack. All you do is hook it up to a tape recorder. Great, right?

The trouble with this setup is that I'd need someone nearby to work the receiver and the recorder. And if there's one thing I didn't want, it was Kirby to get a hint of what was going on. If she didn't know, she couldn't spill, and if she did know, she wouldn't be down there in the first place making the whole thing possible.

So that was out.

And besides, both units were designed on the assumption that whoever would talk to me would talk freely about the disappearance of the three boys. *That* theory was lousy.

I decided the best thing to do was to pick up the best possible portable tape recorder around. From then on I would just have to play it by ear.

It would have to be able to operate under any condition. It would have to have a directional mike that would screen out background noises, like cars passing, or dishes being washed. It would have to record for, say, one hour. And it would have to be completely noiseless.

I still remember what happened when I was using my first recorder years ago. I bought a cheap one to save money. I carried it in an attaché case.

The guy I was taping was out in the kitchen mixing some drinks. I slid the recorder under the couch where he was sitting, started it going, and had the attaché case back by the door on the hall table without him knowing anything about the operation.

He was a cheap actor who was blackmailing a married woman. I had struck up an acquaintance with him in a bar, and I had him convinced I was a beginning playwright with some great scripts. I made up some wild plot and he loved it, and he was trying to interest some people in producing it off-Broadway. I had arranged a double date for us, and he was so pleased with the way things were going that he began boasting about his conquests and how this old bag was financing his vacation trip to Mallorca next month because of a little phone call he threatened to make to her husband. I kept feeding him admiring remarks until he had put enough on the tape to lock him away for a nice stretch or to persuade him to go away quietly. He stopped talking for a second and lit a cigarette. That very second was when the tape chose to reach its end. It began to make that slapping sound each time the reel came around. I can still hear it, *slap-slap-slap-slap*.

He said quietly, "What's that noise?"

"What noise?" I asked. I never was much of an actor, and I defy anyone to say that sentence convincingly.

He looked under the couch. It took some doings back and forth before I could leave with the tape. In the meantime I lost the recorder and two side teeth. The porcelain replacements and the bridge set me back five hundred and seventy-five bucks, and all I could collect from the grateful lady was seven hundred and fifty. The recorder was a mess. It had cost one hundred thirty, so I cleared forty-five bucks on the deal. Lesson for the future: when you buy for your profession, buy the best.

So I went out and bought a four-hundred-forty-dollar Kim.

It would have another use. I would have to drive around the countryside taping rural speech patterns. A recorder looking as impressive as that one did would tend to persuade people I really was a professional. People are funny. If I were to use a fifty-nine-fifty job, they'd think I was some sort of an amateur.

I took the Kim to the office and played with it until it knew me and was friendly. I played with it until I could work all the controls with my eyes closed.

An hour later the phone rang. It was George Foglia.

"How you doing, George?"

"Fine, just fine. If you're not doin' anythin', why don't you drop up for a bite tomorrow?"

"Sure, glad to."

"Wait a minute. I got a place in the country. You know?"

I didn't know.

"Can you make it up there by twelve?"

"Where is it?"

"About thirty miles west of Saratoga."

That would be about two hundred and ten miles upstate.

"Why, for crissakes?"

I could tell George was mad by his silence, but I was mad, too. This waiting was getting on my nerves.

Finally he said, "I got a new set of golf clubs, that's why. You been sayin' how much you wanted to try my new iron. Here's your chance. You can take a few practice swings. It'll limber you up."

I realized he was right. If George said I should take a

few practice swings, he knew what he was talking about.

"Okay. Give me directions."

He gave them. It would be easy. All I had to do was take the New York State Thruway and then cut north. I hung up. The mailman came in with one letter. It was a check in full for the Burger report. The three hundred and fifty dollars made the four-hundred-and-forty-dollar bite for the Kim seem less poisonous. I locked the office. I wasn't interested in any more business. I walked to Central Park and strolled through till I came out at Fifth Avenue and 59th Street. I looked up at the equestrian statue of General Sherman with the bronze figure of a woman striding before him holding his horse's bridle. I suddenly remembered Kirby's remark about the statue after she had been working for me about a month and had taken a sandwich and gone down there for her lunch.

"Just like a Yankee," she said, "to ride that horse and let a lady walk."

I realized I was looking forward to seeing her again. I went home, took a long bath, went out for dinner, and went to bed early.

I left at eight the next morning. By noon I was driving past George's letter box. I made the left turn he had directed me to, and went up the hill on a winding dirt road between two stone walls. By the poor state of the walls I knew that the farmer who had built them was dead long ago. I passed by one abandoned farmhouse, then another. There were several overgrown fields. On the top of the hill was an old farmhouse. But this one was in good condition. George stood waiting for me on the porch.

"You made good time," he said. "I saw you turn in at the bottom of the hill."

He had lunch all ready. Spaghetti, meat sauce, green salad, wine. He made it all himself and was proud of it. "The wine, the wine, guaglio," he said, and pointed out the bay window to the small vineyard. "I made it myself. It's safe to drink it. I took my shoes off first."

After lunch he picked up an attaché case and said, "Let's go for a walk."

We stood on the porch. He flung his free hand out in a big semicircle. "I can see for miles from here," he said. "I own four hundred acres. I got woods an' little rivers an' an old quarry. The road you came up, that's the only way. You come on foot, I stay here with my binoculars, I can see you easy crossin' the fields."

"This where you keep your golf clubs?"

"I got four hundred acres to hide 'em in," he said.

We walked through a little garden planted with plum tomatoes, onions, lettuce, and escarole. He said he would sit on the porch on sunny afternoons when the rabbits were hopping around. "I shoot the goddam bunnies," he said. His face became all red with anger when he thought what they did to his lettuce. "So the neighbors are used to shots all the time. This is deer country anyway. They all got guns. An' they know I'm a gun nut, always doin' my own loadin', weighin' it out grain by grain, an' havin' a ball shootin' at targets. I tell 'em I got a nice little insurance business goin' on in Brooklyn with my paesani, an' I like to get up here an' smell the nice air where it's peaceful."

He led the way through a grove of pine trees, then through a meadow which had once been a cornfield. At the far end of the field a little road led to an abandoned limestone quarry. At the far end, against the rock wall, leaned two life-size human cutouts. They were made of half-inch cardboard.

"There used to be an old movie theater in Vandermill," he said. "That's the nearest town. No one went ever since TV got popular, so they turned it into a supermarket. The manager knows I like target shootin' an' he said I could have these, they was only pickin' up dust in the basement. Who do you want, Greta Garbo or Gary Cooper?"

I picked Gary.

He put down the attaché case, took off the binoculars from his neck and scanned the hills and the valleys carefully. Satisfied, he opened the case.

It was filled with foam rubber. Cut in it, to fit the broken-down machine gun, were variously shaped holes. He pulled out the parts and assembled it easily in thirty seconds. Then he took it apart.

"You try it," he said.

It took me ten seconds longer.

"Once more."

This time I did it in twenty-five.

"Good enough," he said. He took out a drum from the case and clipped it on. He took out a three-inch-thick cylinder of black plastic, five inches long, and screwed it on the thread at the muzzle end. "The silencer," he said.

He showed me where the safety was. He handed me the gun.

"How about a practice swing?" he said.

I walked toward the cardboard cutout I liked, and paused about thirty feet away. I swung it up, pointed it at the neck. I squeezed the trigger. As soon as I felt the faint vibration of the first shot, I began moving the muzzle from side to side, lowering it. The drum took five seconds to empty.

There was very little recoil. It felt like someone was patting me gently on the forearm. The gun went *chug-chug-chug-chug,* very quietly, like a man coughing across a room and trying to muffle it out of consideration for others.

Gary Cooper disintegrated from the top down.

George showed me how to set it for single-shot action. He clipped on another drum, took it off, had me clip it on, nodded. He was satisfied I knew how to do it. I squeezed off one shot. It made a hole in poor Greta's stomach three inches in diameter. The gun coughed quietly once and subsided. Bits of cardboard were floating in the air.

"God," I said.

I took it apart and put it in the case. We walked back silently. At the house George gave me a full drum. I put it in the case. He asked me if I wanted another one. I shook my head. I gave him twenty fifty-dollar bills.

As I got into the car, I said, "That's a terrible thing."

"So don't buy it."

He watched me drive down the road. When I reached his letter box, which was mounted on a cedar post with morning-glory vines blooming all around it, I paused and looked up the hill. He was still standing on the porch. Neither of us waved goodbye.

19

I took the bus down to Jackson rather than the plane. I wanted the extra time for Kirby to worm herself into the town, and if I got there too early, I'd only gum up the works.

So I took one small suitcase, the Kim, and the attaché case down to the Port Authority Bus Terminal. The attaché case had a leather partition in the middle which divided the contents equally. There were two buckles by which it could be attached so that the golf-club side was permanently covered. The empty half had three slots into which I stuck a couple of books on speech, a notebook, and a couple of ballpoint pens. As soon as the bus started down the ramp leading to the Lincoln Tunnel, Mr. Wilson (who had decided he would like to be called Hal rather than Harold) began to catch up on his homework. He also had an excellent reason for keeping the case on his lap at all times rather than placing it in the overhead rack.

I read all the way through New Jersey and Maryland. It wasn't as hard sailing as I thought it might be. It was pretty interesting. *Brid* became *bird* because the effort it took to slide the mouth from *b* to *r* was just too much. So some lazy forebear stuck in an *i* between them to bridge the gap, and it took. The same thing with *thrid*, which became *third*. *Am not* became *amn't* which became *ain't*, which was once used in polite society. It ain't permissible now, although George Foglia uses it all the time. Then I came to the symbols they have dredged out of mathematics and other languages in order to represent sounds not covered in English. I made notes on them. They weren't the kind of notes that any Ph.D. candidate in my chosen field would have on him at this late stage in his career, but it was the only way I could remember all the junk. Later on I would tear them up.

I read grimly on as our headlights drilled across Virginia. Somewhere near the southern border of the state I couldn't take it anymore. I put my book and notes in their proper slots, closed the case, and reached up to turn off the little bull's-eye light that was focused on my lap. I levered my seat back, stretched my legs with a groan of pleasure, leaned back with my hands clasped on the case, and closed my eyes.

I couldn't sleep. I stared at the dark country as the bus cruised at seventy. A sudden thought jumped into my head. I could open the case, spend thirty-five seconds on the contents, and then kill everyone on the bus. Forty-seven people. And the driver wouldn't even turn around. He'd think the studious gentleman in seat 27 was just having a quiet little coughing fit.

It was the kind of thought a psychopathic kid might have. For a second I thought that the most intelligent thing I could do would be for me to get out at Fayetteville, walk to a bridge over the Cape Fear River, and drop in the nine little parts plus the drum, go on to Jackson, pick up Kirby's note at the general delivery window, tell her to pack up, withdraw the money from the Okalusa bank, and meet me at the bus depot in the car. Then we'd drive to Cape Hatteras and I could go surf-casting for sea bass for a couple days while she went on up North and answered the phone. Then back to New York, peeping at keyholes, striking up barroom acquaintances, and reading about the latest electronic devices in *Security*. And not sweat nights about Moran.

But I'd already spent close to three thousand bucks. It would be too embarrassing telling Parrish I'd changed my mind, sorry, I'd pay him back over the next few months. Well, definitely by the end of the year. And then I'd be stuck with two cars—when one is a big enough headache to park in New York.

I knew what Parrish would do. He wouldn't yell. He'd just listen. He'd say, "Okay. Pay me back when you can, Mr. Dunne." And he'd hang up. He'd sort of despise me for the rest of his life. But then you don't hire a man who's thought about your offer first for twenty-four hours, agrees to it, spends three thousand dollars of your money, and then expect to like him when he welshes. The mere thought of Parrish's quiet contempt made me flush.

We rolled into Fayetteville at three in the morning. Very few towns are appealing at that time, and most American cities are way down at the bottom of the list. It looked cold, locked up, hostile. We stopped at the Greyhound Depot. Twenty-minute rest stop.

All I had to do was to walk out with my baggage. I went into the station and had a cup of coffee that was an insult to my stomach and my intelligence. Ten minutes to go. Ten minutes to change my life. And what swung it was that coffee. It was so bad I took it personally. Because it suddenly occurred to me that when this Parrish job would be over, I'd never have to drink lousy coffee at three A.M. in dead little towns in the piny woods again. Never.

I got on the bus and was asleep before the driver started her up.

We got into Jackson at eleven the next morning. I checked the Kim and suitcase at a locker and walked on over to the post office, whistling and swinging my attaché case. People were walking far more slowly than they do in New York, and several of them nodded to me pleasantly. General delivery had a letter for me. From Mrs. Harold Wilson, 412 South Magnolia, Okalusa.

Dear Hal,

Welcome to Dixie! I rented a nice little second-floor furnished apartment for sixty-five dollars. The house belongs to a decaying couple named Garrison. The phone is 516. Phone me when you get this letter and I'll put on an award performance at the bus station like I promised.

(Mrs.) Harold Wilson.

I phoned her right away.

A soft voice said, "Yes?"

"Mrs. Garrison?"

"Yes."

"I'm Harold Wilson, and I—"

Instant warmth. "Oh, *you're* her husband! I declare! We heard so much about you an' the wonderful thing you're goin' to work on down here! She's been pinin' for you somethin' dreadful. You jus' hold on now an' I'll get her for you quicker 'n you can say Jack Robinson! Don't go 'way now, y' hear?"

"Yes, ma'am."

Kirby must have started her performance as soon as she hit the city limits.

"Sugar?"

"Hi, Kirby."

"Darlin'! Jus' get in? I found the most delightful place I ever did see, an' I know you're jus' gonna love it!"

"I gather the landlady is standing right next to you."

"Yeh-uss! I feel the same way about you, honey! I love this lil ole town, evvabody's been so nice an' friendly an' all!"

"Can you cut it short?"

She wouldn't. She went on and raved about the town park with the bandstand and the flowers planted all around it and the swimming pool. She said the grocery man was so nice and so was the boy at the gas station who checked her steering and suspension and found she needed an idler arm and he put it in and he charged her just for the labor and nothing at all for the inspection, and he adjusted the carburetor and timing and didn't charge nothing at all because she told him I was working hard still going to school.

"This is what happens when I hire an out-of-work actress," I said, and immediately realized I had made a serious slip. The local operator might be listening in. Kirby recognized the danger as soon as I did.

"I'm so glad you wouldn't let me go on with those actin' lessons, Hal," she said. "I was beginnin' to hate all those No'th'n girls in mah class always makin' fun of the way I talked."

"I always liked the way you talked, honey," I said, breathing easier. "This bus gets into Okalusa at two-forty. Will you meet me?"

"What a silly lil ole question! Miss Ethelda-Grace, would you like to come for a ride to the bus station with me when mah Hal comes in?"

Miss Ethelda protested, but only weakly. She must be

quite bored. Kirby knew this was the surest way to spread the news over Okalusa that I had arrived.

I hung up with a loud kiss echoing in the receiver. I bought a ticket for the Jackson-Okalusa bus, bought a copy of *Pleasure*, wondered why people thought those colorless bunnies had any flavor, tried to read the third-rate prose, threw it away, and had a better time reading *True Detective*.

The announcer finally called my bus. The friendly driver cut short his conversation with the mechanic and helped with my baggage. I thanked him and he smiled pleasantly and went back to his seat and his conversation with the mechanic.

"Y'ought to make the run to Okalusa just once, Gene," he said. "We grow cotton so high thataway the moon has to go around by way of Tinnissee. The mosquitoes get so big in the swamps outside of town they c'n stand flat-footed an' drink out of a rain barrel. An' the frogs in them swamps along the Chickasaw, why, when they get to bellerin' of a night, they rattle the winderpanes ten mile off."

"You bet, Ray," said the grinning mechanic. He took out a wrench from his back pocket and adjusted the outside rear-view mirror.

"Come down an' eat our catfish," said the driver.

"We got good catfish heah. Ain't no reason to travel a hundred and eighty hot miles to eat yours, Ray."

"I tell you we got good eatin' catfish, Gene. You take our catfish an' corn bread an' some of that white mule them hill boys make up in the laurel, an' you got a good thing goin'." He saw me listening with interest. He swung around and included me in the conversation.

"Mister, you look like a stranger. Lemme tell about our catfish up there in the swamp. One time a cotton-mouth struck me on the face, right here. It weighed seventy-eight pound, coiled. It was bigger'n a bushel basket. It plumb tore away the whole left side of my face, but all they fed me for three days straight was that local catfish from the swamp, an' corn bread an' corn whisky, an' by the end of the week it healed up an' didn't even leave a scar. You see any sign of a scar on mah face?"

I shook my head.

"Mister," the mechanic said, "Okalusa's in Milliken County. An' you can hear anythin' in Milliken County except the truth and bacon a-fryin'."

Ray closed the door, switched on the ignition, and grinned.

"Hold it, Ray," said the mechanic. "You got one more passenger!" In a lower tone he added, "A jigaboo."

Ray opened the door. He said curtly, "C'mon. Step on it. I ain't got all day."

A black man of about sixty began to climb the steps with a heavy old suitcase. Once inside, he gave his ticket to Ray, who didn't wait till the old man could be seated. The bus started immediately and the old man was having trouble with his bulky suitcase in the narrow aisle, which was littered with boxes and shopping bags. It was obviously the bus used by country people to do their serious city shopping in. The old man paused and hesitated when he saw the cluttered aisle. There was an empty seat far in the rear, and there was an empty one beside me. I could almost see his thinking processes.

He would have to ask pardon of ten whites in order to get to the empty seat in the back. He would probably bang a few knees as well with his huge suitcase, and why go through all that humiliation when he could just sit beside me? He looked at me. The look said, Please, mister, are you gonna make a fuss if I sit beside you?

I was filled with compassion for a man who had to think over things like this when a white person could breeze on ahead, saving his mental energy for other matters. I automatically smiled and moved over a bit. He smiled, let out a sigh, and began to stow his suitcase overhead in the rack.

But I suddenly remembered that Ray came from Okalusa. And I was going to live in Okalusa. It was time I went to work.

"Something seems to smell bad," I said to the driver.

The man beside me stiffened. He had been wiping the sweat from his lined face with a clean white handkerchief.

I took a deep, audible breath.

"And it smells worse and worse."

The man's face beside me was expressionless.

Ray grinned. He was driving the bus expertly through the crowded traffic. I could see his heavy, handsome face smiling at me in the mirror above the driver's seat.

"Ain't it the truth!" He pretended to take a long, deep breath.

"Whew-eee!" he said. "It smelled fine till jus' before we left. What could the matter be?" Most of the whites laughed. A few were silent. The Negroes were very quiet.

"Maybe it's your suitcase, mister," he said. He ironically underlined the last word. "I bet y'all got some real overripe hog maws 'n' chitlin's 'n' collard greens in that ole suitcase? It's against the law to carry them things around in suitcases, mister."

I felt the man's body tremble.

"I guess it's too much for me," I said. I got up, leaving my Kim and suitcase in the overhead rack. I picked up my attaché case.

"Excuse me, sir," I said, with great politeness.

He didn't look at me. He stood up to let me go out into the aisle. "Mister," Ray said to me, "it's the Supreme Co't of the Yewnited States that says he c'n sits where he wants. An' there's nothin' I c'n do about it. Ten years ago you wouldn'ta had to put yourself to all this trouble. I'm rightly sorry."

I went back to the other empty seat. Sixteen years ago in Korea, one Elijah Bowman, sergeant, USMC, carried one Joseph Dunne, PFC, on his back down a hill and across a valley enfiladed by enemy machine-gun fire. Private Dunne's thigh had been broken by a bullet. Although Dunne urged Sergeant Bowman to get out and leave him, Sergeant Bowman answered, "You're a marine. I'm a marine." Placing private Dunne eventually on a tank, Sergeant Bowman turned to reenter the fire fight. He was immediately killed by a burst of machine-gun fire. Sergeant Bowman's home was on a farm near Ocala, Florida. He left a widowed mother who had hoped he would come back and run the farm after the war.

Sergeant, forgive me if you can.

I looked out the window. I thought of all the unpleasant things I had done in my life. I decided I had just copped first prize. I saw Ray's face from time to time looking at me in the rear-view mirror. I averted my head. I didn't think I could smile back at him for some time.

After thirty miles the black man got off. Ray turned and said, "Hey, mister, you wanna sit up front? The air's done cleared up."

A few people tittered. I got up. I looked at the faces smiling up at me as I moved up the aisle. I smiled back at them. It wasn't so hard as I thought it would be, but it took some straining. I was going to earn Parrish's money. Every cent of it. I think it was then it really came home to me the things I'd have to do.

Ray said, "You new in Okalusa."

I nodded.

"They got two hotels there. No matter which one you go to, you're gonna wish you had gone to the other."

I smiled and told him my wife had already rented a place.

"Oh, you're married to that pretty Georgia gal! You're

the fella from up in Canada? How come we eveh let a girl like that get away?"

"I worked fast as soon as I saw her."

"Serves us right."

People got off along the highway. The bus became half empty, then there were only five people left. The cotton fields ended. The road ran like an arrow along a causeway with a deep ditch on each side filled with stagnant brown water.

The bus had no air conditioning. The air was stove-hot, and filled with moisture. My shirt stuck to my back. I pulled away from the seat and plucked it away from my sticky skin. The air was almost unbreathable. I had the feeling that if I would pass my hand through the air it would come back with a thin film of oil on it. The leaves of the swamp were all dark green. They were the same color that I had once seen on a boa constrictor's skin. Shiny, sleek, and dark. Nothing was moving in the swamp or in the ditches alongside. The sun kept sucking up moisture from the rotting mass of leaves and decaying branches, and as a result a thin white mist was twisting and writhing above the treetops.

Something brown and thick around as my forearm was moving across the road. Ray accelerated. The heavy bus picked up speed and the wheels went over it. There was a barely perceptible bump.

"Moccasin," Ray said with satisfaction. "Got the son of a bitch! Had a cousin years ago went to the lil pond on a real bad hot day in August. We'd been havin' a long dry spell, an' that pond was 'bout the only place for miles 'round where they was some water. He shucks off his pants an' dives in. They was fo'ty-seven moccasins floatin' in that pond. Know how come I know how many? 'Cause when I come by half an hour later an' I finds him dead with all them bite marks, I went home an' took a stick of dynamite. That's how I know they was fo'ty-seven cottonmouths."

The swamp ended. Cotton fields, miles and miles of them. Signs for cotton gins, cotton-baling machinery, and crop-dusting planes.

Then: YOU ARE ENTERING OKALUSA, QUEEN CITY OF THE COTTON KINGDOM.

Then: CITY LIMITS OKALUSA POP. 28,165 DRIVE SLOW WE LOVE OUR CHILDREN LIONS MEET TUES. 12:30 ROTARY THURS. 12:30.

Negro shacks began to give way to little bungalows. Then suddenly we were riding down a broad street lined with big, old trees and big, old houses. Kids were riding bikes up and down the sidewalks, dogs were running alongside and barking. Lawn sprinklers were turning. The worst of the day's heat was over. People were sitting on front porches gently waving fans and waving at the bus.

We pulled into the bus station. I saw a car with Quebec plates parked outside. My heart, to my surprise, began to beat quickly. I stood up and reached for my luggage.

"This is a nice town," Ray said. "I hope you like it real fine."

"I think I will," I said, reaching for my attaché case.

20

As soon as I walked into the waiting room, I heard a shrill rebel yell. I had just enough time to turn around to see a blonde flash coming fast at me. Then I was hit by Mrs. Wilson. "Hit" is the right word. I was struck by two arms and a shower of kisses. Some of her hair got loose from the silver barrette she was wearing at the back of her neck, and it fell across my face. It had a good smell, of soap and sun. Then she gave me a passionate bear hug. She was a strong woman with good back muscles and she was using every one she had.

People were watching with big grins. Which one was our landlady?

I couldn't afford to be as impetuous as she was, not with my four-hundred-forty dollar Kim in one hand, the suitcase in the other, and the attaché case under my left arm. I lowered everything to the floor while she was still squeezing. "Take it easy," I muttered. She paid no attention. She was carried away by the audience.

I hugged her back. I squeezed just as hard as she had. It started out as a performance for the benefit of the town, but she gave me a kiss smack on the mouth, a direct frontal kiss that forced my lips against my teeth rather painfully. It was a hard, sex-starved kiss from a passionate lady who hadn't seen her husband for one long week and who had been telling everyone how much she loved him.

So I muttered again, "Hey, take it easy!"

"I can't," she hissed. "I told everyone how much I missed you."

So I kissed her back. It started out as a supporting role for my Academy Award friend, but after two seconds it got out of control. I realized the lady was serious. She was pressing her breasts against me. She was wearing a thin nylon blouse of an apricot color, and a thin nylon bra underneath. I was wearing a thin cotton jacket on top of a thin drip-dry blue shirt, and I could feel her nipples bulging into my chest as hard as cherry candy.

I finally pulled away. The first thing I saw was a thin elderly lady staring at us only a few feet away. Her pulse was beating rapidly in her throat. This must be Mrs. Garrison, the landlady.

For the first time I noticed Kirby wasn't wearing her horn-rims. The small of her back was soaked with sweat.

She was breathing quickly with her eyes averted. I put my hand at the small of her back and felt those long flat muscles tense under my palm.

"I missed you, honey-lamb!"

"Me, too." I was stiff and self-conscious. This was good. Canadian males should be embarrassed at public displays of affection. It made me look all the more convincing.

"Gimme one more kiss," she said. She couldn't bear to leave the limelight without at least one encore.

I let her have it. Good as she was, this kiss was sedate by comparison. We both were beginning to realize that the other kiss had far more reality in it than the situation called for.

Kirby broke away. "This is Mrs. Garrison," she said, "and this is mah husband."

"I'm delighted to meet you," she said shyly. "I've heard so much about you."

"I found us a lovely apahtmint," Kirby said. I bent down to pick up my luggage. She grabbed the attaché case, talking enthusiastically about the apartment, the trees, the people she had met, how nice they all were. I let her take the case and I followed her out to the car. I didn't like her carrying it. And that shows you how stupid I was. I thought somehow she'd be less involved if she wouldn't have touched it. As if she wasn't in it already like someone caught in quicksand.

The Wilson car was parked carelessly at an angle to the curb, unlike every other car in the block. The parking meter said *Expired.* Leaning against the meter was a fat cop in wrinkled khaki pants and a dirty white shirt. He wore a western-style gun belt with a pearl-handled .45 low on his right hip. Sloppily pinned above his heart was a sheriff's badge. I could see it was a good one, a Blackinton, made out of 24-karat heavy gold plate with an anti-corrosion finish. They didn't care much for uniforms in Okalusa, but if all their police equipment was as good as the badge, it meant they had a good mayor or police chief. Well, maybe not good, but at least he took care of the boys.

He was wearing a cheap broad-brimmed straw hat. When he saw Kirby, he straightened up and tipped it.

"Afternoon, Mis' Wilson. I expect this is your car."

"Yes, it is, Mr. Hungerfo'd. I want you to meet mah husband. Mah husband, Hal Wilson, soon to be *Doctor* Wilson!"

He shook hands, looked at the angle parking, at the expired meter, and then grinned.

"Mebbe I better let it go," he said. "Mr. Wilson, welcome to Okalusa. Mebbe I better start callin' you Doctor right away."

"I—" I began, then stopped. I was speechless.

"They all take on like that, Mr. Wilson. Pay it no nevermind. You tell Mis' Wilson to park nice an' put in a dime now an' then in the meters, an' I wish you folks have a nice time in Okalusa." He tipped his hat and ambled ponderously away.

We drove past the courthouse square with the iron park benches and the usual statue of the Confederate rifleman. Then three blocks of stores and offices, then the residential district began.

"We have a lot of good houses here," Mrs. Garrison said. "A lot of planters like to live in town, it's so pleasant, an' there are so many things to do, not like those big lonely plantations with neighbors too far away. Mr. Garrison an' I, we owned one, but it got too big for us, an' there was a few bad years in a row. He knew cotton, an' when the guvvamint told him to div—div—diversify, he wouldn't. He said all he knew was cotton an' that was that. So the fourth year came an' we didn't have a penny. So we lost it all, but we did have the town house, an' now we rent it out upstairs an' maybe one or two rooms. We try to get a nice class of people, no children, an' that's why we're glad to get such nice people as you an' Mrs. Wilson."

Several blocks further we stopped at a big yellow frame house. Scrollwork ran all the way around the roof.

"Know what that is?" Kirby demanded. "That's Carpenter Gothic. That's why I picked this house to live in. You know why? Because that's the way the house where I was born looked like."

A wide veranda ran all around the house. A porch swing sat at one end, at a corner surrounded by four old magnolia trees. A huge live oak shadowed the second-story bay window. Kirby pointed to it and said, "That's our window!"

We walked up the walk. Mrs. Garrison thanked Kirby for the ride and left us in the hallway.

We went up the carpeted staircase. The room was big, with the bay window under the branches of the live oak. I stood there and watched a squirrel run up a branch, sit down, and stare at me with a look of astonishment.

Kirby said, "He wants to know what a Yankee is doin' in this house."

I smiled. The room possessed an enormous double bed with a quilted bedspread. Kirby said Mrs. Garrison's grandmother had stitched it together when times were bad after the Civil War. A smaller room to one side had a little desk and a couch. My study. I walked in and put the attaché case on the desk. The study had a worn Persian rug on the floor. It had once cost a lot of money. The room was immaculate. I heard birds in the tree. The light filtered through the branches and made a soft yellow glow on the desk. An old lamp with a green glass shade stood on the desk. I snapped it. It filled the room with a gentle light. It occurred to me that if I were really working on my Ph.D. I could not ask for a better place than this.

Kirby sat on the bed as I started to unpack. "We're in!"

she said. "They love me. I've apologized to everyone for you being a Canadian. They've forgiven me, specially since I told them that when you were in England—"

"Wait a minute," I said. "When was I in England?"

"Three years ago," she said promptly. "You were a Rhodes Scholar and you went to Oxford."

"All right. Go on."

"When you were in England, you saw how badly black immigration was working out. You don't like it, and you're glad that Canada has been spared this problem."

I was amused to see that when she became serious and when she was talking to me she lost her Southern accent.

"I play dumb Southern bunny with the sheriff. I've already asked him for road directions several times when any three-year-old idiot would have understood them the first time, but all Southerners like their upper-class women to look cool, elegant, and helpless."

I moved quietly to the door. I opened it suddenly. No one was there listening. I didn't think that Mrs. Garrison looked the type, but people in small towns have so little to do that even nice people kneel at keyholes to get material for gossip.

I came to the bed. Kirby sat motionless, staring up at me. I bent close to her. Later I could see how my actions might easily have been misunderstood by anyone. Her mouth parted and the color flushed her skin. "Oh Joe, oh, Joe—" she said, and put her arms around my neck.

I pulled them away. Her face flushed with embarrassment.

"From now on," I said quietly, "no confidences in the room. Maybe the Garrisons aren't nosy. We can't assume it. We have to assume that they are nosy, that the room will be bugged. The only time we can talk freely will be in the car, or when we're out walking alone in an empty street. All right?"

"All right." She was looking down at the rug and tracing

one of the arabesque patterns in it with her right shoe. "You wash up. I'll be back."

I had finished unpacking and had changed into a fresh shirt and slacks when she tapped on the door and came in with Mr. and Mrs. Garrison. He was a thin pale man with a full head of white hair and a shrewd, sour face. He congratulated me on my lovely wife. He said he knew a good woman when he saw one. That's why he grabbed Mrs. Garrison.

"When I married Ethelda-Grace," he went on, "she lived on one side of the Chickasaw an' I on the other. An' when I went to fetch her for the weddin' day, why, they'd been a flood an' all the bridges was down. So Ethelda stood on one side, all impatient in her sunbonnet an' umbrella, an' we were married on both sides of the river."

"Don't believe him," Mrs. Garrison said severely. "We were married in a house, like Christian people. Well, we'd best be getting along, Mr. Wilson. You want anythin', you jus' give a yell. I hope you enjoy livin' in Okalusa." They left.

"Nice people," I said. I stood up. "How about you giving me a lecture tour around Okalusa and the suburbs and then we'll go out for dinner?"

She was delighted. When she started the car, she said, "Are we casing the joint?"

"Yeah. We're casing it."

I thought that in my soon-to-arrive retirement it might be fun to build up a good library of books on slang and argot and cant. A man can't go out fishing twenty-four hours a day. Maybe books on English dialects as well. I could skip the queer symbols. It might be very interesting to look up the origin of criminal slang like "case the joint," for example. Why "case"? I remember once looking into the thirteen volumes of the *Unabridged Oxford English Dictionary* when I was killing time in the library of some rich client. When he came in, I asked him how much the set was worth. He told me he had paid three hundred dollars for it.

At the time I thought, who the hell could fork out three hundred bucks, just like that?

Well, I could. In about three weeks.

21

But when I got downstairs I felt as if I had been sandbagged. I had had too little sleep for two nights. That and the unaccustomed heat did me in. I went back upstairs, took my shoes off, and lay down on the sofa for a brief nap. When I woke up it was morning, there was a sheet over me to protect me from the early morning chill, and I smelled bacon a-fryin' in spite of what the mechanic had said about Milliken County.

Breakfast was ready. Thick bacon, cooked brown and crisp, corn bread sticks soaked with sweet butter, and superb coffee steaming on the table. And a tall glass of ice-cold orange juice, freshly squeezed.

"I'm sure glad I married you," I told Kirby.

"Oh, yes. I've nevah regretted it even a teeny lil bit."

We ate in silence. While she washed up, I took out the few papers and books from the educational side of my attaché case. I arranged them neatly on the desk in my study. Beside them I set the books she had taken down in the car. I put out a few pads of long yellow sheets of legal paper. It looked like a serious Ph.D. candidate was about to start work.

I picked up the case and we went downstairs to the car for my delayed tour of Okalusa. I tossed the case casually onto the back seat. It had become such a part of me that she didn't even really notice it. I wasn't worried about anyone opening it. It was locked. But I was getting tired of carrying it around, and I had better find a good place to hide the nasty contents.

The gas gauge was almost empty. "Let's gas up at your favorite station," I said. Several blocks east she pulled into a Texaco station. The guy there came out of a grease pit and gave her the big hello.

"I want you to meet mah husband, Mr. Sanderson," she said, with that eager little thrill in her voice I was beginning to realize she saved up for these occasions.

"Pleased to meet you, sir," he said. He didn't even look at me and I knew he didn't mean a word of it. I didn't blame him. Kirby was something special in those days. I suppose the excitement she felt in playing a role gave her a marvelous coloring. If she were around, I wouldn't waste time in looking at someone else.

He filled the tank, checked the oil, checked brake-level fluid, checked transmission fluid, cleaned the windows till they shone and sparkled. They had never been cleaned like that for the whole life of the car. He liked the front window especially because that gave him the chance to look at her the longest.

I asked her lazily, "Where did you fix the spare?" I had noticed early that morning that it was still flat.

Her mouth opened as she realized she hadn't had it fixed. "Oh, oh. I plumb forgot."

So I had Mr. Sanderson fix that. I noticed a rack of new tires. Below that was a rack of secondhand tires. I smiled. I had just solved a minor problem.

"Honey," I said, making sure that Sanderson was within hearing, "you've been driving out around town. How are the back-country roads?"

"Not good."

"Gas stations pretty far apart?"

She nodded.

"I think I better get an extra spare." Sanderson had

been listening. He tried to sell me the $31.95 special, a wide-track ground-gripper, mud-and-snow tire, guaranteed against all failures for thirty thousand miles. I listened patiently to this poor man's version of Harry Gilbert, Madison Avenue's contribution to the great thinkers of the twentieth century. I didn't want to make any enemies down here unless I had to. When he stopped for breath, I spoke.

"Gee, that sounds great! But I live on a student's budget, and I'm afraid I can't afford it. Would you have anything else?"

"We got some worn ones. They ain't so good, they—"

"If they're cheap, I'll take one."

He sighed and sold me one for four dollars. I picked one with extra-wide tread. He sold me an old rim for another four dollars. When I told him I needed a pump, he knocked two-fifty from a seven-fifty job and he threw in two rusty tire irons for nothing. So I was all set for my taped interviews anywhere in the county, as I assured him with a big, friendly grin.

We pulled out with Sanderson staring wistfully at Kirby. He reminded me of a big dog looking at a delicious bone hanging high out of his reach. I looked at her as we went through Okalusa. She took the barrette out and let the wind blow and whip her hair around her face. I didn't blame Sanderson at all. Here was this beautiful bone and I had very carefully stenciled it *Poison. Don't Touch.* My intelligence complimented me, but my body thought me stupid. I concentrated on the road.

I heard her chuckle. She had a deep contralto amused purr when she did that. I never had known any other woman with that same quality. She was looking at the long row of traffic lights that stretched down Main Street.

"Back home," she said, "there's a little ole town name of Shelby. Shelby's very poor an' they was real proud when they bought ten traffic lights for the main street.

They looked real pretty when they all were green an' red, an' the mayor used to stand at the window at City Hall an' look at them. They cost a mighty big amount. They hadn't been up a week when a twister came down Main Street an' took all those traffic lights an' took them four miles out of town an' dropped 'em in the swamp."

We were in the cotton country. She was looking out the window with her chin resting in the palm of her hand. She suddenly became serious. "I'm gonna sing you a song. You listen careful, now."

> *Oh, I'm a good old Rebel,*
> *Now that's just what I am,*
> *For this Fair Land of Freedom*
> *I do not give a damn!*
> *I'm glad I fit against it,*
> *I only wish we'd won,*
> *An' I don't want no pardon*
> *For anythin' I done.*

She looked at me from the corners of her eyes. She had sung it slowly and defiantly. She went on.

> *I hates the Constitution,*
> *This Great Republic, too.*
> *I hates the Freedman's Bureau,*
> *In uniforms of blue.*
> *I hates the nasty eagle,*
> *With all his brag an' fuss,*
> *The lyin', thievin' Yankees,*
> *I hates 'em wuss an' wuss.*

"That was written over a hundred years ago," she said. "An' the best way to understand the people down here is to realize they mean every damn word of it. Want some more?"

I nodded. She lifted her head and the defiant words came from her long throat:

> *I hates the Yankee nation*
> *An' everythin' they do,*
> *I hates the Declaration*
> *Of Independence, too;*
> *I hates the "glorious Union,"*
> *'Tis drippin' with our blood,*
> *I hates their striped banner,*
> *I fit it all I could.*

"Remember, Joe. They still mean it."

"Joe Dunne is number one," I said. "Are there any more verses?"

She nodded.

"Teach them to me," I said.

She sang two more stanzas. I filed them away for future reference.

We came to a crossroads.

The fields of cotton ended. The road ran through the swamp for three or four miles. Then there was a crossroads, a bridge over a little river bordered with cattails, a few splintered docks, and a little general store with a rotting front porch. Soft drink signs were tacked all over it and probably helped a lot in holding it together. A rusty gas pump was in front. A ramshackle beat-up pickup truck was parked beside the store with the back gate hanging down by one side. A sign was nailed above the side facing the road. It read: BAIT FRESH CATFISH.

Three Negroes who had been sitting on old kitchen chairs on the porch froze as the car stopped. When I got out, two of them stood up and got into the pickup and drove away. One of them remained in his chair. When I was a few feet away, he stood up and said, "Yessuh?"

"Can I get a cold drink here?"

"Yessuh!"

I followed him through the screen door. There were several big tears in it. He took two bottles right off the ice, opened them and handed them to me. I carried them out to the car and handed one to Kirby. I tipped mine back and let the ice-cold fluid run down my throat. I felt the blaze of the sun on my face as the soda went down.

"Why did you stop at this dirty ole place?" she asked.

I looked at her and said nothing. I took another long swallow. She said "oh" in a small voice and sipped hers.

Every time I took another sip, I looked up at the sign above the store. It said ALEXANDRIA POST OFFICE. And where was Alexandria but in Egypt land?

I took the empties and went back inside. The man was now in the back of the store reading a magazine. I had the feeling he wanted to place as much distance as possible between himself and any white person.

"My name is Wilson," I said. "I'm from Canada. I'd like to do some fishing for catfish. I've never tried catfish. I'm staying over in Okalusa. I wonder if I'd be back in an hour with some old clothes could you rent me a rowboat?"

"Ah sure could, boss."

"Thank you."

I got into the car and turned around. Kirby wanted to know what had happened to the drive.

"Tomorrow," I said. She felt left out. I told her I was going fishing.

"I want to come too," she said. "I c'n put worms on hooks an' fan you an' sing songs."

"Sorry." She turned sullen and stared out the window all the way back.

I dropped her at the public library with instructions to charm the librarian. Librarians in small towns are very good at spreading gossip. She brightened up at the assignment. I went home, changed into an old shirt, old slacks, and an old hat I used for fishing, put the Kim on the back seat, and threw in three old shirts. I headed back for the Alexandria P.O.

When I reached the swamp road, I pulled to one side. I would see a car coming for a mile in either direction. As for anyone being in the swamp on either side, I took a look at the impenetrable mass of cypress stumps. No rowboat could maneuver around them and be unnoticed by me. I put the jack under the axle and jacked the wheel up a few inches in case anyone should come by while I was working.

I let the air out of my just-purchased secondhand tire. With my tire iron I took the tire off the rim. I took the attaché case, put it in the trunk compartment, took a look at the road in both directions. No one coming. I took out the contents. I ripped up my old shirts. I wrapped each piece carefully and inserted them all into the old tire. I had been worried about the drum with its eight-inch diameter, but it went in easily into the wide-tread. I mounted it on the rim and pumped it up. Then I bolted it down in the trunk and tossed the good spare on top.

No one would think of looking inside a worn tire that was full of air. The spare on top was an almost new tire, and if some poor guy was hard-up enough to steal spare tires, that's the one he'd grab. I scrubbed off most of the grease from my hands with some weeds, and when I bent down to grab a handful more of them, I shot to one side like a frightened quail exploding out of cover.

But what I thought at first was a snake lying coiled at my feet was only the shed skin of a cottonmouth.

I put my hand on my heart. Boy, oh, boy, nothing wrong with your reactions, Dunne. My adrenalin was A-okay. My heart seemed to be pumping away eight hundred to the minute. I got behind the wheel, wiped my face with my forearm, lit a cigarette, and waited till my chest had stopped its wild hammering and settled down.

22

I rowed the battered old rowboat till I was out of sight. I wasn't interested in serious fishing. That could wait for a month or so. What I was doing in that river winding through the swamp was to convince the Alexandria post office that I was what I seemed to be, a speech expert who liked to fish.

I dropped the small radiator used for an anchor in a little bayou. I baited the hook with one of the worms the owner of the bait shack had sold me in a rusty tin can. I stuck the bamboo pole over the stern and watched the little cork make little ripples in the slow current.

From time to time I scraped a flattened tomato can along the bottom of the boat, emptying the water that kept slowly trickling in through the seams. I had three cans of beer along. I drank them slowly in the increasing, savage heat of midday, dropping the empties into the slow river. I was not a good citizen. I didn't flatten them first. I let the current take them and move them into the swamp. They swirled around a cypress buttress, into the current, banged gently against another cypress, and disappeared among the tangled jungle of vines.

The cork suddenly danced delicately three or four times and then went under with decision. I had caught my first catfish. In the next two hours I caught six good-sized ones. I strung them on a line tied to a screw-eye at the bow. A cool wind blew down the river, drying the sweat. I could hear frogs in the swamp. They wouldn't rattle windowpanes ten miles away, but some of them did have a good deep thrumming note, like a string being plucked on a big bass cello. A bird chirped somewhere. It was pleasant being someplace where there were no truck noises, no sound but the water sounds around the cypress knees, a frog or a bird.

The empty beer cans had disappeared. Maybe the boys were in the swamp somewhere. Maybe they were at the bottom somewhere along this peaceful little river with heavy iron weights tied to them. My forearms were burned red. It was time to go back. I pulled up the anchor and rowed back to the bait shack.

"That's a nice passel o' cats you got theah, boss," he said, with that rich, phony black laughter he saved for whites.

"I like that little river of yours."

"Yessuh. Lakes are fine, but they nevuh go anywheres. Take a river, it goes on, it lahk to work, to ramble around, an' see what's 'round the next bend. An' sometimes it gets real mad an' throws its weight around, but that's in the springtime when the snow melts up theah in the mountings."

I paid him for the boat and the bait and the beer. I handed him the string of fish. "They're yours," I said. His eyes widened with pleasure. "Mrs. Wilson wants to eat out tonight and they'll smell up the refrigerator if I keep them in overnight."

"Why, thank you, thank you." He was delighted. Mrs. Wilson, from the remarks I had heard her make about catfish, would have been delighted herself to make a meal of them, but it was more important for me to please this man than her.

I asked him to join me in a beer. He brought out two ice-cold ones, and he stood sipping his until I pushed a kitchen chair at him. He sat down on the edge of his chair with his knees together, but he had relaxed quite a lot from his earlier stiffness.

"Ah nevuh did see a car from—from—from wheah you

come from," he said. I was glad to see he had dropped the yessuh business.

"Quebec?"

"That's how you say it? From Queeebec."

He chuckled at the sound of the word.

"I came down to do some research on the way people talk around here."

"You what?"

I got the Kim from the car. I set it up on one of the kitchen chairs. "I use this tape recorder," I said. He didn't know what a tape recorder was. I switched it on and while he was asking questions, I taped him without his realizing it.

I played it back. He clapped his hands.

"Oh, Lawd, lissen!"

I bought two more beers and explained how the speech of Northern Mississippi was important to scholars.

I told him I paid five dollars an hour for people to talk to me and tell me stories. I told him if he would tell me how he rented rowboats and how he caught catfish and would tell me a couple stories about the catfish he had caught, I would pay him five dollars right on the spot. He was delighted. I taped him for forty minutes.

"Most city fo'ks nevuh eat the best part of a catfish," he said. "When they breed in the spring, parts of they muscles gits bigger behin' an' undah the eyes. These here chops are lahk jus' solid lumps of meat. They as big as the ball of your thumb, an' they firm, an' white, an' juicy. Man, they good!"

When the forty minutes were over, I gave him five dollars. I told him I paid the hourly rate even if it ran to less than an hour. So he had made from me, if you added the rent for the boat, the worms, the beer, and the five dollars, about twelve dollars with very little effort on his part. Plus the six fresh, free catfish. He was in a very good mood. When I told him I'd like to tape him again, he felt even better.

I began to pack up the Kim. When I was doing it, I said casually, "I hear there's a man around here who tells good stories."

Bait shack was cleaning the catfish. For a moment I thought he had clammed up, but then I realized he hadn't heard me. I repeated it. I added, "If he'd like to make some extra money—"

"Sure, Ah'll tell 'im."

"His name is Moe, or Moses, or something like that."

He chuckled. "That's Ol' Man Mose. He about ninety. He a conjure man. He sell yarbs to iggerant colored people."

"Yarbs?"

"Little plants good for sicknesses. But he smart, Ol' Man Mose is. He can't walk good; you'll have to go to him." He stood up and yelled, "Simon!"

A little kid with a ragged pair of blue jeans ran up from the dock where he had been bailing out my boat.

"Simon, you run to Ol' Man Mose. You tell 'im theah's a gennulman heah wants to give 'im five dollahs a hour jus' to lissen to 'im tell stories. Ah want you goin' so fast Ah c'n play checkers on your shirttail. Git!"

Simon took off like a rocket. We drank our beer till he came back, panting and sweating.

"Ol' Man Mose, he say—he say—" the kid was out of breath. He finally took a deep breath and got it all out. "He say, 'come.'"

I gave the kid half a dollar. His eyes bulged out in amazement. Well, that made two people I had made happy that afternoon. And maybe me, if Old Man Mose believed in an eye for an eye, a tooth for a tooth.

23

I drove slowly for five minutes on a very bad road. Occasionally the crown of the road scraped against the rear end. The fences were usually broken, the sides of the road choked with weeds, and cows stood in the road munching at the grass. The ruts were baked hard by the sun.

At an old oak the road made a sharp right turn. I climbed for a while and then, following directions, made a left onto an even worse road. After a few hundred feet I stopped the car. I was afraid of ruining the rear end. At the top of the hill was a shack where Old Man Mose lived. Sunflowers eight feet tall grew all around it. Oleander was blooming in the sun-baked yard. There was no grass. I stopped near a peach tree with a rotten trunk and called out, "Mr. Mose!"

A thin, black, wrinkled hand came out of the door and beckoned me to approach. It was covered with veins that stood out like ridges. The tendons and muscles and veins had barely enough skin to cover them. The fingers were long, the fingernails were long and sharp. I came up to the door, took off my hat, and entered.

It was dark inside. There was only one room, and across the farther end ran a window four feet across. Several strings stretched across it, each a foot or so higher than the one beneath it. Bunches of herbs were tied to them. Not much light filtered through. On the one plain table in the center of the room stood a kerosene lamp. The glass was polished clean, without any soot deposits. A green glass shade, with little flutings, was mounted on top.

"Those my simples," Old Man Mose said. His voice was strong for a man of ninety. He was sitting in an old rocker. He was very small and had a completely bald head. He had a stubble of white all over his chin, as if he had missed shaving for a few days. He wore an old-fashioned striped shirt held together at the throat with a gold-plated collar button.

"From the swamp?" I asked.

"Some on 'em."

He looked at me closely.

"An' some on 'em from de fields. You interested in de swamp simples?"

I shrugged.

"Wid 'em Ol' Man Mose kin cure faintin' spells an' seizures an' snakebite. You the gennulman what's givin' away money?"

I nodded.

"Ah'll take some."

I went to get the Kim. He watched me as I set it up on the scarred table. His eyes were bright and shrewd. As I worked, I looked around. On an old bureau next to the window sat a squat brown jug with two handles. Around the neck hung several strands of cheap, colored glass beads. From the strands two tassels hung down. Around the open mouth, almost like a necklace, was what looked like a crudely made charm bracelet, with all the charms made from tin. A rake, a hoe, a shovel, a scythe, and another shovel.

Next to it stood a small female figure ten inches tall. It was naked and was carved out of stone. It looked very old and worn. Her pointed breasts jutted out; her stomach was full and distended, as if she were pregnant. She wore a tiny little necklace of blue glass beads. The upper skull of some animal plus its upper jaw was tied against her back. An old string was passed through its eye sockets and then under her breasts. Holes had been drilled at the base of the skull to permit another string to he lashed around her knees. The skull had two enormous fangs, and between them rested her head.

From a nail driven into the wall another weird creation was hanging. It was an old piece of brown leather three inches in diameter. A silver loop two inches across had pierced the leather at the top. Hanging from the ring were two large wire hoops eight inches in diameter. Through another hole in the leather a two-inch length of some hollow-stemmed grass had been forced.

The lower jaw of some small animal which I did not recognize had been wired horizontally to the bottom of the leather. From the end of the jawbone fell three rawhide thongs. On the bottom of each one was tied a snail shell. A small length of worm-eaten wood had been slid onto one of the big metal hoops. It had slipped to the bottom of the hoop.

I turned aside from my staring. He had been watching me with a little smile. I set up the mike.

"We start now?"

"Your time started as soon as you said you'd talk."

His eyes widened.

"First, Mr. Moses—"

"Holt it. This here tape goin' to be listened to by a lot of people up there in Canada?"

"Yes."

"Then ah wants my name spoke. Mah name is Moses Howland Gardiner."

I started the tape. I said, "This is the voice of Mr. Moses Howland Gardiner, taped on the twelfth day of September, in his house in Milliken County. Mr. Gardiner, I'd like to start by asking you to tell me what you remember of your early days in Milliken County."

" 'At's easy. They got more religion an' less morals heah than anywhere else in de world. Over on de upper stretches of de river there's a man that claim he been daid an' come to life. He say he went to heaven for half an hour, an' he met Christ there, an' the man, he tell Christ about the road he had come an' how lonesome it was, an' he ask Christ, if that was really the road to heaven. 'Hit was all grass-grown,' he say. 'Hit must be very few ever go to heaven if that the road,' he say. An' Christ say, 'Yes, that de road to heaven, but that not de only road. That jus' de road from no'th'n Mississippi.' "

He looked at me with amused eyes. He was sharp and deferential. He was reserved and polite. His guard was up. I couldn't sense any opening anywhere that wouldn't result in his pulling in fast, like those little hermit crabs you see on the beach, dragging their shells behind them, like Ol' Man Mose with his rocking chair. I knew if I made a sudden grab he'd clam up solid.

He talked about the way he tended his garden.

"Ah'm a great hand to garden in de moon. Things that grow under de ground, lahk potatoes an' carrots, they want to be planted in de dark of de moon, an' things like beans an' peas that grown above ground want to be planted in de light of de moon. You c'n start potatoes side by side, some planted in de dark of de moon, an' some in de light of de moon, an' those you plant in de dark will be de bes' ever' time. That is de case."

I asked him casually what the things on the bureau were.

"That with de woman, she good luck from Obalufon. Obalufon, he makes de babies take a good shape so they be born healthy, not hunchback nor nothin' like that. That jaw with them big teeth, that a baboon. That come from Africa with my great-great-great-great—oh, I fergit how many greats ago, my grandmamma. Maybe three hundred years ago. It gits passed along from father to son wid its power. I got no son now; he got hisself killed ten years ago by some white man over to Montgomery. So I de only one wid its power. An' that, wid de leather an' old wood from de swamp an' de silver rings, real silver, an' de snails an' de snake's jaw, that a good luck charm 'gainst evil spirits."

"What evil spirits?"

His hands slid over the ends of the rocking chair arms. His palms began rubbing them in a slow, circular movement.

"Spirits in de swamp."

"Do people believe in that?"

"Oh, yes. People goin' in de swamp fo' deer or alligator they come to me fust. Ah lets 'em rub it. It keeps 'em from gettin' snakebit. Ah charges fifty cents an' it works. Ah knows it works 'cause Ah has no complaints. But de othuh conjure men, they gets complaints. Theah's Melvin Robinson, ovah to Gaines Creek. Theah's Dorothy Baker, she's only eighty-fo', she sells love simples. An' down to Okalusa, back of Morgan's Fun'ral Parlor, theah is Preacher Eugene. He blesses with the prayers of the Lord Jesus, but Ah don't hold with that atall."

"Why not?"

" 'Cause mah simples got African power, an' that am de best. Theah's plenty othuh conjure people 'sides those three, but Ah am de best. Mr. Morgan, he used to play 'round heah when he was a baby an' his daddy was a good friend to me, but he went to France in 'fo'ty-fo'' an' when he come back wid de Bronze Star he got too uppity an' one night he was lynched. Mr. Morgan promised me a real good fun'ral, better'n mah burial society, an' he say, regardless what the preacher might say, he bury mah conjure things wid me."

"What does the jug mean?"

He rubbed the rocking chair for a few seconds. He looked at me with a mocking smile. "That's nothin'. That's jus' pretty to look at."

The tape ran on. Neither of us spoke for a few seconds.

"You wastin' your tape, mister."

"Your pay goes on."

I stood up and fingered the swamp charm. I tapped the hanging snail shells. They banged against the wall.

"You interested in de swamp, looks lahk."

I said nothing. I fingered the jawbone.

"That from a cottonmouth. He bigges' one Ah ever saw."

"Did you get all these yourself?"

He didn't respond. "You plannin' on goin' in de swamp?"

"I might have to."

"Nobody to talk to in theah."

I shrugged.

"You want good luck?"

I dug out half a dollar.

"Put it on de table, boss."

I put it on the table. He put it in his pocket.

"Now, you jus' run yo' finger ovah ever'thin' in that charm, an' don't miss none, 'cause that spile the charm."

I did what he said. I put my heart in it. "Yessuh, that'll do it, that'll do it!" He laughed that rich, dark, phony black laughter they use only for white men.

"Mr. Gardiner."

The laughter still went on. "You won't be et by an alligator, or bitten by a cottonmouth, or—"

"You're too old to Uncle Tom it, Mr. Gardiner."

The laughter stopped short.

"Turn that thing off," he said. I switched it off.

"Yo're damn right Ah'm too old. Ah'm ninety-two or ninety-three, I fergit when Ah was born. You heavy, son, you press me inside." He put his hand over his chest. "Ah gives you de ol' darky talk 'cause 'at's safe. But Ah don't have to do that no more."

"That's right, Mr. Gardiner."

"You come into my house an' you done took off yo' hat. You de fust white man evah to do that. You calls me mistuh an' not uncle. An' Ah c'n tell you means it an' you ain't aimin' to sell me nothin'. What you after?"

"I want to know who killed those three boys."

"You know they was heah?"

I nodded.

"You know they was heah an' de sheriff heard 'bout it an' drove up an' came into mah house an' tole 'em to leave Milliken County by sundown?"

"No, I didn't know that."

"An' Thomas, one of de black boys, he from Syracuse, he tole de sheriff to git off mah property because they had done no crime an' Ah hadn't invited him in. An' when he say that, Ah was as much surprised as you would be if Ah was to pick up this lamp here on de table an' throw it at your head. An' that ole sheriff, he turned red like a turkey cock an' he drove off. A black boy tole him to git! He made me so proud! Ah ain't a shoutin' man, but he make me so proud Ah could jus' shout way ovah de highest hill you c'n see."

"And then?"

"An' then de white boy—he calls me Mr. Gardiner too—and de two black ones, they laugh an' laugh. An' they decide to go down to de river an' cotch a passel o' catfish an' cook 'em later. They drove away to de river an' that's de last I seen on 'em, to this day."

I let out my breath.

"You're sure they're dead?"

"Ah'm sure. You fixin' to do somethin' 'bout it?"

"Mr. Gardiner, as you know, I'm only a speech expert."

He sailed ahead like the *Queen Elizabeth* riding over a rowboat.

"Now, there's Mr. Isaiah Thomas, he lives mebbe a quahtah mile down de road from Ryerson. Ryerson, he pretty old to be ridin' 'round Milliken County in a bedsheet. But thutty, fo'ty years ago he used to be pretty spry. Now, Mr. Thomas, he heahs three, fo' cars turnin' in to Ryerson's place 'bout three in de mawnin'. Ryerson ain't sociable. He don't lahk no one. Mr. Thomas, he go out and walk down de road. After a while they all come out of de house an' go to de melon patch with a flashlight an' then they all go back to de house an' then drive away. Now that ain't much, you say. People like melons, they go git some. 'Specially when they gits 'em de same night de boys went fishin'. 'Pears to me effen Ah was you, Ah might feel a hankerin' fo' a big juicy slice of melon. Ah jus' might."

I said nothing.

"Do you know when I can visit Mr. Thomas?"

A strange look came over him. I realized that he now was seriously regretting being so open. It was the easy money, the courtesy, and the feeling that I was a white who wanted to do something. He had temporarily forgotten that whites were not to be trusted; and that, even if I were an exception, I might start something official in which he would be swept up helplessly.

"Mr. Thomas?"

He was playing for time while he planned how to get out of it. I've often seen the same look on stool pigeons who were willing to talk some but not too much.

"Mr. Thomas," I said patiently.

"Mebbe you bettah not see him."

"I could say I've talked with you."

Yes, he was probably thinking, your big ofay mouth could get both of us into serious trouble; you're down here for a few days and we have to spend our lives here.

"Mr. Thomas would be 'fraid Mr. Ryerson would see you, an' Mr. Ryerson owns Mr. Thomas' land. 'Sides, de white folks would git to talkin' 'bout you seein' me an' seein' him."

I didn't want to push him anymore. It was clear that he had gone as far in that direction as he would go.

I nodded and stood up.

"You goin' to see Mr. Thomas?"

"No, I don't think I need to."

A wave of relief swept over his face. I gave him five dollars. As I was packing up the Kim, he felt apologetic.

"You wants to know 'bout de brown jug?"

"Yes."

"That is a shrine of Oya."

"Oya?"

"Oya is de Goddess of Death. Ah'll git her a new necklace in town. She might want to look nice befo' she steps out."

24

I got in the car and drove away. I felt as if I were trying to run across a field covered with two feet of molasses.

I was getting mad at the slow approach I had to make to everything. I'd never had to look for murderers when I left the police. It was always adulterers or swindlers or con men or missing persons. Sort of safe. I wanted to get all this over with, and here I was, taking careful little dance steps in front of Old Man Mose, as if we were some kind of birds in a mating ritual. He had not felt much like joining me. He was interested, that was all. No, that wasn't it. He was very much interested, but not enough to get up and waltz around the dance floor with me.

But I would have to be careful. There would have to be a lot more careful spinning of fine wires all over the county. To each wire I would tie a little wooden float. And then I would wait to see which one bobbed down. I would have to go around setting my lines and making sure I would have an easily handled fish under the float that was bobbing. Not an alligator. The country was full of alligators. You could get killed with alligators. I preferred it the other way round.

I parked at the curb and dragged out the recorder. I climbed the stairs up to the porch slowly. I went down the hall and then began to go up the staircase. I liked the smell of cooking that hung over the stairs. I suppose the old carpet covering the stairs had been absorbing all the food smells that had ever come out of the kitchen. There was fried chicken and ham hocks and black-eyed peas and pork roasts and catfish and corn sticks woven into that carpet. I took a deep breath just as Mrs. Garrison came out of the kitchen and looked upwards at me.

"Good smells, Mrs. Garrison."

She beamed.

"My, my," she said, "doesn't that machine get awful heavy?"

"It sure does."

"Now you set that thing right down there on the landin' an' come down for coffee, y' hear?"

She went back into the kitchen. I set it down and went downstairs, flexing my fingers. I was going to play the serious scholar.

A tall glass of iced coffee waited for me on the kitchen table. I sat down and sipped it. She had a big old electric fan mounted on a wide windowsill. It swung slowly back and forth and made a sleepy hum that I liked. It was very relaxing just to sit there after the heat of the back roads, listening to the fan and her amiable gossip.

"You what?" I asked.

"I said, I never heard a tape recorder, Mr. Wilson." I went upstairs and brought it down. I started it at Old Man Mose. I might get an interesting reaction from her. Old Man Mose began to tell the story of the man who died and went to heaven.

Her mouth turned sour.

"That'll be Ol' Man Mose," she said. Her hand made

a wiggling motion of distaste. I kept the tape running a little while longer, but when I saw she was not interested, I shut it off.

"He's a *bad* man," she said.

"Him?" I faked all the incredulity I could muster. I was the wide-eyed innocent, believing all people were basically good. "That nice old man?"

Mr. Garrison came in with a surprised expression. "Good afternoon, sir," he said. "I could've sworn I heard Ol' Man Mose in here—"

"Mr. Wilson has him talkin' heah on his machine."

He let out a breath.

"You talked to that ole devil?"

"Sure," I said. "A very nice, amusing old man, I thought."

" 'Ole man' is all I'll go along with you with, Mr. Wilson. He's a hard man, an' I've seen the niggers shake hands with the minister after church on Sundays an' then head straight for his house an' come out with love potions an' worse. They're all a mite scared of him. Once in a while people who offend him, they jus' take to their beds an' lose weight an' stop eatin'. When the doctor can't help them, they send to Ol' Man Mose an' maybe he'll take off the curse an' maybe he won't. It gen'rally costs plenty. But when he gets money, people get better. Sometimes I think it's poison he gives 'em, 'an sometimes I think he really puts on a curse. He must have a lot of money buried somewhere under the floor of his house. He don't use the bank at all."

"You seem to know him well."

"He an' my dad grew up together. They were born practically the same month. They ate together in the kitchen. Ol' Man Mose's mother was our cook. The boys swam together an' stole watermelons an' pecans together an' went fishin' together. An' my father told me somethin'; it's true for me an' if you live here long enough, you'll find it's true for you. It's like this: Equality isn't safe. Now you take Ol' Man Mose. He loved my father an' my father loved him. My father remembered him in his will. But if my father had taken him into his family and raised him like a white man, he'd a murdered my father in three days. They always do just that when you get to favorin' 'em."

"Al!" Mrs. Garrison said suddenly. "The card!"

"What card?"

She pulled out the kitchen drawer. It was filled with pens, old bottles of dried ink, bills, bank statements, and old greeting cards. She rummaged through it and tossed something on the table. He read it aloud.

The Chickasaw River Country Club requests the pleasure of your company for a dance, to be held Saturday, August 27. 8:30 p.m.   R.S.V.P.

"Now, Al," she said, "that jus' came in the mail this mornin'. We never go, but that nice Mrs. Wilson, I thought she'd love to go. We'd get you in 'stead of us as our guests. Now that would give me much pleasure, Mr. Wilson."

It would give me a lot of pleasure, too. What we had been lacking was circulation among the upper classes. Acceptance by them would gain me some more respect—maybe some resentment—among the poorer people. But any suspicion about me would be deflected when they'd hear about me at the country club. So I said I'd be delighted. I called Kirby and she came downstairs with her eyes sparkling at the news.

"Now you wait right here. I'll call Rich Cravens. He's the club secretary." She dialed while Kirby played the thrilled young housewife.

"Richard? We're fine, thanks. Yes, we got the invitation, but we're not goin'. Now, Richie, you know we're gettin' too old, but we'd like to give our invitation to a nice young couple stayin' with us. He's a professor an' Mrs. Wilson's a nice girl from Georgia." She covered the mouthpiece and whispered, "He says he heard about you…Why, thank you, Richie!"

She hung up and beamed. "He says he'll be delighted!" Kirby hugged her. I excused myself and went upstairs to take a shower.

Things were moving well in that direction. I put on my pajamas, spread the sheets on the couch, and picked up a fifteen-dollar book on regional English dialect transformation. I was too tense to sleep. I never took sleeping pills or tranquilizers. I was finding out that books on obscure dialects had the same effect. After a few minutes I dropped the book on the rug and turned out the lamp on the end table.

In a few minutes Kirby came in quietly and tiptoed across the room. I heard the shower running. I tried to make my mind a blank, but I could just see the water running over her breasts and down her flat stomach. Her skin would have a golden light full of high spots because of the soap and water.

I lit a cigarette and interlaced my fingers at the back of my neck. I tried to think of other things—of standing up to my hips in the warm green water off Marathon Key trying for bonefish, or of the hammerhead shark that used to drift under the pier north of Clearwater and scare away all the small fish.

I stared at the ceiling. There were no interesting patterns on the ceiling I could trace to hypnotize myself to sleep. Maybe Old Man Mose had a juju I could use. He might even have a simple. And I would bet it would be just as effective as a tranquilizer. And organic. There would be no chemical residue left in my tissues to raise hell with my chromosomes. I must have chuckled because Kirby called out from her bed.

"What's funny?"

"Oh, nothing."

She got up and came, pulling on a blue robe of some thin material. Her hair was not in curlers.

"Oh, come on," she said, sitting on the end of the couch and lighting a cigarette in the dark. "You know you can't jus' laugh an' tell your wife nothin's funny. It just ain't friendly."

"I can't sleep."

"I thought you were a hardened veteran."

"I am. I still can't sleep."

Her behind felt warm and firm on my toes.

"Joe, what's going on?"

"One reason why you're getting so much money is that I won't have to tell you anything."

"Are we in danger?"

"Not with normal luck."

"Am I supposed to fall into a relaxed sleep with that answer?"

"For five hundred a week you can afford to sleep lousy."

She disregarded that. "Joe. Am I being some kind of an accessory?"

That was an interesting legal point she was bringing up. I didn't think she was one, either before, during, or after. The state would have to prove she had full knowledge of what was going on and what my purposes were. I could protect her by not letting her know. If they'd ever give her a lie-detector test, she'd come out ahead. The trouble was that she would now want to know more than ever what was going on, and if I wouldn't tell her, she was smart enough to piece it together from keeping her eyes and ears open. And as far as Milliken County was concerned, they wouldn't give a damn about legal definitions. A shotgun poked into a car window after we'd been run off the road would be a duly constituted court.

"You're not any kind of an accessory." That was legally debatable, but it was my position.

She made little circles with her toes on the rug.

"Joe, if I'm more than camouflage, I have the right to know what kind of a situation I'm in."

Sure she had the right. I had thought, however, that I could buy her silence and make her keep her fears to herself for five hundred a week. She was more than camouflage. Her advice in most matters was excellent. And perhaps the legal boundaries as to being an accessory were getting very thin here.

She exhaled slowly.

"If I wind up being dragged before some judge or other, I have the right to know what I'm doing."

"Who pays what I'm paying for legal services?" I burst out. "Goddammit, you knew that when you started!"

"All right, Joe. I'm a woman and I just changed my mind."

"And I'm exercising my male privilege and I don't feel like answering."

"All right. New topic. How are things going?"

"Lousy. Thanks for asking."

"My pleasure. Good night."

She stood up and looked down at me for a moment. She was hurt and she was mad. The blue robe hung open. Her breasts were pushing against the thin white nylon nightgown. The walls were thick, the bed in her room was solid; it had a firm box spring and a good mattress. The Garrisons were not hanging around the hallway eavesdropping, and their bedroom was downstairs and at the other end of the house.

I wanted to pull her back and pull her nightgown up and kiss her knees. Just for starters.

But it was better for her to go away hurt. It would force her to keep her mind on her work. And I was a man expecting to run fast pretty soon. How does that old proverb go? *He runs fastest who travels alone.*

Scarcely an original thought. But it had pith. Pith is a

stupid word. You can make bad puns with it. But pith it had, nevertheless.

I watched her walk back to her room. I watched her close the door. Then I watched the thin slab of golden light at the bottom of the door. Then it went out.

Dunne, you son of a bitch. You were noble. But try to sleep now—if you can.

25

Next morning I was about five miles west of Okalusa, drinking a Coke in a gas station. I heard a faint roar far down the road. It quickly became a scream. I shoved open the screen door in time to see a yellow blur go by. The noise bursting from its twin chrome-plated exhaust pipes was so high-pitched that it sounded like the blare of a bugle. I had never seen a car go so fast outside of a racetrack.

"Jesus Christ Almighty," I breathed. The owner of the gas station hadn't even gotten off his chair.

"That'll be Ray," he said calmly.

"The bus driver?"

"Yep. He cain't do over sixty with the bus or he'll git fired, so on his days off he goes up an' down here considerable faster. He built that car hisself outta junk parts."

Ray was someone I might get involved with in a business way someday. He chatted away. I drank the rest of my Coke thoughtfully, paid for my gas, got into the car, and looked at the speedometer. After all, Milliken County's specialty was forcing strangers' cars off the road into a ditch and shotgunning them.

The number at the extreme right end said 110. I had best make sure it was telling the truth. I got out and had the guy get her up on the lift. The king-pins, the linkage, and all the front-end steering was okay. The tires were good.

The lift hissed and she came down. He refused my offer to pay for his services, and I drove off with a wave of my hand.

I drove to a road that ran straight as an arrow through the swamp. No side roads, no intersections, just a deep, wide ditch on both sides. No deer could make a sudden leap out of the bushes and wind up going through my windshield, flailing around with its razor-sharp hooves.

I wanted to find out what I had under me and what it would do when I might ask it to sit up and stretch out.

I pushed the accelerator to the floorboard. She picked up speed like frozen glue, coughing like an old man with bronchitis. Then she began to go to work. Reluctantly. At fifty the steering began to wobble a little.

It could do eighty-three. Eighty-three wasn't bad. But it wouldn't do in Milliken County, where the kids began to fool around with Wolverine push rods and Mickey Thompson pistons at an age where Northern kids were graduating from stickball games into poolhalls.

The gas station man had told me that Ray's yellow rocket had a big 401-cubic-inch Buick engine mounted on a '31 Ford Model A chassis. It had a Hilborn injector atop a GMC 4-71 supercharger, and all that power was being transmitted to the ground via a pair of M and H Racemaster 9.00 by 15 tires.

Eighty-three? What I needed was a simple Ford chassis with a Chrysler engine cunningly hidden inside it, and some of the glamorous accessories hanging around at the Mille Miglia.

And with that I might be able to walk away from anything the county could produce. The only trouble was that I couldn't see how a poor scholar like me might have such a jalopy. So I would have to live with that 83 m.p.h.

albatross slung around my neck with the hope that I would play my cards right, and ease out of Milliken County as easy as a ripe apple falling from a tree—when the time came.

26

Two evenings later we drove to the country club. Kirby was driving. Washboard roads and mud can tire your back and shoulder muscles when you spend all day on them.

I slumped down in the seat beside her and looked at the top of the magnolia trees that were sliding by overhead. They lined the winding drive that led to the club. Every hundred feet another lamp lit up the dark green leaves. A moon hung low on the horizon like a big yellow balloon.

"How did it go today?"

"Umm."

"No, really."

"All right. I'm getting sick and tired of going into crossroads grocery stores where the blacks who come in take off their hats and wait to be spoken to by some tobacco-chewing slob who lets them know he's going to finish reading the paper or serve some white first who came in after them. It sort of spoils the air."

"An' all you want from now on is beautiful people?"

I waved a hand.

"Just bring me beautiful people," I said.

She was wearing a green dress. I had never seen the dress. She looked like a million dollars in it. I rolled my head against the back of the seat to look at her again. Her hair was exactly the same color as the low yellow moon.

Kirby parked in the lot back of the club. It had a graveled surface raked in neat parallel lines. Trash bins were placed at regular intervals around the edge. It was full of Caddies and Jags. The patio was filled with tables, each one with a hurricane lamp and a candle burning inside. Trees in the patio were festooned with lights.

As soon as we stepped through the French doors opening into the club, a man came up and greeted us. He had the most sincere handshake I had ever encountered up till then. I thought I had left those kind of greetings behind when I eliminated Harry Gilbert from my circle of associates.

"And you must be the Wilsons!"

My hackles rose. They're the small hairs at the back of your neck and you can actually sense them sort of stirring when you're angry if you can bend your mind to it next time you feel mad. I guess it's an inheritance from our animal days when we used to erect our fur to make us look bigger and more threatening. Since I wanted to make everyone like me, I was glad those pre-dinosaur days were over. Else he would have known right away that I would have liked to sink my fangs in him. There must be something prehistoric in me which can't stand the Harry Gilbert sort of person. I don't know why it is. I will admit it's a serious defect; lots of people don't object to that warmth even though it's produced by forced draft. They even feel flattered.

I suppose it's because I don't like being handled as an object. Because that's what these people do, they regard everyone as a sort of a bolt that moves along an assembly line. You take the bolt, shove it through a properly machined hole, twist a nut onto the other end, give it nine turns with a wrench and there aren't any problems from the bolt. It's even supposed to like being treated like the other bolts. And it's supposed to love the sensation of having a nut squeezed against it.

I haven't been machined. I don't want to be treated as a great guy when I might be a son of a bitch. I don't give out love when I'm stroked that way. I'm not a cow's udder to yield milk when someone smiles at me. As far as the country club was concerned, I might very well be harboring evil thoughts.

But I put on a very convincing smile when he was pressing the flesh.

"I'm Rich Cravens the third," he said, and beamed.

"Third what?" I asked, puzzled. I was pushing it, and Kirby nudged me warningly. She was right. I had better ingratiate myself and not try to be funny.

"Why, Rich Cravens the third," he repeated carefully. He explained that his grandfather had the same name, and so had his father. That made him the third, he went on. I listened patiently while he made it clear.

"I'm the club secretary. Mrs. Garrison told me to take special care of you two fine people, an' that is what I'm goin' to do, you can bet on that! You come 'long now, y' hear?"

He took Kirby by her left hand and me by my right. He still hadn't let go of it from the time he had begun to shake it. He must have been operating on the principle that if seizing one hand is good, grabbing two is better.

He took us into a huge room. There were handsomely draped curtains at the windows and on either side of the French doors, and three big chandeliers with thousands of crystals. Buffet tables lined one wall. Chairs were grouped around low tables filled with fresh flowers in vases, and two bars were busy working. People wandered in and out with drinks in their hands, nodding pleasantly as they passed.

He draped a heavy arm around my shoulders. I don't like to be touched. I held back an impulse to throw it off. He put his arm around Kirby. That one I really wanted to fling away.

She sent me a quick warning glance. I rearranged my face into a shy, amicable look. He took us to the bar and presented us with mint juleps in iced silver mugs, introduced us to the few couples at the bar and waved a fat hand and disappeared.

After two juleps I found myself talking to him once more. He had circled around the room and had returned with a tall red-headed man and a thin, sulky, dark woman. She had short black hair, a deep cleavage, and several necklaces.

"I looked all around," Cravens said, with one heavy arm draped around me once more and the other arm around the shoulders of the red-headed man. "An' I brought two of ouah members ovah. Mr. an' Mrs. Owen Brady!"

Brady looked at Cravens with distaste. Mrs. Brady looked at Cravens' arm as if it were a snake. He took it off and clasped his hands together and stood there, flushing. No one said anything. I felt affection for the Bradys.

Kirby said immediately, "I think this place is simply marvelous!" I could recognize her instinct for saving situations. Mrs. Brady gave her a sour look.

Cravens said, "Mrs. Wilson, we're real proud of the club. We think we're pretty advanced in just about everythin' we do here. We—"

"Sure," Mrs. Brady said. "Where are the black members?"

"Well," he went on, "I'm an upholder. That's what I am. I'm an upholder of tradition."

"Of course."

"I mean, I can't allow any niggers in here. An' I'm not prejudiced. I want you to un'er'stan' that. I am not at all prejudiced. It's only that I've got to stand in with the old traditions."

"You betcha," Mrs. Brady said. "Then how come they're out there parking cars and in here serving drinks?"

"Oh, well," he beamed, "anytime any one of them

wants to work here, they're welcome if we have a job openin'."

Mrs. Brady cocked an amused eye at me.

"Richie boy," she said, "you know what you are? You are stupid."

Brady looked amused but embarrassed. Cravens said, as if in total explanation, "Mrs. Brady is from Milwaukee, Wisconsin."

"Well, for Christ sake, what other Milwaukee is there?" she demanded. She turned to me. "I ask you, don't you get tired of people who always tack on the state? You ask them where they're from and they say, 'Los Angeles, California.' Or they say something you never knew, like 'New Orleans' —now hear this startling news—'Louisiana.' " She turned back to Cravens. "Come on, Rich, give the man credit for knowing some geography!"

He said uneasily, "Well, folks, I got to circulate."

Mrs. Brady folded her arms and stared at him as he disappeared. When he was mingled with the dancers, she said feelingly, "Jesus."

She turned to me. "What do you think of *that*, Wilson?"

I grinned. Kirby said to me, "Darlin', would you like to get me a puffectly delicious sandwich, honey?"

Mrs. Brady stared at her, loathing stamped on her face. I murmured, "Excuse me," and left for the buffet table.

Owen Brady was standing there eating a roast beef sandwich.

"What do you think of our local fun an' games?"

"Nice people."

He had a wide, friendly smile. I liked him.

"An' what do you think of our local Babbitt?"

"He seems very pleasant."

"You know, Mr. Wilson, under that bland no-offense position which you feel you must assume, I seem to sense that you think he's a pain in the ass."

"No comment."

A small man entered the room. He moved across the floor, stopping and chatting from time to time. He emitted a feeling of power the same way that radiators give off heat. He would give that impression, I felt sure, even if he were alone in a room, but what made it very clear was the way the people he talked to would hold themselves. Their upper torsos were always bent a little toward him, as if they were on the verge of bowing.

"Who's that?"

Brady had been idly shaking an ice cube around and around in his glass.

"Who?" His back was to the man.

"The one everyone's groveling in front of."

"Why, I can answer that without turnin' around. That is A.B.C.—Amory Blanding Carlyle. He's small an' has smooth white hair. Am I right?"

"Yes."

Brady turned.

"He important?"

"You might say that. He owns the best farms, the best plantations. He owns the best banks. He controls all the political patronage in northern Mississippi. No one goes to the legislature down in Jackson or goes to Congress from around here or sits in the governor's chair without his lil ole permission."

"He looks like it would spell trouble if he was crossed."

"Understatement of the year. He isn't the best educated man you ever saw, an' he's a damn sight smarter than nine tenths of the college grads around here. An' just about everyone down here's afraid of him."

"You're not joking?"

"A man who controls the patronage controls the tax assessors. So he can break any farmer or property owner or industrialist he wants. Any black man who starts out in business an' does too well or shows signs of friendship to the NAACP will find it's real hard to get along. The labor or health inspectors will keep findin' violations. An' when he wants to renew licenses, he'll run into all sorts of trouble. He doesn't like women. He doesn't like men, either. He doesn't like food. He only likes politics."

I watched the deferential smiles flowing around A.B.C. as he approached us.

"Look at the bastard! He's as well-adapted to the Southern rural environment as an alligator is to livin' in a muddy river."

Brady went on, eyeing A.B.C. sourly. "Now, an alligator is downright interestin'. Sometimes, after a good meal, it'll set on a bank and open its jaws wide. There's a little bird that hops inside. An' this bird pecks at the lil bits of meat between those long, sharp teeth. The alligator lets them clean out what they can find."

"And these are the birds?"

"Some are. Some would like the honor."

Brady went on about alligators. He knew a great deal about them. I listened, fascinated.

Brady filled his glass and went on.

"A man like A.B.C. has got to keep his power base in line. He does it pretty easy. He does favors for those poor whites, an' they vote for him an' keep the blacks from the polls. It works all right for everybody. If the blacks ever get to vote, they'll just jerk that nice comfortable rug right from under A.B.C. So to keep settin' on it, he sort of helps along the White Citizen's Council."

"With money?"

"You're damn well right, with money. Here's the old son of a bitch now, sneakin' up on us."

"Evenin', Owen."

"Evenin', Amory."

"How's my lib'ral opposition?"

"Fixin' to get you one of these days."

"Anytime you want to spread around what the Voter Registration nigras say 'bout me, go right ahead. You jus' write a big long letter to the papers."

"You know they won't print it, Amory."

"Goodness me! Why won't they?"

"Any other jokes for tonight?"

"Nope. You might consider printin' leaflets an' stickin' 'em in all them rural mailboxes, Owen. No one'll read them 'round here, 'cept you and eleven others."

"I'm glad you pay it no never-mind, Amory. You'd have trouble with them big two-syllable words I'd be usin'."

A.B.C. grinned. He turned to me. "Evenin', sir."

"Good evening."

Now that he was close, he had the same feeling of power held in check that Parrish had.

"Visitin', sir?"

"Yes, Mr. Carlyle. I'm doing research in Southern speech for my Ph.D. project."

"You're the feller goin' around tapin' my dirt farmers?"

"Yes."

"Any time you want to tape a Southern reactionary politico, you tell Owen here an' he'll arrange it. I hope you like it down here?"

"Yes, sir. I like the people very much. Everyone has been helpful."

"Yes." He had wide, pale eyelids. The little blood vessels glowed in them. "We're a hospitable people. Owen, you come on over on the seventeenth an' bring Mr. Wilson along. I hear there's a Mrs. Wilson."

"There she is."

He looked at her dancing with Cravens.

"A handsome woman. I hear she's from Georgia."

"Yes, sir. It's a Northern victory, but since I'm Canadian I hope you'll forgive me."

He clapped me on the back. "You be sure to bring her,

now!" He left and resumed his slow, triumphant tour of the room.

"He's got a sort of charm," I said.

Brady gave me a dry, ironic look.

"Remember those three kids who were killed down here?"

"Those Voter Registration volunteers, you mean?"

"Yes."

"Sure. But how do you know they were killed?"

"Oh, come on, Wilson. This is the South, and this is Mississippi, it's not Connecticut or Wisconsin. The last night they were officially in existence, if that's the approach you prefer, they were arrested by the sheriff for exceedin' the speed limit inside the town limits of Okalusa. That isn't plausible, because these VR people are very careful not to give any police officer the slightest excuse to get picked up. Now, the word I get around here is that the sheriff held the boys until he got off a few phone calls. While the kids were in the cells, he went out an' broke the right-hand bright light bulb in their car. They paid their fine an' he released them. Two cars were waitin' for them three miles south of town; they recognized the car because of the single headlight, an' forced it off the road. The sheriff followed a minute later. When the FBI came by an' asked to look at the police blotter, there was no mention on it of the arrest. Nothin'. An' why?"

"Why?"

"Your friend and mine, Amory B. Carlyle, had told the sheriff not to enter any arrest on the blotter without askin' him first. Without any official record of the arrest, it's awful hard to prove any official connection with the murders. That's Amory's charm for you. You just keep your head out of his jaws."

"Ummm."

"You don't sound convinced."

"Well, local gossip, you know. People like to believe lots of powerful mysterious people control all sorts of power."

"You think mine is a typical case of the conspiracy theory of history as applied to Milliken County?"

I didn't think so at all, but expressing doubt about something is a fine way to get someone to spill more.

I shrugged my shoulders.

He shrugged, too. Maybe he thought he had been talking too much.

"Your funeral," he said, not knowing how close he was coming. He sipped his drink. "How's life up in Canada?"

"It's all right, I suppose. Good fishing. When I have some extra money—which is hardly ever—I fly up north and hunt caribou. Aside from that I find this Southern environment much more interesting; the cooking, the people. Things like that."

"It is better down here. I tried livin' up North for a couple years outside Milwaukee. My wife's home town. Couldn' stand the cold an' those cold Northern faces an' lookin' at TV all night an' no one sayin' 'thank you' when I held the door open for people. Missed the warmth an' the friendliness you'll find down here even between a man who'd shoot his sharecroppers for votin' but who'd go out huntin' coon with 'em. It's a complex thing out here. Don't know where it's goin'. You show you've got good intentions towards blacks—that's the new word, right?—and they'll back off. They don't trust us. Why should they? They can't level with us. Too many centuries of deviousness between us. An' we remember what happened when they ran the legislatures the three, four years after the Civil War. The feet on the desk, the bribes, the corruption, the arrogance. But in a way I can't blame them. Not after two hundred years of slavery. That's what it came to in eighteen sixty-five. An' I'll take some of the blame. Well, that's enough of a speech. We ought to shoot us a couple turkeys up in the hills next weekend."

"I think I'd like that."

"Good. I'll phone you in a day or so an' we'll make it definite."

He shook hands decently. I liked him. I liked the idea of rambling around the woods with him hunting turkey.

I turned toward the buffet table and began to assemble a heaping plate of rare roast beef, slices of onion, little plum tomatoes, and pickles. I filled another plate with tossed salad.

"You like spiced crab apples?"

Mrs. Brady was standing next to me. She was a bit unsteady but holding it very well. She must have had at least four drinks by then. She put a hand on my arm to steady herself.

"Sure, thanks."

She reached out, grabbed a fork, speared two crab apples, and shook them off onto my plate. The juice splashed onto the sleeve of my jacket.

"Ooops!" she said.

"No problem."

" 'No problem!' Listen, buster, it's a problem. Say it's a problem. Say I'm a drunken bitch. But don't stand there and be bland. Be honest!"

"And frank and spontaneous."

She speared another crab apple and dumped it onto my plate. She said, fluttering her eyelashes, "Oh, Mr. Wilson, Ah think you'll find these puffectly delicious!"

"You don't have much fun living in Okalusa, do you?"

"I don't have much fun living period. How could you ever marry a Southerner?"

I noticed that a few couples were listening with that here-she-goes-again look.

"She's a great girl."

"All right, she's a great girl, but what about that awful,

cloying Southern accent? How can you stand it? You seem intelligent, but admit it, buddy, you certainly screwed up on that one." She dumped two more crab apples on my plate humming, "puffectly, *puffectly* delicious!"

"I'm going to get a demerit from you," I said, in a jolly tone, "but I like her accent."

"Don't talk to me the way people are supposed to talk to drunks, goddam you!"

This was the time when a good husband should appear and take her home. He wasn't around. I could tell from the way that the nearby couples were edging away that she was close to her lift-off time. I couldn't see any way to ease out gracefully.

Kirby saved me again. She appeared at my elbow. "Mr. Wilson," she said, "you dragged me here sayin' you were goin' to dance with your wife. Who's your wife?"

"You, baby."

"Dance with me," she said, lifting her arms. I put my plate down.

"Excuse me," I said to Mrs. Brady. "Duty calls."

"Funny, funny," she muttered. She waved a hand without a ring but covered from wrist to elbow with about thirty narrow silver bracelets.

"Take him," she commanded. "But I'll be waiting for him."

Kirby smiled at her but muttered "Yankee bitch," under her breath.

I grinned. Kirby had strong back muscles. I felt them flow like live little things under my palm. I didn't want to talk about Mrs. Brady. I found her a bore. She was like a million other bored country-club wives. They were the ones I had to catch in compromising situations up North, and I didn't want to handle another one down here. I was holding something unique in my arms and I wanted to concentrate on it.

"Ummm," I said.

"She must be quite a handful for poor Owen."

"Yeah."

"What should poor Owen do?"

"He ought to be a little mean. Open the door on the hinge side once in a while. But it's too late. Now he's stuck with her till she sleeps with one too many visiting firemen. The local code demands that he kill the both of them."

"Will he?"

"My guess is that he will, then commit suicide."

"I think you're right. I've been digging up information on him while you were talking to him and the witch."

"He seems a nice guy."

"He is. He's also the town liberal. Contributes to the American Civil Liberties Union and the NAACP. Has local black lawyers over for dinner."

"How come no flaming crosses on the lawn?"

"Old family, over here ever since the first settlements were cut out of the woods, around eighteen hundred five or so. They fought the Indians and were the first traders. His great-uncles fought in the Civil War; one was a governor, another one a senator. You can get away with a lot with that background."

"I like him. We're shooting turkey maybe this weekend."

"No, you're not."

I looked at her.

"Honey," I said, "don't tell me what to do. You're lovely to look at, delightful to hold, and a great typist. Let's keep it—"

She pressed her face against mine and nuzzled her nose against my neck. I smelled her skin. It was like a garden after a shower.

"Town liberal," she murmured. "You're too friendly. Pick a fight. In public."

I kissed the top of her head. No one looking would have guessed that we were having a serious strategical discussion.

"You're right," I murmured. I should have thought of it myself. Maybe the languorous Southern night was ruining my brain. The dance ended. I let Cravens take her for the next dance and stood there, trying to figure out how to get rid of my new friend. Publicly. And loudly.

Mrs. Brady suddenly ran her arm around mine and pulled me out to the patio. I was about to break away when it occurred to me that here, properly handled, was something I could work up into a nice situation.

There were wicker chairs with deep cushions scattered around the patio in groups of two, three or four. She steered me to two chairs, sat down, and hitched her chair so close to mine that our knees touched. She leaned forward and put a hand on my knee, gently stroking it. People noticed. Good.

"This is the most goddam boring town in the world," she began. "You and me could liven it up. I don't mean that literally. This goddam liquor affects the choice of words. But my mind is clear. What I mean is that we could liven it up for each other. And discreetly. Oh, so discreetly. For instance, I hear you do a lot of driving on the back roads. And every week or so I drive the hundred and sixty miles to Jackson, take in a movie, go shopping with the girls, and have myself a hysterically exciting time generally. We have a summer camp out on the river, where we go weekends. Never during the week. I'll be there tomorrow."

"During the week?"

"During. You could drive past Alexandria, take the second right, drive six miles, and turn in at a sign reading *Brady*. About two would be just right. I'll be there dusting. I'll be wearing one of those shirt dresses. And nothing else. I'll be airing the bedding about then. You can try out my Northern speech patterns as adapted by a Southern environment."

"I don't notice any."

"Oh, yes, I'll say, oh, oh, oh, ohhhh!"

Somehow she made the cry of a woman having an orgasm, Southern-style, sound very funny. It sounded well-bred as well. It was an obvious dig at Kirby's diction and I suppressed a smile. But she cried out so loudly that people nearby turned to look. She paid no attention.

"Oh, those Southern ladies," she said, with disgust. "You know, you can make any Southern lady as long as you don't tell her what you're doing?"

I laughed.

"Then," she went on, exhilarated, "you could use me for a control. Then you could continue along the road, looking for poor but noble peasants while I finish airing out the bedding, which now really needs shaking out. Your aroma will be in them. But I'll be very pleased with myself. About three hours later I'd go home to hubby, and we will have passed a pleasant and rewarding day. You could use an hour's break in your dusty progress through our red-clay roads, and I could use whatever screwing you'd care to hand out. What do you say to that, Wilson?"

I thought it was a very good idea with not too much wrong with it. Being placed in close contact with Kirby every night was putting a big strain on my self-control. I was sleeping badly. Mrs. Brady looked like an expert bed mechanic, and she had sketched out what seemed to be a very workable scenario. I idly twirled a swizzle stick and looked at her.

"Well?"

I could see Brady walking toward us, smiling. It was now or never. She put a hand on my arm and looked at my face in an intent, pleading manner.

I waited till he was about five feet away. I picked up her arm and threw it away as if it were a filthy handkerchief I had accidentally picked up.

He saw the gesture and his smile clicked off. I stood

up and shoved my chair back so hard that it toppled over on the flagstone patio. Several people turned.

"Brady!" I said.

All the hum of conversation stopped. I went on. "Brady. Do me a favor. Take your wife away from me before she gets herself slapped."

She sat there with her hands clasped on the table like a nice little schoolgirl.

"Who's going to slap me?"

"If your husband won't, I will!"

"Look here, Wilson," Brady said. "There's no need to talk that way."

"Oh, yes there is. She's been insulting my wife all evening and I'm getting tired of it!"

"Come on home, honey," he said. He took her elbow. She tugged it away and hitched her chair closer to the table.

"Lemme alone!"

But he pulled her to her feet and clamped an arm around her waist. It seemed to me she was yielding. I felt sorry for the poor guy. But it was beginning to look as if nothing was going to happen. I had to step up the pace.

"Mr. Brady," I said in my best Ph.D. candidate style, "the Japanese make a doll. The doll has a round bottom packed with lead. You push the doll and it lies down on the floor. But the lead makes it spring right up. You know what I think? I think you have a real life-sized dolly in your house."

He couldn't let *that* one pass. And sure enough, he let her go and walked toward me. The patio was silent and the French doors leading to the dance floor were filled with people who had heard the last few sentences. They were standing with drinks in their hands. Behind them I saw Kirby biting her lower lip and looking pale. I hoped she wouldn't bite too hard when the action started.

"I must ask you to apologize," Brady said.

"Apologize, hell! I'm getting tired listening to a phony liberal like you bullshit me!"

Well, shoot the works. We'd see what would happen now.

He was looking at me with his mouth a little open. He was in too close. A good fighter would be staying much further away. I could get in fast with a good short right. I had to make him look good. If I creamed him too fast, I would look like a louse.

I said something vulgar. He had no alternative after that. He wouldn't ask me for another apology, not if he lived down South.

I saw his muscles begin to bunch at his right shoulder. When I'm very tense, everything seems to go slow-motion, the way it does when you're in a car and know you're going to be in an accident.

His right arm pulled all the way back. It was pathetic. He should have lifted his elbow and hooked. He might have made it. He weighed enough and he could have pivoted enough to dump me easily.

Instead, it took him two seconds to get the stance he wanted. I would have to help him.

"Now see here, Brady," I said, lifting a warning finger. It looked as if I weren't taking him seriously. That would be sufficient explanation for a beholder why such an amateurish swing could have connected.

His fist caught me on the side of the jaw. I snapped my head around a fraction of a second before he hit. It looked to the audience as if he had a powerful punch, but he was too far away and his feet were badly placed. And I drained out whatever force he might have put into that swing by rolling with it.

Only an expert boxer would have known I was throwing the fight. I stumbled backward, tripped over the low cocktail table, and smashed into the wicker chair. I felt one of the chair arms crunch.

I struggled to my feet, cursing loudly. More people appeared, bless them. Brady was standing there, looking surprised and pleased. I let him hit me again. I took a strange kind of masochistic pleasure in it. I felt guilty about the whole setup, and I wanted the guy to carry away a couple nice memories. This time he hit my left cheek, right over the jawbone. I spun around like they do in movies and fell into a flower bed. I could have made a fortune wrestling on TV. I got up, brushing the dirt from my knees. Now I had a big audience, most of whom had seen me decked twice. He was dancing on the balls of his feet and feeling pretty good.

"Apologize!" he demanded.

When I was a kid, I lived on 53rd Street between Tenth and Eleventh Avenues. That's a tough Irish longshoremen's neighborhood, just a block off the North River docks. My father was a longshoreman. He was killed when a heavy crate slipped out of a sling.

You fought. If you were going to the seminary and become a priest, you were excused. Otherwise, you fought.

Ex-pugs used to teach boxing at the Catholic Youth Organization gym. I learned to come in fast with a low crouch, ready to drop one hand to protect the family jewels. "Don't waste time," Jim O'Neil told me. "Don't waste energy being a ballet dancer. You're gonna fight ten, fifteen rounds, you save your energy. And suppose one night," O'Neil said, "s'pose one night you run across a guy in the street, he wants to fight. All right, suppose he's as good as you. That fight is gonna run on half an hour if no one calls the cops. The guy in better condition is gonna win. But if you ain't in good condition, chances are you ain't gonna be fightin' in top condition. So don't waste energy."

O'Neil taught me how to cover my face and still see what was going on. He taught me how to tighten my stomach muscles against a belly shot by grunting just before the impact. He taught me to smack them over the heart and kidneys until they would drop their guard and then come in high for the convincer.

So I watched Brady dance around for a second. I sighed inwardly.

Then I hooked a hard left into his solar plexus.

He opened his mouth in pain and surprise. I hooked another one, and he dropped his guard in order to bend over to relieve the pain. I had my opening. I hooked a hard right at his jaw, but he turned his face into it, and I knocked out three of his front teeth. I wanted to say, "Brady, you damn fool, I didn't mean it." He spat them out as if they were grains of rice and stood staring at them. The blood began to pour through his lips and run down his chin.

Mrs. Brady kicked me on the ankle. I backed away. She followed me, swinging. I covered my face, wondering where the hell Kirby was. I needed protection and she could give it to me.

Mrs. Brady told me what she thought of me for knocking out her husband's teeth. I silently agreed with her. Still, it was hard maneuvering backward around the oleanders in their tubs. I was beginning to look ridiculous, and suddenly I saw Kirby appear again in the French doors. I felt a surge of relief that showed in my face, and Mrs. Brady turned around to find out the reason. Kirby came up in a few long strides.

"You leave mah husband alone, you damn Yankee!" She was three inches taller than Mrs. Brady and ten pounds heavier.

"Don't you dare touch me!"

Kirby pointed to Mr. Brady. He was holding a sopping red handkerchief to his mouth.

"Get him to a doctor, you damn fool," she said conversationally.

The sheriff appeared in the doorway. His hat was

tilted to one side and one khaki pants leg was crammed inside one boot. The other leg hung down outside the other boot. His hands were in his pockets.

Mrs. Brady turned to him and yelled, "I want him arrested!"

He ignored her and walked up to Brady, pulled the hand away from the mouth, and peered inside. Satisfied, he grunted. "You'll live, Mr. Brady."

He turned to me. "You all ri'?"

I nodded.

"Well. It seems like y'all traded punches, an' Mr. Wilson here was a bit luckier. Why don't y'all start dancin' an' Mr. Brady, have your wife drive you to the doctor 'n' get patched up, an' le's all forget the whole thing."

"I want him arrested!" screamed Mrs. Brady.

He turned to her. "That's for Mr. Brady to say, ma'am. Mr. Brady, you wan' Mr. Wilson arrested?"

Brady shook his head.

"*I* want him arrested! My husband is in shock and he doesn't know what he's saying!"

The sheriff stood there, puzzled. I had a good contact there and I wasn't going to let him talk her out of it.

"Sheriff," I said, "I'll be happy to go along with you and let the judge decide."

He gave me a grateful glance. "You comin' of your own free will?"

I nodded. I turned to Kirby. "You drive the car back," I said. She nodded. Her eyes filled with tears. She flung her arms around me and sobbed. For a second I thought it was for real, but then I heard her whisper softly, "How'm I doin'?" An actress with a farewell scene.

The sheriff ran his hat through his big brown hands three or four times. Finally she finished milking the scene. I walked out with the sheriff, getting dirty looks from everyone.

27

As we stepped outside, Carlyle joined us.

"Evenin', LeRoy."

"Evenin', Mr. Amory."

"How you been?"

"I been fine, Mr. Amory. Just fine."

"Fightin' crime?"

"Yessuh."

"That your crim'nal?"

"Well, sir, not 'xactly."

"He doesn't look so dangerous to me, LeRoy. I saw it all. Just one of those Saturday night country club exercises."

"Yessuh, but Mrs. Brady, she's carryin' on."

Carlyle turned to me. He looked at my jaw critically.

"He hung a nice one on you," he said.

Good for you, Brady! I thought.

"I wish you would have punched him through the window, Mr. Wilson. An' his wife, too. She's a mean woman an' bad-mouths everybody. If she was mine, I'd give her a couple backhand slaps an' she'd settle down nice. She keeps tellin' everybody how much better things are up North. An' she keeps talkin' the same way to the niggers. If his family wasn't so big 'round here, he'd have to keep his mouth shut an' keep hers closed for her. Or sit up all night with a shotgun. It did me mighty good to see you dump him, Mr. Wilson."

"Always glad to oblige."

Carlyle said, "You fight very well."

"Thanks."

"You don't box."

"I don't have time to be a ballerina."

"Ever fight professionally?"

"No."

"You've been around more than the usual college professor."

I didn't like the way the conversation was going. He had a pleasant smile, but his pupils seemed to have a yellow glow, almost as if they were wolf's eyes, with a curious, shallow intensity. You could very easily believe that he would rip out your throat without any personal animosity back of it. He would drink your blood and then fall asleep and sleep very well. I don't want to give you the feeling that he was a psychopath. There was something not quite human, yes, but there was no sign that he might go out of control like a crazed dog with rabies running down a street snapping and biting at everything he saw.

"I had to do lots of things in order to save enough money for tuition."

"I had to do them too, Mr. Wilson. Do you find it gives you a sort of contempt for anyone lucky enough to be born rich?"

"Contempt, no. A little envy and a little pity."

"Pity!"

"Sure. They'll never know if they could have made it on their own. They'll carry that problem all their lives. And I don't have to worry about that. I got here by my own efforts. No one helped me. It might not look like much to a man with a great deal of wealth, like you, Mr. Carlyle, but it means a lot to me to be able to come down, on a project of my own, and collect tapes in order to get a Ph.D. And if I'm lucky I'll publish it in book form, and I'll become famous. In a very small circle, of course. Maybe not more than fifty people will understand what I'm doing. But they're the ones whose respect I value the most."

The little fire went out of his yellow pupils. They looked

dead. He thought he had smelled live meat for a little while, but I must have convinced him I was nowhere. He tried again.

"You let Owen look good."

I didn't like that one. Right over the plate.

"The least one can do for a friend?"

This one had to be fielded right.

"I liked him in the beginning, Mr. Carlyle. But he got on my nerves soon enough. And I didn't come down here to play with other men's wives. I probably wouldn't have reacted so violently if I hadn't been drinking, but I have rigid standards."

I may have pushed too much. The tiny little blaze in his eyes seemed to flare up again. He was extremely sensitive to tone and to nuance, damn him, and something must have struck him as a little bit off.

I didn't like the drift at all. It reminded me of an afternoon several years ago. I was swimming between two cays down in the Bahamas. They were about five hundred yards apart. I took it slow. When I was a little over halfway across, a shark's fin broke the surface about a hundred feet away. I was alone. I kept swimming at the same speed. Sharks become excited when they sense an irregular rhythm in a fish's progress. It signifies to them that it is in distress and probably injured. And it's the same with humans. So I kept the same steady pace. The shark kept swimming in concentric circles, gradually nearing. It was a hammerhead and about fifteen feet long.

It came closer and closer with each revolution. When it was about ten feet way, the shore was seventy-five feet distant. At fifty feet it brushed against my legs. Its skin was harsh as sandpaper and it was only later I discovered that it had neatly removed the top layer of skin and left the exposed layer oozing lymph and some blood. I thought it would turn and come in for the final charge, but for some reason it had held off.

Sharks were unpredictable. I felt the same way about Amory Blanding Carlyle.

I got in the Olds. The red flasher on the top was still turning.

"Good night, Mr. Amory."

"Night, LeRoy. Night, Mr. Wilson."

"Good night, sir." I arranged my face in a pleasant smile. I kept it frozen into place while he stared at me with a cool smile. It only took the sheriff a few seconds to turn the car around, but they seemed like hours under that icy, calm stare. I didn't like him. Not one single bit.

"Now you take Mr. Carlyle," the sheriff began.

I wouldn't, not even with a $30,600 owner-driven Rolls-Royce thrown in. How would you like living in a house with a full-grown cobra roaming around it who could sense your footsteps from the other end of the house, and who might come slithering over for a close look? You wouldn't like it, and it made me a little uneasy with A.B.C. in the same county.

"Seems a smart man," I said admiringly.

"Remember them No'th'n niggers come down here with that white boy from Ha'v'd? Stirrin' up folks 'n' all? Nothin' I could do 'gainst their constitootional rights, which I am sworn to uphold', but it don't hurt to keep track of 'em. So's to protect 'em. How could I keep track? Mr. Amory, he jus' drove 'round the county 'n' tole everyone who owed him money or whoever might be lookin' for a loan from his bank or whoever worked for him to keep a lookout, an' whenever them three boys drove by a farmhouse or gen'ral store or a gas station, someone would phone me at the police station. An' Mr. Amory, he had me stay at the police station keepin' track of them boys twenty-four hours a day until they disappeared."

"You knew where they were all the time?"

"Put it down on the county map with a red tack. Place 'n' time. We could figger where they was goin' next jus' by lookin' at them red tacks. Like huntin' rabbits. Once you know how a rabbit thinks an' moves, you don't have to follow his tracks, you jus' go where you know he'll be comin'."

Three rabbits and a cobra.

Amory sure didn't give me a good feeling. I felt as if a hot little jet had suddenly opened up in my stomach.

"When these kids came down an' started makin' trouble, Mr. Amory checked 'em out."

I played admiring.

"How did he do that?"

"The FBI an' the state police up where they came from. They didn't have no records anywhere. Maybe they was too little to get their pictures took. But they all had their draft cards. I do believe they jus' took off an' went to Sweden or one of them countries that takes draft evaders. Sooner or later they are goin' to write their daddies an' fin'lly we'll be shut of these reporters who come down an' nose around."

"Yes. We don't like those draft evaders in Canada."

"Then he asked some ex-CIA people to check out the boys after they disappeared. They got an office up in Washington. Two nice ol' country boys from around Biloxi. They was dropped from the CIA because when they was in Thailand or maybe Malaysia, I forget which, they run across some Russian agents an' they got rid of 'em without askin' permission. So the king down there, he told 'em to get out. They come to Washington and opened their own agency. That was six, seven years ago. They got branches all over now."

I wasn't convinced that A.B.C. had asked the two nice old country boys to check out the disappearance. That smelled like a little smoke screen for my benefit. He might have asked them to check out the boys' background.

LeRoy's juicy little piece of information wasn't tasty at all.

Some agents get dropped when their kill rate seems excessive or undertaken without prior consultation. Psychopaths do manage to get through the screening. They're brilliant actors, and extremely intelligent, or they wouldn't wind up being considered for the CIA to start with.

They're the kind of people who get satisfaction from killing people. Very useful in wartime, but apt to be embarrassing in peacetime, unless very, very carefully held in check.

He lit a cigarette and offered me one. I took it and thanked him. He tossed his cigarette lighter back into the glove compartment. I saw a blackjack, handcuffs and a shiny pair of brass knuckles.

"I have to tell these reporters to stay off our back roads at night. People down here, they got somethin' on their mind, they don't call me. They get their rifles and settle it themselves. People up No'th, they don't understan' that." He sighed. "Mighty nice of you to come along so peaceful, Mr. Wilson."

"Not at all. I don't like to put you in the middle and have a hysterical woman screaming at you."

" 'Preciate it."

"Those brass knucks," I said. "Confiscated?"

"Nope. Bought 'em."

"You use them?"

"Sure."

I must have looked startled.

He grinned. "Look, Mr. Wilson. Y' ever cruise Niggertown Sattidy night. You get a call from some bar. There's a big thing goin' on. Ten, maybe fifteen, smashin' up the furniture. Not enough to shoot anyone about, an' I'm alone. I look 'em over. If they ain't got no switchblades, or they ain't got a Sattidy-night special—"

"What's that?"

"That's what we call the twenty-four-ninety-five thutty-two caliber pistol you c'n buy over at Meridian. Well, if they ain't got one of those, I like to use the knucks. Trouble with the blackjacks, they got too much lead in them, an' if you gets too excited, you might fracture a skull or two. With the knucks, you maybe break a jaw or nose, but ain't no one dyin' on you in the jail."

He sounded friendly.

"You got to the club pretty quickly," I said.

"I was cruisin' close by. We got two cars coverin' the nigger bars in Okalusa and we keep one close by the club on Sattidy nights. Some hysterical lady phoned an' said you was killin' each other. How does it feel to hit a real rich feller?"

"Pleasurable."

He chuckled. "You ain't been born rich, Mr. Wilson?"

"No."

"That makes you 'bout the only barefoot boy in the country club."

"Not anymore, I'm afraid. No more invitations."

"Now, if you was talkin' off the record, Mr. Wilson, what do you think of our rich folks?"

"They bore the living bejesus out of me."

He laughed.

"Mr. Wilson, I never could understan' how a grown man could stand around eatin' them itty-bitty crackers with an itty-bitty dab of cheese at the parties they give. An' them martinis with them olives, godalmighty, is that a drink for a grown man? How's a man gonna get a good grip on his woman later on in the evenin' with *that* under his belt?"

I laughed.

"How you comin' along with your project, Mr. Wilson?"

"Not too good. Nobody interesting."

"You'd do pretty fine to tape some of my friends. They're interestin'. They're a little cracked, some of 'em. There's one man who collects snakes' heads for bounties. Others. Tell you, Mr. Wilson, you come on down to *our* country club. It ain't got a golf course, it ain't got a swimmin' pool onless you want to take a dive right into the river, which I wouldn't advise, with all them moccasins. An' once in a while a 'gator comes pokin' along. It ain't fancy, but a man c'n let down his hair an' bay at the moon an' eat catfish 'n' hushpuppies 'n' drink the best white mule you ever curled a tongue aroun'."

"I heard about *that* white mule. It'll heal your face without a scar."

"Oh, you bin talkin' to Ray."

"That's right. We met on the bus."

"Yeah. He tole me. Lissen, Mr. Wilson, you want to come out? We'll be real pleased. You talk to the boys an' if you want, you come next time with your machine."

"I'd like that very much."

"All right. You won't be able to drive back because you will be paralyzed. But we got a cot to sleep on till it's safe for you to get in yore car. So you be sure to tell that nice Mrs. Wilson not to sit up an' worry. You are goin' to be all right in the sheriff's custody. You come on over tomorrow night 'bout eight. You go past that nigger bait shack at Alexandria. Then you go right 'bout four miles to the right along the river road. Then you see a shack built out over the river on pilin's."

"I'll be there."

"No point takin' you to the judge. Mrs. Brady'll cool down when she sobers up. But if she don't, will you come on over tomorrow to the jail an' post bail?"

"Sure."

He sighed with relief. We drove home in silence. He was a good, fast driver.

My car was parked in front of the house. Our light was on upstairs.

"That's a fine woman you got, Mr. Wilson."

"Thank you, Sheriff."

We shook hands. He had a firm, cool grip. I watched

him drive away. Much against my will I found myself liking him. Life could be simpler if we could hate our enemies. But life kept producing enemies who were easy to like.

Oh, the hell with it. I was tired. When I got upstairs, Kirby was gloating over her performance. She told me she was the hysterical woman who had phoned the sheriff.

"You?"

"Baby, I played all them organ stops tonight. I am *good.*"

She was. She was damn good. But I was still smart enough to go to bed by myself.

28

It was a beat-up sign, all right. It looked like it had been scavenged from a pile of secondhand lumber. Someone had nailed a vertical post to it and had then lettered the words CATFISH CLUB PRIVAT.

I turned in and drove a hundred feet. The winding road ended in a cleared space backed by cypress. There were five cars jammed together. One had the red dome light under which I had ridden earlier. The parking area was bordered by several badly trimmed logs. Then came a bank which sloped down to a dark-brown liquid which swelled up here and there.

The swellings were old cypress knees. A board sidewalk had been built over the swamp. I followed it toward the Catfish Club.

The Club was a shack with weather-beaten gray wood sidings. It rested on top of several rickety pilings. The river slid among the pilings with a little hissing noise that had an unfortunate resemblance to a snake's warning.

Beyond each piling a tiny whirlpool formed, which drifted downriver with the current. The sky was getting dark and there was no wind.

I stood for a second on the top edge of the clumsily built walk and looked down into the mud. It moved just underneath me. It heaved upward. I gripped the railing hard.

Then it hopped. It was only a frog. I let my breath go out. Down there was the kind of country I'd feel comfortable walking through if I were five feet up in the air. Or wearing iron pants.

The sound of voices came from the shack. I knocked.

The sheriff's voice said, "Now, Vince, you see who that can be."

Vince opened the door. He wore a dirty apron and had long hair and a sour face. He held a frying pan in one hand and scratched the stubble on his chin.

"It's that feller from up No'th," he said, looking at me coldly.

"You invite him in."

"I didn't invite him here and I'll be dad-blasted effen I'll invite him in," Vince said.

The sheriff came to the door. "Come in, Mr. Wilson," he said. "Vince ain't got good manners, but he sure cooks good catfish."

I stepped in. Vince went back to the old iron stove and slammed the pan on top of it with a big clatter. The three men sitting around the scarred old table seemed embarrassed. They nodded to me and settled back in their old kitchen chairs.

"Vince is all right," said the sheriff. Vince was muttering to himself as he scrubbed away at the pan with some steel wool. He didn't notice the sheriff make circles with his forefinger in the air. "He's a damn good cook. He's Tom's cousin here. Tom here, he's my depitty."

Tom grinned and nodded. He was a heavy man of

forty who was patting cornmeal into little round balls and stacking them upon the table. The sheriff opened the door of the old icebox in the corner and took out an old enameled dishpan filled with pieces of fish.

"Fresh catfish," he said. "Have yourself a seat, Mr. Wilson. We'll be eatin' in half an hour."

I looked around. The men were shy and grinned at me. Several old kitchen chairs were sprawled around the shack. Three of them had one or two back-slats that had disappeared. Wire held them together. A calendar was nailed to a wall. It showed a hound baying at a treed raccoon.

"That calendar is 'bout eight years old," one of the men suddenly volunteered.

Next to the calendar was a crudely built shelf formed from an old orange crate nailed to the wall. On it were three mason jars filled with a colorless liquid. Several empty jelly glasses stood next to it.

"Will one of you gennelmen do the honors?" said the sheriff.

One of the men stood and filled the glasses. The white mule went down smoothly.

The floor was full of cracks. Some were very small, two or three were an inch wide.

The drainpipe of the icebox ended between two big cracks. The sheriff noticed my glance at the floor.

"I laid the floor myself," he said. "Laid it when I was feelin' no pain." He took a cheap tin pie plate filled with cigarette butts and shook it out over another inch-wide gap in the flooring. I could see a few white flecks floating past on top of the dark water.

"Nice, huh?" he said. "The garbage what don't get et by the 'gators or the fish ends up in the Mississippi three, four days from now. Makes housekeepin' easy. Now, this here's Ray, you remember him. He's the bus driver."

"Hi, Ray."

"Hi, Mister Wilson."

"This here's Joe Sam."

"Hi, Joe Sam."

"Wooo-woooo!" said Joe Sam. He leaned back and howled.

"Pay him no never-mind," said Ray. "He got some bounty money an' he's been drinkin' all day."

I looked puzzled. Ray explained.

"Up a ways," he said, "we got plenty of timber rattlers. The county gives four bits a snake. Now, the county auditors want proof, right? They'll take the snake's head, or the rattles with two inches of the tail. But if you kills 'em all, why, you dries up the revenoo. So Joe Sam he captures 'em alive an' he cuts off the rattles and two inches. Then he lets 'em go so's they can breed. I'm sure glad I ain't lumberin' up there. I'd never get no warnin' an' them snakes'd be so mad they'd take off after me."

Joe Sam giggled. He called to Ray, leaned over and whispered in his ear, and slapped Ray on the back. Ray grinned and turned to me. "Joe Sam says to tell you this if you promise not to tell no one. He says he c'n trust you 'cause you're a guest of the sheriff. You promise?"

I looked at the red-faced, giggling Joe Sam.

I held up my hand. "I promise," I said.

"Joe Sam," Ray added, "Joe Sam has improved that system. He don't want no pissed-off rattler goin' around with a pain in its butt bitin' them loggers, some of 'em is kin, so he jus' kills all the males and cuts of they heads, but the females he keeps in a barrel till they give birth. He feeds 'em till they gets big enough, then he kills the brood."

Joe Sam bent over and slapped his legs.

"Hoooo!" he said, gasping for breath. He beckoned Ray over. Ray listened.

He turned to me. "Joe Sam wants you to know that he ain't greedy. He says fifty, sixty tides him over until the railroad starts hirin' section hands come spring. What he means is, he ain't touched. Vince is touched. He's all right, but he's touched. Look, look at 'im!"

Vince was hefting the heavy frying pan. "Now, Ray," the sheriff said. "You stop bein' mean. An', Vince, we got us a guest here an' I aims to do him proud." He filled my jelly glass again with the whisky.

"You just soak your tonsils in that an' let me know how it goes down, Mr. Wilson."

It went down pretty good. It was smooth and had a lot of quiet authority. A warm glow began in my stomach and began to spread outward.

I watched Vince as he dredged the catfish.

"Vince don't talk much," the sheriff said.

Vince took a big jackknife out of his back pocket and opened it.

"You're not gonna use *that* goddam rusty knife again!" Ray said.

Vince turned and looked at him.

"You shut up, boy!"

"Aw Sheriff, I ain't too particular 'bout dirty plates an' all but that's the knife he cuts off snakes' heads with."

I must have looked puzzled. I thought it was Joe Sam who was in the bounty business, but Joe Sam leaned over and poured more whisky into my glass. "I borry it," he said. "He keeps it mighty sharp. Hit don't offend me none. But other people is delicate." He snorted with pleasure.

Vince lifted his head. He rattled off a monologue which it was obvious the others were waiting for.

"This here," he began, "this here knife is—is—" he hesitated and scratched his head with the point of the knife.

Ray prompted him. "This here is a fine silver steel blade knife with a moth—"

Vince held up his hand. "This here is a fine silver steel blade knife with a mother-of-pearl handle, brass-lined, round joint tapped and riveted tip top an' bottom, a knife made under an act of Congress at the rate of thutty-six dollars per dozen, there is a blade fo' ev'ry day of the week an' a handle fo' your wife to play with on Sunday, it will cut cast iron steam steel wind or bone an' will stick a hog frog toad or the devil an' has a spring on it like a mule's hind leg!"

Ray chuckled. "He bought that knife from a peddler maybe forty years ago an' he remembers ev'ry word that man said when he stood by the co'thouse square that day. Mr. Wilson, I believe we are ready to eat."

There was a platter of catfish, a platter of just-baked hushpuppies, a pound of sweet butter in a cracked blue plate. I ate and drank with pleasure. The sheriff filled my glass up again. That made three of them in less than twenty minutes.

I sipped it. After a while I unbuttoned my shirt. There was no wind and it was getting hot.

"We ain't got air conditioning," Joe Sam said. "Ain't like the big club."

"I like it better here," I said, and I meant it. Everyone was eating and no one was trying to get next to anyone to make a deal or line up someone else's wife or see how much another woman might have spent for a dress. They were all eating and drinking and enjoying it.

These people were brutal murderers and yet they could be marvelous company. They could tell stories beautifully, they knew how to hunt and fish, they knew how to live. I wished I was down there for pleasure. It would easily be possible to have a great time.

"Pleasure havin' you here," the sheriff said.

I crammed more hushpuppies into my mouth enjoying the crispness and the firm succulence of the catfish.

"You read 'bout them civil rights workers come down here, evvabody been lookin' for them?"

I was in the middle of a long swallow of whisky. I finished it and wiped my mouth carefully with the back of my hand while the sheriff told Vince he better keep some paper napkins for people who had been better brought up.

"A headline or so," I said.

"We get along fine," he said. "Pity them other Northerners came down. They shoulda stayed at home under their own vine."

Joe Sam dredged around in his teeth with a fork tine. "Sometimes in this wicked world," he said, "a man dies because he can't do nuthin' else but."

"Amen, brother," the sheriff said. "I'm a great big friendly ole country boy, but I don't like to be crowded. Them civil rights workers *crowd*. They don't know what it's like down here. Hell, you get two Northerners arguin' 'bout somethin' an' they'll yell back an' forth for ten minutes seein' who'll make the first move. Down here they don't talk. They move fast. Hell, we was raised on guns an' keepin' down niggers, an' we're used to all that violence stuff they keep talkin' 'bout on TV. Hell, Mr. Wilson, it's Southern towns got the country's highest homicide rates. It's Southern boys take home most of the Congressional Medals of Honor. Them civil rights people from up North they don't know that. We down here we purely don't like outside influences."

He filled my glass again.

He chuckled. "Here's a song a nigger prisoner was singin' today." He sang:

> *If I had the guv'nor*
>   *Where the guv'nor has me,*
> *Before daylight*
>   *I'd set the guv'nor free.*
>
> *I begs you, guv-nor,*
>   *Upon my soul:*
> *If you won't gimme a pardon,*
>   *Won't you gimme a parole?*

"Now, ain't that just a great song? They's great people, but they oughtn't to take up with radicals. They stupid but friendly, an' them outsiders they don't understan' they nothin' but animals. They nice animals, but they animals."

"The more I see them down here, the more I believe you're right."

I took a sip and announced I was going to sing. I sang "Oh, I'm a Good Old Rebel" all the way through and added the last two stanzas Kirby had taught me:

> *Three hundred thousand Yankees*
> *Is stiff in Southern dust;*
> *We got three hundred thousand*
> *Before they conquered us;*
> *They died of Southern fever*
> *An' Southern steel an' shot,*
> *I wish they was three million*
> *Instead of what we got.*

The sheriff joined me for the last stanza.

> *I can't take up my musket*
> *An' fight 'em now no more.*
> *But I ain't a-goin' to love 'em,*
> *Now that is sarten sure;*
> *An' I don't want no pardon*
> *For what I was an' am,*
> *I won't be reconstructed*
> *An' I don't care a damn!*

They loved it. Joe Sam filled up my glass again so fast that it slopped over and soaked into my pants. He was apologetic. I took the jug and spilled some on his and said we were even. He was pretty drunk by then and thought that was funny.

The evening went well. There were hunting stories;

there were surprisingly few obscene stories. It was quite a change from a typical evening's drinking session up North. Finally, I knew I was so drunk I couldn't sit up. I cradled my head in my arms. But the sheriff took me to a cot in the corner.

"You're not used to drinkin' this much," he said.

"Nope," I said. My lips were numb. "Great food. Great people. Can't stay awake 'ny more. Beg pardon." He stretched me out.

"Don't you worry," he said. "Couple hours from now you'll be able to drive home. If you can't, one of the boys'll drive your car. Don't worry 'bout a thing."

I nodded and closed my eyes. The room was circling around and around, and I got up and vomited out the back window into the river.

I made my way back, waving aside the offers of assistance. I was embarrassed at my inability to handle the liquor. I closed my eyes again. My mind was working along nicely. I just couldn't give any orders to my body. It was willing to perform, but all the muscles had resigned for a few hours.

A violent headache made an appearance. I groaned. The sheriff's voice said, "Y'all right?"

"Oh, God," I said, "I want to die."

"You'll live," he said.

I fell asleep but woke up. It must have been only a few minutes later. The level in the jug was about the same and they were still in the same positions. Someone was saying, "Man, I sure could go for one of Ole Man Ryerson's watermelons, right now!"

Joe Sam said he had one cooling in his refrigerator. I heard him leaving and the door closing and the roar of the car starting. I fell asleep again, and I woke up again when he came back. I smelled the fragrance of a ripe watermelon being sliced open. Joe Sam said, "The professor want any?"

The sheriff said, "Let him sleep."

I determined to stay awake. I kept my eyes closed and began snoring very lightly. It must have had a soothing sound, because Vince grunted, "He won't want none fo' hours yit."

They chatted about dogs and inconsequential things. And then Joe Sam said, "This here's a great watermelon. An' no wonder, lookit the manure he got fo' nothin'."

There was a sudden silence.

Then the sheriff said in disgust, "Well, shut your mouth, you goddam fool."

They were silent a few seconds. Joe Sam suddenly said, "Give the perfessor a piece." They had a lot of trouble waking me up, but they finally did. I ate a slice and fell back again on the cot. In a few minutes I was really asleep.

29

Next morning I swallowed three aspirins and looked through the phone book. I found a Sam Ryerson on Saw Mill Pond Road. I went in the bathroom and shaved. Through the open door I could see Kirby sleeping.

She was stretched out on her stomach close to the edge of the bed. I wondered idly why people who sleep that close to the edge never fall off. Her long hair was more rewarding to think about. It flowed over her right shoulder and down to the floor. The thin sheet that covered her followed the lines of her rump very carefully.

Even though my head was throbbing as if it were the big bass drum being pounded in a circus parade, I felt a sudden passion to get into the bed.

Instead I went downstairs, got into the car, and leaned over to open the glove compartment. My head began to throb again and as I fished for the county map, I began to sense that something was unusual. I got the map, closed the compartment, put the palm of one hand on my forehead, and pressed hard. I guess I was trying to compress the headache into a smaller space. It did feel a little better. I took my hand away and then became aware of a little nagging tension at the base of my spine.

It took my white-mule-damaged brain a few seconds to realize the reason for that. The car was parked with both right-hand wheels on the curb. Either Ray or Joe Sam or Vince had done it. I began to remember that I had been dragged upstairs by two of them. I got out of the car. There were no dents or scratches. I got in again, spread the map over the steering wheel, and found Saw Mill Pond Road. It was fifteen miles north of Okalusa. It was a good county map; it showed property lines and owners.

Ryerson's farm was only a quarter of a mile from an unpaved road that ran westward for eight miles. This road ended at the main highway from Memphis to Jackson. The Ryerson farm would be just about thirty miles north of Alexandria—thirty miles away from where the three boys had last been seen. It would be natural for searchers to prowl through the swamp near Alexandria. But all they would turn up would be frogs and water moccasins. Who would ever think of a remote farm thirty miles away?

I decided to account for my appearance. First I stopped at a roadside stand two miles away, drank a Coke, and taped the old black woman who ran the stand. Near the farm I found a utility lineman on a pole. He came down and gave me ten minutes.

Then I drove up to Ryerson's place.

His house was halfway up a long, gentle slope. At the bottom lay a pond. A few plump Herefords were standing in the mud up to their hocks, drinking. They lifted their dripping muzzles to stare at my car.

Back of the house, and sweeping around to its left and down to the road, was a thick stand of long-leaf yellow pine. Halfway up from the road to the house was the watermelon patch. It was about a hundred and fifty feet down the slope from the house. Even from the road at the bottom I could see the big green cylinders of the melons.

I drove up the road to the house. A small gray-haired man with gold-rimmed glasses and worn blue denim coveralls stepped onto the porch.

"Good morning," I said.

He stared at me coldly.

I was surprised. Up to now I had received only courtesy from Southerners. True, when they discovered my real purpose I expected that to end, but in the meantime—I shrugged.

"I've been taping people of Milliken County," I began, but he cut me off.

"Saw you talkin' to the 'lectric feller on the road. Talkin' in that machine you got there on the back seat."

"Yes, sir. I wonder if you'd mind talking into it. I pay five doll—"

"Where you from, mister?"

"Canada, sir."

"Lived onct up t' Chicago. I hates No'th'ners. Runnin' this way, runnin' thataway like cow-critters. Don't have sense enough to walk slow."

"Well, Mr. Ryerson, I'm a Canadian. And I walk slow."

He looked at me impassively. Then he grunted.

"Won't talk. Talkin's a waste."

"All right, I hear you have good watermelons. How about selling me one?"

"I never turned away one o' God's images yet, even if they's Yankees. An' some on 'em is dreffel pore likenesses. You follow me, now."

He stepped off the porch. I followed.

But he didn't head for the patch. He walked toward the barn.

"How'd you hear about my melons, mister?"

"I ate one last night. The sheriff told me you grew it. I said to myself, I better get one all for myself and my wife, and when I was taping down the road, I suddenly remembered your place was here."

"You the feller from Canada who married a Georgia girl?"

I admitted it. He seemed to soften. "I'll git you a good one. Been aimin' to sell these in town, an' I'll give you first crack."

"Won't we get fresher ones in the patch?"

"No, mister. They ain't puffect yet. An' you wouldn't like to go in theah anyway."

"Why not?"

"Theah's plenty dry-lan' moccasins come out of the piny woods an' lie around under the vines waitin' for frogs."

I felt the back of my neck tingle.

"What's a dry-land moccasin?"

"You fellers up No'th call 'em copperheads. Now you take a look at these here beauties."

He slid open the door of the barn. He had backed in an old flatbed truck. He had spread straw over the bottom and set melons on it.

They were beautiful melons, if all I wanted out of life was a beautiful melon. I had thought he'd take me up to the melon patch, where I could amble around, rejecting this one and that one, finding another one somewhere else in the patch that I preferred, rejecting that one upon close examination, and finally picking one after I'd gone over the whole patch.

By then I'd have seen where there was any seriously disturbed ground.

It was a good plan, but that wasn't the way it was working out. There was nothing wrong with the melons on the flatbed. If I were still to insist upon looking through the patch, he would get thoughtful. He would know damn well what he had planted up there besides melons.

I might have tried it and gotten away with it if I had built up a reputation for being an eccentric. If I had pushed the absent-minded professor bit, always demanding perfection from the gas-station attendant, demanding super-cleanliness from the landlord, super-service from the shops—I might have gotten away with the search for the super-melon.

But I had carefully built up a picture of myself as a real sweet, reasonable kind of guy. No. I would have to work out something else.

He cut out a hunk from one end of a melon and gave it to me. I ate it. It was superb. I bought the melon, paid him sixty cents, shook hands, and drove away. There was one consolation. There were no dogs around the house.

I drove home slowly working out my next step in the campaign. By the time I turned into my block, I had solved everything. I came upstairs whistling. Kirby was out shopping. I cut a big chunk off one end and put the melon in the refrigerator. It was still so big I had to cut it in three pieces to be able to slide them in.

I sat down and cut my end into one-inch-thick slices and began eating. They were warm and still oozing with the sweetest pink juice I had ever had in a melon. I spat out the black seeds into an empty plate. I spread out the *Okalusa Star-Clarion* and bypassed the editorials denouncing the invasion of the state by a gang of Northern long-haired radicals who had come down under the guise of bringing freedom to Mississippi Negroes.

At the bottom of the editorial column was a little box listing the moon phases, sunrise and sunset, moonrise and moonset. I studied them all carefully. I needed the information for some early morning navigation.

30

Sunrise was at 5:47. I put the paper down, ate some more melon, and studied some more. Moonrise was at 8:11. Moonset, 11:47.

Kirby came home twenty minutes later. I cut her a slice of melon and put the groceries away as she ate.

"Pack a small overnight bag for yourself," I told her. "We're leaving tonight for Jackson. You better go and tell the Garrisons you're going to take in the sights in Jackson while I get my tape recorder fixed in New York."

She went downstairs. I packed my big leather camera bag with the Leica, the special lenses, the tripod, and a bellows extension. The Leica was loaded with light-sensitive film. I packed a small bag with a couple of shirts, underwear, and socks. Kirby came upstairs and said, "All right, boss. What's next?"

"Next is we'll be leaving about nine tonight. I'm going to be up all night and so will you. We'd better catch a couple hours' sleep."

I took a shower, put on my pajamas, and lay down on the couch to try and grab three hours. I heard the water drumming for her shower, put the image of Kirby soaping herself out of my mind, set the alarm for 8:45 P.M., and fell asleep.

The alarm went off. I shut it off and padded into the bathroom for a quick shave. Kirby had heard the alarm, turned off the light in the bedroom, and had just as promptly fallen asleep. I kicked her mattress as I went by. She opened her eyes, smiled, and swung her long legs over the side of the bed.

She stretched her arms as far as they could reach, and then yawned. I was shaving and the door was open. The pale blue cotton of her nightgown was stretched tight across her nipples. She opened her eyes and looked at me.

She said very softly. "Well?"

I said curtly, "We won't have time for coffee. We'll eat on the road." Then I closed the door and cut my chin shaving.

We went downstairs quietly. I carried the Kim. The Garrisons heard us coming down and came on the porch to wish us a nice vacation down in Jackson.

"Don't know it they c'n fix that tape recorder in Jackson," Garrison said.

"I don't think so," I said. "I have a feeling I might have to take it to New York. At any rate, Mrs. Wilson can sightsee down there if I have to go to New York."

They told her what to see in Jackson. A good conversation. He would remember it.

I stopped at a roadside restaurant south of Okalusa. We sat in a quiet corner booth. We ate country ham and black-eyed peas and grits. The ham was thick and succulent and had been fed on fallen nuts. It was nine-thirty. Over two hours to moonset.

Kirby told me of an uncle of hers who raised mash-fed hogs. He was a bachelor who collected empty thread spools and slipped them over nails hammered into a wall of his house. When he had filled the whole wall with spools over the nails, he set an old-fashioned sewing machine in front of them. The sewing machine was operated by a foot treadle.

He ran a cord from the machine in and out of those thousands of spools and led it back to the machine. Then he sat down and pumped the treadle. He was perfectly happy for hours as he watched all those spools revolve.

I told her my uncles were famous only for drinking up

their paychecks on Friday nights. I told her that didn't make anyone eccentric in my neighborhood; it made you normal.

She leaned back and laughed. She stopped short and came up to meet my mouth. I put a hand on her breast and she strained against me. If I would have had a couple drinks, I would have pushed her in the car and driven back fast. I probably would have torn off her blouse in the car and ripped off her skirt going up the stairs and we would hit her bed stripped.

Instead I took a deep breath and pushed her into her corner. I slid away and drank a glass of ice water. I filled up the glass again from the pitcher and drank again. Somewhere I had once read that any passion could be extinguished by quickly drinking five glasses of water. I was pouring out my third glass and beginning to see the truth of the proverb when she spoke.

"I had no idea I got you heated up so bad," she said.

A little drop of blood was running across down her lower lip. As I watched, it fell onto her blouse. I had kissed her so hard that one of her upper teeth had cut into her lip. I dipped my napkin into the pitcher and reached across to rub out the bloodstain.

She took the napkin. "Better stay away, boy," she said. "I don't want you goin' up in smoke."

I crossed my arms and watched. I felt my face getting red. This blow hot, blow cold was not my style.

"What you goin' to do now?"

I looked at my watch. Thank God, the moon would be setting in fifteen minutes.

"Let's go."

I paid the check while she got into the car. The waitress took the money and brought the change with that relaxed courtesy which always came as a pleasant shock after New York.

I came outside putting my wallet away just as the big

gray Olds pulled in. I cursed under my breath. I walked straight ahead, not looking at it, hoping he wouldn't notice me in the darkness. But he saw me. He was sharp.

"Want an escort to town?" he called out.

"And take you away from a cup of coffee? Not me."

"Had my coffee. Saw your car and thought you might like an honor guard."

"No, Sheriff. We're going to Jackson."

"Pretty late to be drivin' a hundred sixty miles," he observed genially.

"When I want to go somewhere," Kirby said, "I *want* to go somewhere. Immediately if not sooner. I want to wake up in a nice air conditioned room. I want to sleep late. I don't want to hear dishes bein' rattled downstairs or hear a nice ol' man clearin' his throat an' spittin'. Now, honestly, Sheriff, I do like the Garrisons, but they're the *noisiest* damn people I ever did see. My husband thinks he's back to N'York to repair that silly damn tape recorder of his, but he's really givin' me a two-day vacation jus' sleepin' late an' eatin' in a good French restaurant, which I hear Jackson has got." She leaned over and nibbled at my ear.

"Mrs. Wilson, if I could work it, I sure wish we 'llowed ladies to come down to our club."

"I'd be jus' as pleased. But I'd be in the way there. I'd want to start scrubbin' the filthy mess you men always make of housekeepin', an' then I'd order ever'one to start shavin' and sayin' ma'am to me. Honey," she went on, turning to me, "I'm gettin' so sleepy, I'm goin' to curl up in the back seat. You drive careful, y' hear?"

"She wears the pants," I said. I waved goodbye to the sheriff while she got in the back seat. I pulled out and headed south, toward Jackson. And away from Ryerson.

I drove five miles, checking the rear-view mirror. No one was following. I pulled over, got out, took out the jack, and put it by the rear end in case anyone became curious. I took a dime from my pocket and loosened the screws holding the glass in place over the light above my rear license plate. I unscrewed the bulb just enough. I put everything back in place and got in. Kirby woke up as I was turning the car around.

"Something wrong?"

"No. I just want to tiptoe north. I think I'll take a few side roads. I want to bypass that son of a bitch."

"He's a puffectly nice man," she said.

"He is," I said without sarcasm.

As long as you're not a civil rights worker. I'd feel pretty safe in my house knowing he's out there riding around in that big Olds of his. If I had a kid who'd get drunk in some highway bar, I'd feel pretty good that the sheriff would see he got home all right without driving. I'd feel confident he'd know when to relax the law and when he could step outside it. You don't challenge the political structure of this county and you get pretty good protection. But every once in a while I wonder what he'd do to me if he found out what I was really up to. Or what his friends would do after he'd arrest me, for, say, not having my rear light working. He could very easily remove my gun and then drop me outside my house. And guess who'd be waiting down the block in a car without lights? Some of those guys from the Catfish Club. And guess who would investigate the crime? It's pretty near perfect. Every time I thought about it, I felt my spine roll up like a window shade.

She got into the front seat and watched the dark road a while. Then she fell asleep again. Her head slid across the back of the seat till it rested on my shoulder. She had handled the situation well. I met only two cars on the back roads, and when I was a mile from the Ryerson farm, I woke her up. She slid behind the wheel.

I told her I was getting out soon.

"Remember the exact location where you're dropping

me," I said. "The sun rises at five forty-seven. You drive south on this road to the crossroad. It's two miles south. Make a right and go three and a half miles. That will put you on the main highway. Make a right and go north, away from Jackson."

"Why do I go north?"

"That'll take you away from Okalusa and the chance of seeing our friend. You be back here exactly at five forty-seven."

"Taking pictures?"

"I'm a big one for nature studies a little before sunrise."

"An interesting hobby."

"A good shot of a cross-grained red-bellied pushover will gain me fame and fortune. I've worked out the time. If you stay at a steady thirty-five, you won't attract attention and you'll be back here just right. Wear my hat. Put your hair underneath and take off your make-up. Turn out the dashboard lights and a casual look at you will give the impression you're a man."

"But I'm not."

And didn't I know that.

But I let that remark pass.

"Joe," she said, "wouldn't it be simpler for me to find a little road and just park till it's time to come back?"

"It would be very simple. But suppose someone sees you and pulls over to see what the matter is? People are helpful around here. Suppose some kid thinks no one is around and stops to strip the car, and finds you inside? You keep movin' at a normal speed on a highway and no one'll give you a second look. It's cars on these back red-clay roads that attract attention. And don't stop moving. Don't go to a ladies' room. You went to the ladies' room in the restaurant."

"You're terribly observant."

"So you won't have to go again."

"Ladies have enormous tanks. Don't worry."

"Okay. Let me out here."

She stopped. I got out and told her to push in the headlight beams. I didn't want those powerful lights sweeping over the Ryerson farm as she made a U-turn.

"Take care, y' hear?" I nodded and closed the door gently. I watched her turn. A good girl. A clever girl. She handled the meeting with the sheriff very nicely. We made a good team. If I were to stay in the private detective business, I would have used her a lot. A few months ago a millionaire had come in. His ex-wife used to get drunk and allow herself to be blackmailed by gigolo after gigolo across Europe. Hotel after hotel overcharged her. Paris jewelry shops sent padded bills. What he wanted was a very shrewd woman operative to keep her out of trouble. He would have paid very well, and I regretfully declined the job. I had no one who could handle it. And all the time I had Kirby typing fifteen feet away!

I watched the car disappear down the road. I nursed the bitter wisdom of hindsight. I sighed and turned toward the dark mass of the pines.

31

I walked upward through the pine grove, dodging the branches that whipped at my face after I had pushed through them. The needles were fragrant, and so thick that it was like walking on a luxurious wall-to-wall carpet. Occasionally I broke a dead twig. It made much too loud a snapping noise. I thanked God that Ryerson didn't like dogs. I bumped into several trees, but my sense of direction was pretty good. In five minutes I came out on the farm just below the melon patch.

I walked back and forth through the cultivated rows

between the melon vines. Nothing. I got on my knees and felt carefully at the ground. It just felt cultivated. Nothing. And there I was with a fifteen-dollar pair of slacks being ruined on the damp ground. There were no cleared areas. Full-grown melon vines that had taken months to reach their growth. And you can't transplant melon vines without a severe cutback being necessary. All the vines looked full-grown and healthy.

There went a perfectly good theory. Shot to hell. I began to think I must have misunderstood what they were saying back in the club about manure on the melon patch. I had been drinking quite a lot. Probably I had misunderstood what had been said.

I was about to call it off and go sit down in the pine woods till sunrise and wait for Kirby when I realized that in the center of the patch was a pile of weeds about two feet high. It looked as if someone had pulled all the weeds in the patch, saved them, and then had thrown them on top of the pile. But the pile measured about eight by four feet. Thirty-two square feet. You could grow a lot of melons in thirty-two square feet. It seemed a shame to lose all that valuable space just to get rid of some weeds. Why didn't Ryerson walk a few more feet and throw the weeds under the pine trees?

I had the time, I had the place. I had nothing to do till sunrise anyway. I kneeled down and carefully shifted the pile of weeds to the nearest open row. I wadded big clumps in my arms. I was smart enough to take off my jacket, so all I ruined was my shirt. My pants were already filthy. In five minutes I had the plot all cleaned up.

By now my eyes had adjusted to the starlight. It was enough for me to see that the soil underneath had been freshly turned over. I got on my knees and began shoveling the dirt away with both hands. Four inches down I smelled the same penetrating stench I had not smelled since Korea.

The Chinese had made a mass grave in the next valley which we took in an offensive three weeks later.

I began breathing through my mouth. That way I avoided smelling. The stink was something you finally got used to in Korea but only after a few days on the line. But I wasn't going to get any few days here to adjust. I would only have till sunrise, which was now only thirty-five minutes away.

After two minutes of this primitive digging, my hand struck something smooth. I braced myself and slid my fingers along it. It was a shoe.

I slid my fingers upward. The shoe was attached to a foot. I reversed my position and began digging where the head would be.

Two minutes more and I had a face.

I took a fountain pen flashlight from my jacket, bent over the face with the jacket over my head to shield the light, and turned it on.

It was the face of a white man. It looked as if it had been beaten with a heavy iron chain. All the front teeth were loose. Everything else was a mess. In five minutes I had all three bodies side by side. Two blacks and a white. The blacks had not been beaten. But three weeks in the damp soil was a lot of time. I turned aside and vomited up my dinner.

I opened the camera bag. I took out the Leica and attached it to the focusing bellows. I had practiced a few times. I screwed the Leica into the tripod attachment. I straddled the tripod over the face of the white boy. It wasn't that I didn't believe in democracy. It was just that the kid's father was paying for everything. Let him be first.

As I worked, I could hear Farr's voice droning on as if he were giving a lecture to the three dead boys.

"Here's a lens designed for available-light photography. It uses aspheric lens elements which eliminate all spherical aberration. This job we have here is very interesting. I consider it a challenge. Now, notice the lens. It has an angular field of forty-five degrees. It has six elements. It's got a click-stop diaphragm with half F stops. Forget it all. Just take a reading all over the thing to be photographed—" "Thing" is right.

If I can do it without vomiting again.

"If your meter reading shows extremes to one side or the other, average it out. Take a few shots with a larger and smaller stop just in case you get rattled and think you're going crazy. You have plenty of film and it's cheap."

Nothing to do now but wait for available light.

I sat back on the pile of dirt I had dug out like a dog panting after a valuable bone. My pants were damp on the seat. I would have given twenty bucks to be able to smoke. Anything to take that smell away. My mouth was dry from breathing with it wide open.

Time crawled. The three boys lay stretched out with their terrible faces upturned to the stars. I didn't feel any rage or pity. They went down knowing what they were getting into. They play rough in the South. Honor to their courage. But no pity.

Farr had said I could start shooting as soon as I could make out the F numbers on the lens housing from a distance of two feet.

Not yet. I could see the outlines of the camera all right, and there was a faint tinge of gray and pink in the east on top of the ridge.

I stood up and stretched. I heard a deep croak just behind me. Part of my mind said it was a frog, but another part made me whip around and crouch, flinging up my arm to block any blow which might be coming down at me. My foot stepped on a soft mass which wriggled and let out a strangled croak. I almost went five feet in the air with my legs racing wildly, just like in one of those old Mickey Mouse cartoons. But it was just another one of those goddam frogs. This one was only a little one, about three inches long. I had squashed it flat. I felt sorry for it.

I leaned against a tree trunk. My pants were too damp to sit down. Time crawled some more. I tried to feel warm by thinking of going fishing for hammerhead shark in my brand-new cruiser, which some lucky salesman didn't yet know was mine.

Finally I could read the numbers at two feet.

I shot one roll of each face. I had a problem I hadn't foreseen when I wanted to shoot the teeth. How to keep the lips back?

I finally picked up some small twigs from the underbrush under the pines. One across the hinge of the jaws kept them open, and three between the lips.

I forced myself to work slowly even though the light began to increase. I had a bad moment when I began to reload the first time. The film kept slipping out of the take-up spool. I found my fingers began to tremble with annoyance. I wanted to smash the camera against a tree and then race down the slope and get the hell out of there and go home to safe New York and blackmailers and extortion artists. At least they didn't have the local cops on their side.

Instead I counted to twenty slowly. I got a grip on myself. I fed the film in slowly and correctly.

In ten minutes I was finished. I packed everything away in the camera bag. I shoved the dirt back, stamped it flat, and dumped the weeds as evenly as they had been placed there by Ryerson. It looked the same to me as when I started, but I didn't have a farmer's eye.

I did have enough of one to see my footprints all around. I tried smoothing them out, but my attempt to cover them up made marks just as obvious. I wasn't working in sand. I had damp soil to deal with. That's what comes of being a city boy. You live your life on concrete. You never think of footprints.

If Ryerson saw them—and I had to assume he would—he would think they were there because of the mass grave. He would think so because they wouldn't be anywhere else. He might think someone was stealing watermelons, but he was no fool. He was bound to get very thoughtful and probably he would phone the sheriff.

The sheriff might think the FBI had been up there. The sheriff would work his contacts in Jackson and find there were no FBI men around. He might even find out there were no Department of Justice men around either. So it might be a local boy not in the club who might be after the reward. And it might be a stranger in town.

Me.

32

What might work would be a good smoke screen. I remembered listening once to a sergeant lecturing us on guerrilla tactics.

"You wanna hold up tanks," he said, "you gotta remember tanks are so vulnerable the jockeys are nervous. They get nervous about anything. We was in the Ardennes in forty-five and I heard a couple Tigers coming down the road. We was buildin' an antitank barrier across the road and another ten minutes we would finish. I swiped ten soup plates from a house and I laid them across the road in a row. Nice and even.

"The tanks came up to the plates. They stopped. They couldn't go around because of the houses. They stopped fifteen minutes wondering what they was. They thought maybe they was some new kind of mines. Every time the hatch would open, I'd let them have a spray. So we built our barrier."

I had to think of something like that for Ryerson. Something unusual. Something weird.

I went back in the woods and scrabbled around. I found the flattened green frog. It looked like a Rorschach blot. I got a branch about four feet long. I went back to my little garden plot. By now I knew it as well as the five people whose guest I had been at the Catfish Club. I shoved aside some of the weeds and dug down. I reached for the face I remembered and pulled loose one of the loosened teeth. I covered everything up again. I sharpened one end of the branch with my pocket knife and split the other end. I jammed the sharp end right into the middle of the weeds in the dead center of the plot. Dead center. Pun by Dunne. I put the frog in the cleft end. I unraveled a thread from my sock and let the tooth dangle from the frog's mouth.

I tried to put myself in Ryerson's muddy farm shoes. He would come across my artwork. Probably not next day, and not the day after. He had a truckload of melons, and it would take him about two days to sell them. So he would be coming up in about three days. Say two to be careful.

He would puzzle his head about it. He would probably connect it with the most unusual thing that had happened recently, and that would be my appearance looking for watermelons. But he would also know that I'm a nice Canadian and a friend of the sheriff's: wasn't I down the night before at the Catfish Club lapping it up with the boys?

Since he was so stubborn, he'd hate to tell anyone about it. But after a day or so he'd give up and tell the sheriff. Wasn't it the sheriff who arranged for the murders and the burial? So off to the sheriff he'd go.

The sheriff would be smarter. He would most likely

think it unlikely that I was involved. The sheriff in turn would kick it around for a couple days. He'd try out his conjure man theory. But since there were several in the county, and since they all kept themselves well-behaved—except maybe Old Man Mose, who had hosted the three boys—he'd be sort of paralyzed.

That Old Man Mose would do such a thing he'd find most unreasonable. People in subjection their whole lives don't suddenly go around looking for trouble. So he'd drop that line of approach.

But it would trouble him. He'd kick it around a few days, hating to take it upward to A.B.C. People hate to pass bad news to a superior. The superior gets mad at the news, and some of the anger rubs off on the poor guy who brings them gloomy messages.

And sooner or later he'd go to A.B.C. And A.B.C. himself would order a quiet little check on me. It was simple common sense. He probably would use those two nice ol' country boys who'd been kicked out of Thailand for excess enthusiasm. They'd report there *was* a Harold Wilson at McGill, all right. If they weren't too careful.

I might be marked okay. So they'd look elsewhere, probably backtracking on Old Man Mose.

But by then—and that would take about two weeks—I'd be four or five days out of the country, buried so deep they'd never find me.

It looked good. The whole situation looked good.

And the juju would shake them up. I'd like that. When things get turbulent, the bottom gets stirred up. Things come up. I'd make sure to hang around the boys as soon as I got back from New York. Sometimes a watched pot boils.

I took one last look at my work. It didn't look like anything a nice Canadian fellow might do. But I had no time to lounge around and admire my work. I ran through the pine woods. I came out of the underbrush bordering the road just as Kirby rounded the curve a hundred yards ahead. I got in fast and crouched down in the back.

We took back roads all the way to Jackson. We came to the airport by 8 A.M. I parked next to the terminal and changed in the car to some clean clothes, packed the camera equipment in my suitcase, since I didn't want anyone noticing that I had a very good camera which could take very good pictures I might not have any right taking.

I bought a ticket on the 8:40 plane to New York via Atlanta. I sat drinking coffee in the airport restaurant with Kirby till it was time to board.

When the announcement came, she kissed me goodbye. "Shall I go home an' make moan about the awful expense of the trip?" she asked. "An' how you have to go all the way back to New York to get that damn thing fixed so you can go on with your project?"

"Good idea."

"To hear is to obey."

"You'll cry, then."

"Oh, I'll cry."

It was time to board. I lugged on a perfectly good tape recorder. I could see her behind the big plate-glass window. She dug her fists in her eyes pretending to cry. With my forefingers I drew lines from the corners of my eyes downward.

She laughed and waved.

FASTEN SEAT BELTS. I did and leaned back, relaxed. For the first time in years I had someone who did the right thing at the right time. I could leave her in that dangerous town and go away with full confidence in her ability to handle anything that might come up.

And although I don't like flying, I found myself whistling as the jet gathered speed for the takeoff. The man on my left glared at me. Tough luck, buddy.

33

At 10 A.M. I was ringing Farr's bell. I rang it five times. No answer. I held my finger on it until he spoke on the intercom.

"Go away," he said. "Or drop dead. Notice you have two alternatives."

"Dunne."

"Oh, the box Brownie man. Come up."

Upstairs there was someone in his bed. The sheet was pulled over her head, thus revealing her gold-painted toes. He noticed my gaze.

"Last night we thought it was funny," he said. "You know last nights. Your life is full of last nights."

"Not lately." I gave him the three rolls.

"How'd you make out, you think?"

I pointed to the toes.

He leaned over and tugged them. "Out," he said.

"I wanna stay."

"Out, honey."

"I'll make coffee and cover my tiny ears with my paws, I promise."

"Oh, Jesus," I muttered.

Farr became insistent. It finally got up, dressed, and went downstairs sulking. It wasn't the same one I had seen there last time.

"How come you always get the same type?" I asked.

"You know any normal female who wants to spend her life with her mouth half open, licking her lips so they'll photograph with highlights?"

"Nope."

"So don't ask."

"The brain that's attached to that body isn't very smart."

"It breathes," he said, "leaving the mind unconfused. Enough for me. All I want. Want me to develop these right away?"

"Yep."

"Will you make some coffee?"

"Yeah. I'll cover my tiny mouth while I do it."

I made coffee. I sat at the kitchen table drinking and staring at the white walls. I stood up and moved along sipping it. Like most bachelors, he had a quart of milk which had turned sour, like mine always did.

I looked at the beautiful twelve-by-fifteen shot he had made a few years ago of a dark forest in winter with a white mist settling down over it. That was my favorite. The other one I liked was the shot next to it—a little girl into whose hands someone had just placed a baby fox. I smiled at her astounded, ecstatic expression.

When he opened the door of the darkroom, I jumped.

"Well?"

"Not as perfect as I would have made them. But good."

I let out a sigh.

"Can they be enlarged okay?"

He nodded. I asked him to pick out the best.

"How soon?"

"Twenty minutes," he said.

He went back in again. I phoned the unlisted number Parrish had given me.

"I'm back."

"How soon can you be here?"

"Where are you?"

"28 Battery Place." That was near the southern tip of Manhattan.

"An hour from now."

"I'll give orders."

"One second. My name's Nelson."

"Nelson. Right."

The time to begin laying a smoke screen was now. He hung up.

I drank two more cups of coffee. I looked through Farr's magazines. I memorized the two photographs on the wall I liked best. The chances were very good that I would never see them again.

He came out with the enlargements.

"A little grainy," he said, "but seeing the available light you had to put up with, damn good."

"What do I owe you?"

"For making me chase that furry thing out of my bed, a couple drinks."

"Right. Thanks."

"If you see that nudnick having hot chocolate in the luncheonette downstairs, tell her to come back, will you? It takes her about thirty-five minutes to heat up the top of her spinal cord for the day."

"Her what?"

"The top of her spinal cord. You aren't listening carefully, Joe. Not like you. She doesn't have a brain, unlike higher-developed animals like you and me."

I said goodbye, went down two flights, and went right back up. I said, "I've never been here, you haven't seen me for a couple of months, and as far as that girl is concerned, make up some sort of a plausible lie if she asks about me. Okay?"

"Okay."

I paused.

"Okay, Joe. I said okay."

"Yeah, I know." I hung around a moment; although Farr didn't know it, it was goodbye forever. I couldn't let him know. So I finally said, "Well, Bryan, thanks."

She was sitting in the luncheonette. I went in and jerked my thumb upward.

"Oooo," she said. "I had three hot chocolates and then I found I didn't have any money!"

"Surprise."

"Yes. So can you please loan me sixty cents?"

Such a pathetic little con.

She misunderstood my look.

"Like I'm short."

Yeah, baby. Short on everything. I gave the counterman a dollar bill. He gave me the change. I shoved the forty cents back. As I turned to go, I saw her pull the coins across the counter. I lifted her hand, shoved the coins back to the counterman, took her elbow, and escorted her outside. I pointed up to Farr's studio.

"Doncha ever talk?"

The less she knew about me or my voice, the better. The more untypical a description of me she might give, the happier I would be.

She started to say something, but I had just caught the eye of a cruising hackie. He pulled over. I got in. She started to say something again, but I had closed the door. I wasn't going to give a destination that she might hear.

She poked her head in.

"Say, listen—" she began. I pushed her head gently and rolled up the window. The hackie watched all this with interest. She began talking through the glass, but I said, "Let's go."

"Where to, Jack?"

"Downtown."

She began to bang on the window.

He took off fast. Halfway down the block I turned around. She was still standing in the street with her hands cupped to her mouth and yelling. I waved. Women were always communicating with me through glass these days.

"Forty Wall," I said.

When we got there, I gave him a good tip. He deserved it for the jackrabbit start.

34

Parrish's office wasn't at Forty Wall. It was at 28 Battery Place, several blocks away to the west. I got out at Forty Wall, walked into the lobby and out the side entrance. The more misdirection the better, and what cabbies didn't know didn't hurt me.

In five minutes I was pressing the elevator button. On the thirty-second floor I told the receptionist my new name for the day. She sent me right in. He met me at the door of his office and looked at the big manila envelope under my arm.

He held out his hand.

"Maybe you better not look," I said. "Just give them to the dentists."

"Let's have them."

I let him have the envelope. He opened it and slid the photographs onto his desk. That's the worst part in a missing persons case—when the realization hits that all hope has to be abandoned. But Parrish took it very well.

"I'm going to get in touch with the dentists this afternoon," he said. "I'll have my men fly up to Syracuse and to Boston. I'll let you know by six tonight."

I went downstairs. Nothing to do till six. I sat on a bench in the Battery and watched the harbor traffic. I ate a hot dog. I took a ferry to the Statue of Liberty. I probably would never have the opportunity to see the lady again.

I ate another hot dog on the way back. I sat among my fellow Americans, drinking the overwatered orangeade and listening to the mothers screaming at the kids trying to climb on the railing.

I went ashore and watched a little kid at a drinking fountain squirting water at pigeons. I watched people with cameras taking pictures of each other. "Hold it," they cried. "Smile!" The people smiled and exposed their teeth.

I got up and turned my back to the happy tourists. I looked up at the mass of tall buildings across the park. It seemed impossible that there were streets down at their bases big enough for cars and people to wriggle through. Look at the buildings, Dunne. Play with those toy building blocks awhile and get out in one piece. If you're lucky. And if I had a decent run of luck I'd get out. Hurry back, Parrish. Let's get this goddam waiting over with.

I bought a bag of stale popcorn. Where was the hot butter and salt they used to have when I was a kid? With the greasy butter staining the paper bag yellow? They gave me a plastic bag and cold popcorn. The hell with those improvements. I thought of those ripe mangoes waiting for me down on the Central American coast and my mouth watered. I ate the popcorn out of boredom. And then it was five to six.

I dumped out the popcorn for the pigeons and walked across the park. I was admitted immediately into his office. As soon as I saw the packet of fifty dollar bills on the desk, I knew I had the right boys.

I picked it up.

"Twenty-five thousand in fifties. I thought you'd find that denomination easier to handle." The packet was four inches thick. I hefted it.

"Where are the bodies?"

I was prepared for that.

"I'll let you know as soon as I come to collect the next installment."

"You don't trust me?"

"As far as keeping the location to yourself for a week or two more? Frankly, no."

"I'll keep it confidential."

"You might. But I don't want to imagine that you might get impatient and start off on your own. What you don't know keeps me a little more relaxed."

"Suppose—"

"Suppose I get knocked off while I'm working for you?"

"Yes."

"Give me a sheet of paper, please."

He gave me a piece. On it I wrote, *John Cushman, 970 Madison.*

"That's my lawyer. I'll give him the information in a sealed envelope. I'll tell him as soon as he is convinced of my death to hand it to you. And he'll put it in a bank vault, so there's no point trying to get it from him."

He looked at me. I picked up the cash and stowed it in various pockets.

Then he shrugged. "Fair enough."

I took the elevator down.

It wasn't fair enough at all. J. Cushman existed, and he was a lawyer, and he was at 970. I knew that because I had noticed the name on a brass plate in the lobby. But he wasn't my lawyer.

I had no intention of getting knocked off in phase two of the operation, to use a clean word for a dirty piece of business—and I was beginning to feel a bit superstitious about assuming I might be. I had never felt that way before, but then I had never killed five people at once for money before.

I went to bed early. I spent a restless night. I was the first customer in the bank next morning. I changed the fifties into five five-thousand-dollar bills, and put them in my safe-deposit box. Later on they could be taken across the border. I could even wear them in my shoes. A four-inch-thick packet in a shoe would attract far more attention.

By 10:15 I was airborne. I almost resented paying

extra for the Kim, but it was a business expense, after all.

I could take it off my income tax.

I made up a little play. Here I am, drifting in the green water of the Gulf Stream. I'm wearing a big, broad-brimmed straw sombrero and a pair of shorts and some sunglasses. Nothing else. I'm very tanned. Swimming out to the launch, with his attaché case clamped between his teeth, is a U.S. Income Tax investigator. I watch him paddling closer with all my delinquent tax records in his jaws. Just before his office-pale hand is about to come over the transom, I punch a button. My twin marine Chryslers start up with a roar, and I leave the poor Fed bobbing in my enormous wake.

It was a nice fantasy, and I fell asleep smiling somewhere over Virginia.

35

When I walked into the terminal waiting room, I saw Kirby waving at me. She gave me a passionate homecoming kiss that mixed her perfume and her hair and body smell in one swift shock. Then she took my small overnight bag from under my arm. It weighed much less now that all the camera equipment was in my closet. I let her carry it.

"Does everything work now, honey?"

"It does now." Loud and unconcerned in case someone might be casually listening. "It was just a broken sprocket in the driving gear."

"You mean, you poor baby, you had to travel all that way for just a lil ole wheel?"

"That's it, baby. How was Jackson?"

She hugged me with her free arm as we walked to the car. "Ummm! Marvelous! I bought a new dress. Now you tell me if you like it, an' don't you dare fib. An' I had my hair done. Do you like it?"

We were outside now. We could drop the *Ladies' Home Journal* dialogue. All the time she had been talking I had been looking at her face. I tore my eyes away to look at her hair.

"It's always beautiful."

The trouble with that remark was that I downshifted from the light casualness we had been using since I met her.

She fell silent. I put the things in the car.

"Do you mind if I drive?" she asked. "I love driving."

"Sure." I sat beside her. I looked at her knees. Better find a distraction. The daily Jackson paper was on the seat beside her. I picked it up. Nothing special on the front page. Sunrise had been at 5:41 that morning.

There were times when I wanted to read a good simple book on astronomy and find out how the hell people could predict things like sunrises and high tides. I wanted to take a course in celestial navigation and find out how a man could take a sextant, a star or two, and a few books, and find out exactly where he was on an unmarked ocean. That was a bigger mystery than anything I had ever worked on.

When I went down to Central America, I decided to take a sextant and a good text on navigation with me. The chances of finding them down there would be pretty small. If I went through New Orleans, I probably could pick them up pretty easily.

I turned to page 3. Nothing special. But the fourth page had something interesting on it. In column four, near the bottom, a one-inch story.

OLDEST INHABITANT OF
MILLIKEN COUNTY DIES IN FIRE

Moses Gardiner, negro, ninety-two, died yesterday in a fire that totally consumed his home. He was the oldest resident of Milliken County. The funeral will take place tomorrow. The body rests at Morgan's Funeral Parlors, Okalusa.

I didn't feel like talking. When we reached Okalusa, I left the Kim in the car and told Kirby I had to go out and do a little work.

I headed for Alexandria. I went up the river road, and then up the red-clay roads to Old Man Mose's place.

I could see the stone chimney still standing. The iron bedstead still stood, but it was black and twisted from the heat. An old man was poking in the ashes with a stick. I got out and walked up to the house. I smelled gasoline. At the base of the chimney I found what I was looking for—several pieces of curved glass. I picked them up. One of the shards had EPSI engraved on it. I smelled it. Gasoline. Pepsi Cola bottles filled with gasoline and with a rag wick make effective Molotov cocktails.

Oya's shrine lay in the ashes. The jug had been smashed. The copper symbols had turned gray in the heat and fused together. The swamp shrine was burned except for the moccasin's jawbones. They were shining in the ashes. I put them in my pocket.

The old man prodded at an old can in the ashes. Heat had expanded it and some bean gravy was leaking out of it. He put it in a sack. Then he saw me for the first time. Before he could arrange his face into the usual amiable deferential look, it flared up with hatred.

"Seems a shame," I said.

"Yessuh, boss."

The yessuh-boss routine.

"Accidental, I suppose."

"Yessuh."

I kicked the pieces of the Pepsi bottle. One of the pieces clunked against the chimney.

"How accidental?"

His eyes drifted down to the glass. He walked over to my car and looked inside. He came back.

"You de gemmun what give Mose money to talk into that machine?"

"Yes."

"What sense in that? No sense in that at all. Better sense givin' money to a youman."

I took out a ten-dollar-bill and gave it to him.

He folded it carefully several times till it was the size of a postage stamp. His thickened yellow fingernails neatly creased the edges till they were knife-sharp.

"Don't wants de ole woman to git it. She gits her hooks onto this, it is *gone*. Gone." He took off his dirty gray hat and tucked the money into the sweatband. He put the hat on, smashed the crown flat with the palm of his hand.

"Las' night, 'bout two, Ah hears cars comin' up de road. That don't happen 'round heah. Fo' cars. One, two, three, fo'. Ah goes to my porch an' Ah lissens. They stop heah. Ah heah de door crack open, pow! Lahk that!" He slapped his palms together hard.

"Mose don't have no gun. Evvabody knows that. Ah has one, Ah has a twenty-two pistol. Ah flattens de bullets so they'll open up when they goes in, an' it'll tear up a cracker jus' as fas' as it'll tear up black folks, an' Ah lets evvabody knows Ah has one.

"After they knocks down Mose's door, they goes in. Ah takes mah gun an' Ah goes out an' hides in de co'n neah mah house. They comes to git me Ah gits me one or two fust. But they stayed at Mose. After maybe ten minutes they comes out. Then Ah sees de fire start up de sides of de house lahk lightnin'.''

"What did you do?"

"Ah didn't move, Ah didn't want to be caught lookin'. The cars go by an' one stops at mah place an' someone goes up and bangs on mah door. Ah keeps quiet an' he opens de door, cause Ah neveh locks it, an' he calls out mah name, an' then he goes away."

"Who was it?"

"Ah dunno, boss."

"You don't know."

He figured he had already risked too much.

"You sure now?"

His face closed and became impassive.

"Yassuh, boss."

"You planning to go to Mose's funeral?"

"It's neighborly."

"Aren't you getting tired of going to funerals of black men who've been killed by whites?"

His jaw trembled. He turned his face away and then began to walk. He walked a few feet and then turned toward me and said, "His name Vince. Now they ask you who tole you you say you dunno an' they gonna know *Ah* tole you. An' they come fo' me you come to mah fun'ral?"

"No. You just flatten a couple more twenty-two's."

"You tryin' to tell me sumpin'. You tryin' to tell me— what you tryin' to tell me?"

"I don't ask anybody to do anything that they don't want to do. You told me it was Vince who came up to your house. You own a twenty-two. Use it."

He took his hat and turned it around a few times and put it on. He said, "Next mawnin' de sheriff come over to Mose's house. He say he ain't gonna permit lootin'. He stood there till they wrapped up Mose in a blanket an' took him to de fun'ral parlor."

"Did you get a look at Mose?"

"No one got a look 'cept de sheriff and de undertaker."

I thanked him. He stood there looking at my car. I

kept seeing him in my rear-view mirror until I rounded a bend in the road. He would do well to take out that carefully folded ten-dollar bill and buy himself some cartridges. A shotgun would be even better. I would hesitate approaching someone with a shotgun. With a .22 I wouldn't mind taking a chance once in a while. Shotgun holders get respectful attention from me.

I drove to the black part of Okalusa. There were a few well-kept houses and neat lawns, but the main business street was full of potholes. Morgan's Funeral Parlors had a beautifully polished black hearse in front. There were no whites around.

I walked in. In the center of the room was a good oak coffin, well made and well varnished. It had gold-plated brass handles. The faceplate was screwed into place with nine large brass screws.

I took off my hat.

"Yes, sir?"

It was a voice that knew how to talk in funeral parlors. It blended with the thick brown wall-to-wall rug and the heavy brown drapes that were arranged in loops across the walls. Discreet lighting flowed down softly from concealed spots attached behind silk valances. There were bowls full of gladioli on the tables. I hate gladioli, but funeral directors adore them. Perhaps because they have a rigid, stiff look about them; perhaps because with so many blooms on one stalk the wilted ones can be discreetly removed day by day.

"May I see Mr. Mose."

"He is in the coffin, sir."

I looked at him. He was a pale brown color and blended with the rug and the drapes. His eyes were brown and hooded. He moved silently. He reminded me of an enormous, brown Siamese cat.

"I knew him. I admired him."

"Yes, sir."

"I'm from Canada, I'm down here on a research project on speech patt—"

"I know."

In small towns everybody knows everything about everything.

"I was very sorry to read about this. I wonder if I could see him for the last time."

"I think you had best remember him the way he was."

I silently agreed.

But I was putting parts of a puzzle together. Everyone knew by now that Old Man Mose had helped me with my speech project. When word would get around that I had been to the funeral parlor, I'd get credit for being a good friend of his.

And there was always the chance that I might be able to provoke some interesting conversation out of some blacks along the line.

People in stressful situations talk when they sense a friendly ear. Morgan had been a good friend of the old man.

I took the arc of charred snake jaw out of my pocket.

"He would have liked this placed in the coffin with him."

"Yes, thank you." He held out his hand. I dropped it in. He set it on the coffin and folded his arms.

"He had a very impressive face," I said.

"Yes."

"If this were Africa, that's the kind of a face I would associate with a king."

"Yes. Some of us were kings. In Africa."

He did not get any friendlier. My remarks seemed to make him more abrasive.

I thought it would be best to move on to another topic.

"I wonder how I can persuade—"

"You can't. I had a little talk last night with a gentleman

of your color who called at my back door. He wore a white mask as well as three of his friends. They said it would be healthy for me to see that my client was buried with the coffin sealed."

"Ummm."

"You know something, Mr. Wilson? You remind me of a snapping turtle. Once when I was a boy I poked a stick at a snapping turtle. He caught it and held it in his jaws. I said to an old man—I believe you use the word 'darky' —I said, 'He won't let go till it thunders.' And the old darky—"

"Try using the words 'old man.'"

He shot me a quick, inscrutable glance.

"And the old man said, 'Ah kin so make 'im.' He got an old lard can and put some rocks in it and shook it in front of the turtle. It made a hell of a racket.

"'That's thunder,' he said to me.

"'It don't sound much like thunder to me.'

"'At's right. Hit sound lak thunder to him. Tu'tles can't tell no diff'rence.'

"So he kept banging away at the can. I kept watching. And the old man turned to me and said, 'Hit'll take a little time. He got to think 'bout hit. Sooner or later he'll let go.'"

"I'm the turtle?"

"And I'm banging away on the lard can."

"I'll still hang on for a while yet. That's a beautiful box."

He looked at me. "Box" is the trade word.

"Yes. It cost a lot of money. Most of our poorer people join burial societies. They pick out a nice coffin and then the number of cars they want. They think a dignified death a sort of a compensation for a humiliating life."

"Understandable. I should think that a defiant death would be a better compensation."

"Yes. You would. You don't know what it means to live

out there with the law like a lawn mower going back and forth chopping off anything that pokes its head a little higher than they like."

He was becoming more and more icy. I knew he had slammed shut a door which was never open more than a crack.

"Would that be all?"

"For now. Thank you."

"Not at all, sir. Good afternoon." He paused a second and played it careful and added, "sir."

36

Funeral parlors always have someone on night duty. And how can it be the owner when he has to save all his energy and be bright and sympathetic during the day?

I parked two blocks away. It was 2:30 A.M. It was a Thursday night. I thanked God for that. Thursday nights are always slow nights everywhere. People have spent all their money by Thursday; payday is Friday, when they can begin to vomit and strike each other on the head again. So Thursday nights are always good nights to find a table in a good restaurant or an empty seat at a popular bar. Or park in Niggertown and walk to a funeral parlor.

There was no one in the street. A few doors down from where I parked, a counterman sat in Larry's All-Nite Café with his elbows on the counter spooning soup and reading a comic book. There were no customers.

Inside the Morgan Funeral Parlors a single light bulb was burning. I pulled open the screen door and a little bell tinkled. It was very discreet and subdued, like Mr. Morgan. I cursed quietly, but the sound was almost inaudible. I stepped in and took off my hat. The coffin was still resting on its two trestles. I came up close and looked down at it.

The faceplate was still in place. Nine big fat screws. I slid a fingernail into one of the slots. A dime would fit in nicely. But they were really in tight. No fooling around with a dime on this job.

"Yessuh?"

I turned. A man came forward, looked at me with silent curiosity.

"I would be grateful if I could look at Mr. Mose for the last time."

"Nope. Nossuh!"

I took out a five and laid it on the coffin. He was impassive. I took out another. His eyebrows lifted a little. People in Southern towns didn't go around spreading money this easily. One more. His tongue came out and touched his lips and then went back in again. One more. That was almost a week's pay on the local wage scale. That was a lot of money for a little effort and not too much risk. He began to warm up. He looked quickly over his shoulder.

And one more.

His hand scooped them up decisively.

"I's gonna get a screwdriver," he whispered. "Now anyone come you say you was gonna kill me effen I din't do what you say."

"Okay."

He disappeared and came back with a long screwdriver with an amber plastic handle. The screws were in tight. It took both hands and a lot of little grunts and shoulder muscle before he could start one. It began to turn with a little squeal. "Phewie," he whispered, "they puts 'em in with one of them 'lectric things. Zoom!"

I held the screws as he took them out.

I wondered what the hell I was doing there. The old man was dead. What was the difference how he had died?

Maybe I shouldn't have come. Word might reach the sheriff I was fooling around with things which were not exactly what a Canadian speech expert should be doing. And if the sheriff heard, so would A.B.C.

I was guilty of doing something which no professional should ever do. I was becoming personally involved; I was breaking a very good rule. I had kept to it damn carefully as far as Kirby was concerned.

It would be smart for me to stay away from Old Man Mose now that he was dead. But I was beginning to hate these people; I wanted to know exactly what they had done to him. I would take a good look and put the data away in the J. Dunne filing cabinet, next to the drawer labeled "Vengeance is mine, saith the Lord."

You can call it childish.

I wouldn't have done it the first few days down in Okalusa. But there was something about that Southern way of handling dissenters I was beginning to get angry about. And it didn't matter too much now what I did; I was getting real close to earning my money. I could go ahead and take the chance. Even if A.B.C. heard about it later and whistled up his bloodhounds, I was sure I could lead them up a shallow riverbed or two and then split across a rocky surface and be long-gone Joe by the time they caught on.

He took out the last screw. He put down the screwdriver and lifted the faceplate.

I squeezed the handful of screws.

Mose had been badly beaten.

Mea maxima culpa.

"Put it back."

He picked up the screwdriver. "Mistuh, you never saw nothin'."

"Right."

To whom do I apologize?

"What I mean is, you might git talkin' someday, an' if

you ever talks about this, I am cooked. I am daid. You gonna bite yo' lips fo' me?"

My palm was wet. I turned it over and looked at it. I had forced a couple of the threads into the skin. I wiped it with a handkerchief and promised to bite my lips.

"I 'preciate that." He walked to the door and held the clapper of the little bell. When I walked out, not a sound came from it.

The counterman had his head pillowed in his arms. No one was in the streets. A slight chill had come in the air and even the bugs that had been bumping into the globes of the streetlights had gone. It was a slow night in Okalusa.

I opened the door of the car and a voice said behind my ear, "Good morning, Mr. Wilson."

Not many people say good morning before they slug you. Although I felt like leaping up and switching ends like a bronco, that thought deterred me. I said very calmly, "Good morning to you," before I turned around to see who the pussy-footing bastard was.

Naturally it was Mr. Funeral Parlor.

Any funeral parlor director, I was beginning to feel, could give points to an Apache when it came to approaching nervous people. Or people who might feel guilty about something. Like me.

"There's something about Mose that attracts you enormously," he said.

"The relationship of Southern Negro vowels to the Herefordshire dialect," I said.

"Yes. You taped him. You visited his house this afternoon. You came here later. You found him so interesting you came again."

"Looking for souvenirs."

"Looking for souvenirs, as you say. I hear you found a couple."

"I was hoping that some of his juju might have survived the fire."

"You'd like a pocketful of conjure things?"

"I'd like a souvenir of Old Man Mose. I admired him."

"I hear you found a couple."

"They were all burned, I'm sorry to say."

"Glass doesn't burn."

I was leaning back against the car and he surprised me with that one.

"I kicked around a couple chunks, yes."

"Shards."

"Congratulations on your vocabulary."

"Shards is a good word. And now you're here for the second time."

"I insist on paying my last respects."

"No doubt. But somehow that's not the kind of behavior I associate with a Ph.D. candidate."

"We vary in our personal qualities."

"Did you see anything interesting when you took off the faceplate?"

"What faceplate?"

He looked at me.

"I only came in once, during the afternoon. I stood with head bowed, in respect for a very old man who had told me some old stories in order to help me for my doctoral dissertation, and then I left, period."

"Period. So if the issue should ever arise, say, in conversation with law-enforcement officers, or even in a court somewhere, will it still be period?"

I was getting annoyed.

"Look here, Morgan. I came about four this afternoon. I stood by the unopened coffin a minute or so with my hat in my hand. Then I left."

"Name, rank, and serial number."

"It'll have to hold you."

"And you never talked to my night custodian."

"Oh, come off it."

"You feel contemptuous. How would you like some cracker to come racing by at four A.M. with a half inch steel ball bearing in a rubber slingshot and let go at your twelve-by-eight plate-glass window with gold-leaf lettering? I can't get window insurance. Or walk out and find all your hearse tires slashed? Or be handled the way they handled Mose?"

"I suppose I'd hate it. And now, if you'll excuse me—"

He backed off enough for me to get in. He took the door handle and closed the door by pushing it gently shut and then releasing the door handle. If I had been ten feet away, I don't think I would have heard it.

"Oh, Jesus," I said, under my breath.

"Oh, Jesus," he repeated. "You try running a good business where the law, the tax structure, the newspapers and most of the rural whites and a great deal of the city ones are lined up solidly against you. You just try it. Try it just a week. And then let's talk about it."

I should have gone to his house, sat over a couple drinks for a few hours, and entered deeply into the question of black-white relationships. He was all primed for it and it would have been very interesting and I would have learned a lot. We might have hammered out some constructive solutions and we would have parted with a lot of mutual respect.

But I wasn't down in Okalusa to develop my sociological imagination. Or whatever they were calling it these days.

I was very sleepy and I had to figure out how to get some incriminating statements from several people who had casually added arson to their list of achievements.

An immature choice, perhaps. But I was stuck with it.

37

Kirby stopped the car at the river. I had everything ready in the trunk. She never had known about the machine gun. I had taken it out of the spare tire the night before and assembled it without her seeing me. Coming out, I had stripped in the car down to swim trunks and a pair of sneakers. I pulled my things out of the trunk, closed the trunk lid quietly, waved goodbye, and slid down the bank with my props for the evening performance.

Anyone in the bait shack might have heard the car stop. But since it started again in ten seconds, it was nothing to get excited about. Even if you lived in a small Southern town.

I unrolled an air mattress I had bought on my trip to New York. I could have bought it in Okalusa and saved carrying it down on the flight, but it might have attracted some attention.

The mattress was made of strong rubberized nylon. It wouldn't tear on a snag of a sunken cypress stump or even on a sharp, broken branch we might drift over.

Twenty deep, long breaths filled the mattress. My chest ached. I wasn't in such good condition as I thought.

I couldn't see the river. The moon was behind a heavy, cloudy sky. If I looked down, I could see a black mass moving slowly to my right. I guessed it was shifting at about half the speed of a normal walking pace, about a mile and a half an hour.

About thirty yards away was another black mass—the trees of the opposite shore.

I set the recorder in the dead center of the mattress. It sank a bit in the middle but still rode high.

I picked up the machine gun. I had wrapped it in a small piece of canvas so that Kirby would have no idea what it was. I unwrapped it and screwed on the big black silencer. It was about the size of a quart bottle of beer. I clipped on a full drum of cartridges. I took out a rubber contraceptive from the little pocket of my swim trunks and covered the muzzle with it in case it would be dumped into the water. It was an old trick I had picked up in Korea.

I put a thick, absorbent towel on top of the gun. I was ready. I waded into the river up to my knees. The bottom felt soft and muddy. I went above my ankles in the mud and I felt it oozing into my sneakers. The water was cool. I pulled the mattress from the bank into the water. As soon as it was free of the shore, the current began to tug at it like a dog pulling at a bone. I pushed it out into the river till the water reached my shoulders. Then I kicked off from the bottom. It was a pleasure to kick free from the bottom mud.

The mattress began to float downstream. The night was hot. It pressed down like a thick wool blanket. From the swamp on each side came the deep bellow of bullfrogs and the *gloink-gloink* of the smaller frogs. The same kind that I had hung up for my personal juju. I smiled when I thought of old Ryerson's face when he came upon it. The croaking of the bullfrogs sounded as if someone were plunking at a giant cello.

Somewhere downstream a fish jumped and splashed back into the water. Fish don't jump for the sheer joy of living, the way colts will race around a pasture. They jump because bigger fish are after them. The alligator is not a fish, but it eats fish. It eats moccasin eggs too, which made me feel a slight affection for it, but the thought made my feet feel very vulnerable. I suppressed a strong wish to hurl myself on the mattress. But if I did, there wouldn't be any assurance that the recorder would remain dry. And if the recorder didn't work perfectly tonight, I might as well pack up and go home.

Mosquitoes whined out of the swamp and settled on my sweating face and neck. I settled down to two hours of drifting, punctuated with irritated mutters and slaps.

Something slid off the bank to my left and went into the black water with a loud splash. I didn't want to hang around and find out what caused it. I gave several strong scissor kicks and the mattress picked up speed. Whatever it was, if it was used to the water, it could swim rings around me if it really wanted to, I took the chance that it might not be too interested in me. At least, not enough to follow me.

A minute later I felt a smooth, round object slide along my thigh and grab at my trunks. I thrashed wildly to one side and kicked as hard as I could. The result was a stubbed toe and a ripped pair of trunks.

I had gone over a submerged cypress knee with a broken stub sticking out of one side. My sneakers saved my big toe from a bad bruise when I kicked out. I felt my heart throbbing away like an engine racing out of control.

We city boys panic easily in the country. It would have been simpler if Kirby had driven me close to the Catfish Club. But we might have been spotted by some member driving to the club. Or she might have been recognized on her way back to the main road. Too risky.

I kicked for another five minutes. That wasn't smart. I gained a little time. But the later I got there, the better. More of them would be there and they'd be more liquored up. What I was trying to do was understandable but stupid: to get out of that black water as quickly as possible.

As soon as I realized what I was doing, I stopped kicking. I was ashamed of myself. That kind of panic activity was the way you lost. Panic action was what got you dead in Korea, and it could do the same down in Mississippi. I had always had pretty good control of myself, but this was the first time I was after five people, any one of whom would have shot me without a second's hesitation if he knew what I was up to. It was true that the North Koreans and the Chinese would have done that too, but then I had a lot of friends around me who would have helped, and a war is where the more people you kill, the easier it is to get a medal hung on you.

My mind was getting stupid.

What did I mean by thinking, "if he knew what I was up to"? A tape recorder and a machine gun and drifting down on their Catfish Club? What would he think I was up to—looking for bait?

The thing to do was to play it cool, just drift. Detach the mind and send that adrift. Another forty-five minutes and I would be at the club, ready for a night of fun and games. Just don't think about the swamp, Dunne. Think about dozing off under a coconut tree somewhere on the Honduras coast. And some girl in a loose white blouse is bending over you with a tall glass filled with cracked ice and gold rum and lime juice.

But the image wouldn't stick. It kept dissolving and all I saw was masses of thick-bodied moccasins coiled up all along the river's edge. I tried to remember whether moccasins were night-hunters. It was either rattlers or moccasins who hunted at night. And this was a hell of a time to forget who did what. I hoped to God it was rattlers. That would leave the day to the moccasins, if that were the case, and I wished them Godspeed with their sunlit pursuit of frogs.

I carefully placed the idea of alligators somewhere in a back room of my mind. I thought I had succeeded, but the door suddenly opened and I could just see the way the water curled around the eye ridge. I could hear Brady idly chatting as we stood on the patio holding drinks and sipping before Kirby correctly decided that he and I should become public enemies.

He said, "Now next time you get to a zoo, take a good look at an alligator. They're as well adapted for livin' in the water as these Southern politicians are for survivin' in Democratic Party primaries.

"You might say both species have it made.

"The alligator has a heavy eyelid. Look and you'll see a ridge around it. This ridge makes the water curl off around his eyes so he can really get up speed when he's on the surface, and it works so good that he can make time and not blind himself. Now look at that inner lid. That's for underwater precision work. That inner lid slides sidewards. He can see through it, because it corrects for underwater refraction of light so he can strike accurately underwater. Any civil rights worker coming into a little Southern town is like a swimmer decidin' to take a healthy invigoratin' little swim in a swamp filled with hungry alligators. Neither one of them is goin' to have much of a chance."

"Brady, you son of a bitch," I muttered. I hated his vivid phrases. I got some sort of shame-faced satisfaction from knocking out his teeth.

Then I got thinking how much it would cost the poor guy for three artificial teeth and bridgework. I once had two teeth knocked from my upper right jaw by a gun barrel in some nighttime discussion. It cost five hundred seventy-five bucks. Probably front teeth were more of a problem. Maybe eight hundred? I would send Brady that and a brief note of apology.

This kind of rambling kept my mind off the river. I decided to go on with it. How could I send Brady the money? It had better be postmarked Toronto.

But how could I send a letter from Toronto if I were going in exactly the opposite direction? I could enclose eight one-hundred-dollar bills in an envelope and a note, wrapping it well so that the bastard couldn't hold it up to the light and see what was in it, the bastard being my friend Moran up in Toronto, with a request that he mail the letter to Okalusa.

But he would probably steam it open to see what he could learn that might be useful or profitable. Goodbye, eight hundred smackers.

No. Moran was out.

It would be better to send the envelope to the postmaster at Toronto with an International Reply Coupon and a note saying that I collected postmarks, and that I would be grateful if he would cash in the IRC for a pretty Canadian stamp and mail it to me.

"Me" would be Brady, of course.

Yes. That would work out fine. I would—a slimy tendril from a water-edge plant wrapped itself around my leg. I almost whipped myself onto the mattress to escape. And to hell with the recorder.

I had just about enough of these encounters. I had seen men break down and cry in Korea when they had had too much. One or two more little encounters like that lousy little weed and I would drop the whole thing.

Except that for half a million bucks I would plunge my naked arm into a bushel full of moccasins. With reasonable assurance that I would survive, of course.

These little mental exercises to take my mind off nighthunters and inner eyelids for underwater precision work were not working too well. And it wasn't doing much good to think of tall glasses packed with crushed ice fed to me by an amiable mestiza while I swung back and forth in a hammock. The hammock would be made of nylon and not out of sisal. Sisal scratches. There would be a double jigger of rum in the glass and a teaspoon of sugar. The juice of a lime would have been squeezed by the strong hands of the lady, and she would hold the glass up to the sky and let me watch the pale green lime juice trickling every which way through the fissures of the cracked ice.

I had just about exhausted all of these little fantasies. I don't think I could have produced any more of them as a defensive wall against any more nighttime surprises from the swamp. I had had it.

Then I floated around a bend and saw the lights of the Catfish Club.

38

A few kicks and I was under the pilings. Light poured down in narrow gold slabs through the cracks in the flooring. If anybody upstairs would take a look down he might see me, especially if I moved.

I had to rely upon habit patterns: no one ever looked down at a floor as a matter of course. And I made doubly sure by maneuvering the mattress so that it would be directly under the table, the way I remembered it.

Someone said, "Aw, not on yore filthy pants."

Joe Sam added, "Wipe that goddam knife afore you cuts the fish. Jus' once. Jus' wipe it once."

Back in Okalusa I had cut a slit in each projecting corner of the mattress. Then I had run a piece of clothesline through each slit. When I had the mattress nicely positioned under the floor, I made the lines fast to four pilings. Now the mattress held firm against the current.

The water was up to my chest. Inside the recorder it said, in four languages:

>   *vor nasse schutzen*
>   *protégez contre l'humidité*
>   *proteger contra humedad*
>   *keep dry*

If they considered keeping it dry important enough to repeat it four times, who was I to disagree? I wiped my hands very carefully. Then I lashed the mike with another length of line to a piling so that it was directly under one of the cracks. I faced it upward. It was a dynamic directional mike with low impedance. I didn't know what it meant, but I hoped it meant good.

The Kim's controls were like a piano keyboard. I pressed the *start* and *record* keys simultaneously. It was like spanning a small octave on a piano. It made a tiny *click!* which was drowned by the gurgling noise of the water coiling around the pilings. I reached up and turned the *on* switch in the mike. There was a faint rustle as the reels turned. It was the sound a snake makes as it moves over dry leaves.

I settled back with my back against a piling and listened.

The sounds of plates. Knives and forks. I could smell fresh hushpuppies. Then the tinkle of glass, probably the jug against a glass rim. Then a gurgling sound.

"I don't hold with that ungodly stuff," Joe Sam said.

"You still talkin'?" That sounded like Vince.

"That squashed-up frawg an' that tooth a hangin' from it. More I think 'bout it, more I think we shoulda done somethin'. Like make the sign of the cross afore we touched it."

I suddenly noticed something shining. I looked down. I had forgotten that the voltage meter was illuminated. I threw a quick glance upward, half expecting to see a curious eye peering down, but there was no one. I pulled an end of the towel over the meter.

"You keep talkin' 'bout it, you gonna vex me, Joe Sam."

"Cain't help it. I cain't git it outta my mind. That there frawg stuck in that stick is a power!"

"Joe Sam, you shut up!"

"Vince, you know Ol' Man Mose, he kept a pocket full

o' fish scales? When I wasn't no bigger'n 'at frawg, he kind o' squeaked an' rattled them scales in his hand an' right then I wished I was dead. I purely don't think we shoulda gone to his house. Then he used—"

"You talk some mo', you gonna rile me."

"Then he used to have a lil bitty ol' dry-up tuttle, jus' a mud tuttle 'bout the size o' my thumb, the whole thing jus' dry-up and dead. He used to take out that tuttle an' put it in the palm of his hand an' sot down an' say:

> 'Little bunch o' pepper,
> Little bunch o' wool.
> Two, three pammy Christy beans,
> Little piece o' rusty iron.
> Mumbledy-mumbledy.'

He used to make my hair creep all ovuh the back o' my neck when he do that. For a fact."

"What's that 'mumbledy—mumbledy'?"

"How should I know? It's African. I'm sure glad I didn't do nothin' to Ol' Man Mose."

"You scairt?"

"I ain't scairt o' doin' what we done with them No'th'n niggers, an' that white boy 'cause he ain't no better'n a nigger, but Ol' Man Mose, he's diffrunt."

Vince said, "Aw, you believe in that nigger voodoo."

"I ain't sayin' yes an' I ain't sayin' no. All I say is, it don't hurt none to go up there an' make a sign. I got me a mind to go up right now."

"Sit down, you damn fool."

"Ain't goin' to sit down. You think jus' because you threw that stick an' that frawg way into the piny woods the power'll stay away? You got to fight power with power. An' killin' Mose ain't the way to do that."

The sheriff spoke. "I don't give a damn 'bout power or voodoo or hoodoo. Don't believe in spirits or hants. That's for ol' ladies an' niggers. All I believe is when someone knows somethin' you don't want him to know, you make sure he don't talk."

"I'm sure glad I didn't do nothin' to Ol'—"

"Aw, shut up." This was Ray.

"It fair sickened me to my stomach, the way Vince went at Ol' Man Mose."

"Why doncha try puttin' your lips together an' not movin' 'em for a while, Joe Sam?"

"I don't like you beat 'im with chains. All you had to do was shoot 'im."

"Chains teaches 'em a lesson."

"How does it teach 'em if they're dead?"

Ray interrupted. He said, "You think mebbe we should bury 'em somewhere else?"

"Yeah," the sheriff said. "No tellin' if Ol' Man Mose din't tell somebody. We better go tonight an' take 'em somewhere else. Joe Sam, you get that ol' tarpaulion outta your garage. You go git it an' meet us back of my house."

"Why that tarpaulion? It's a good one."

"You want your car all smelted up with them boys? They're ripe. Now you go git it, y' hear?"

Well, that was enough to convict. Maybe not in front of a jury of twelve good men and true in Okalusa. But enough for the only jury I cared about. It was sitting at 28 Battery Place, high above Manhattan. I knew what he would accept as convincing evidence. And I had it on that silently circling plastic reel.

I had better begin work. I reached out for the stop key, but just then I heard a car turning off the road. Then it stopped. Doors opened and slammed. Two or three people were coming up the walk. I cursed silently.

They knocked.

"Who's at?"

"Andy 'n' Boone."

" 'Bout time. Come in."

They walked in.

"Put it down easy, now," said the sheriff.

Andy or Boone put it down easy. I heard glasses. Then the sound of a liquid being poured.

"How much we owe?"

"Aw, you know how much."

"Okay. You fellas want a drink?"

Jesus. The local bootleggers making the rounds.

The chairs scraped. Damn them, I hoped they weren't settling down for the night. They talked. From the sudden way the Catfish Club had dropped the topic under discussion, I was sure that the newcomers had nothing to do with the three boys. If they were settling down for an evening of hard drinking, I was out of luck. The next meeting wouldn't be till Friday.

In that week, if A.B.C. was as smart as I thought he was, he might be making me, as they say in the profession. That is, he would have traced me, and found out who I was.

I couldn't afford to wait that long.

So that created an ethical dilemma. If the night went by and those two bootleggers were still there, should I drop half a million bucks just in order to avoid killing two bystanders? Who might not have been involved in this particular killing, but who might have approved of it?

I listened to them talk about the new girls at Mike Gillen's Motel and Truck Stop. There were four cabins in the rear, each one fitted out with a whore from Jackson or Mobile. The girls were rotated every two weeks by the local syndicate. The Catfish Club began to compare the current batch to the previous ones. It was decided that the new ones weren't so hot. This news was very interesting but not worth half a million.

Half an hour passed. I was tired of standing in one place. My legs were becoming cramped and chilled. I didn't dare move. I might make some noise that wouldn't sound fishlike. I might step into a hole on the river bottom and make a man-sized splash.

They talked about the new liquor tax man down at Jackson; about the Air Force plane that had flown low over their mountaintop still a year ago, and how Boone had shot at it and put a bullet hole in a wing, and how the FBI and Air Intelligence swarmed all over the mountaintop looking for the saboteur. Only it was the wrong mountain. This was also interesting information, but Parrish wouldn't pay five cents for a reel on Federal Liquor Tax evasion. Should I kill them?

They might deserve it for having the Catfish Club for a customer. I suddenly felt an agonizing pain stab my left calf. With my city boy reactions I almost let out a yell, but I gritted my teeth and forced myself to remain motionless. It took a second before I realized it was only a muscle cramp.

I bit my thumb to keep from moaning. When the spasm passed, I kneaded the calf with all my might. The cramp finally went away. I was beginning to lose patience. I picked up the gun and started to wade ashore. But suddenly there was a lot of chair scraping and "see y'alls." Then the door opened and Andy and Boone walked out and drove away.

I went back and put down the gun and took a deep breath. Thank God. God would take a more lenient view about five deaths than he would about seven.

I didn't know what the sheriff said next. My attention was turned in another direction: someone was coming down the walk. It swayed and creaked. Then he ducked under the top railing, dropped to the mud, and came toward me. It was only later, when I played the tape, that I heard the sheriff tell Vince to get some mud, and smear it over their license plates.

All I knew at that second was that a man was coming toward me. I thought at first that he was going to urinate, but when he came off the walk I knew I was wrong. And the chances were very good that he would see me and the mattress. There were just too many bars of light coming down on me and the equipment.

I could have gotten him with my machine gun. But the silencer didn't mean that it functioned in complete silence. It meant that it didn't go off with an ear-shattering *blam! blam! blam!* It made a sound which would carry over a hundred feet or more on a quiet night, and even further in a narrow river with high banks. It was all right for night ambushes, or to pick off a patrol without alerting the main body, but the sound of the gun below the Catfish Club would certainly alert the men above. That and the splash he would make when he would fall into the water. And he might scream.

They had guns above and they knew how to use them. I might even get knocked off myself.

It would be better for me to handle Vince without the help of Hiram Maxim's noble invention, the silencer.

So, as soon as Vince ducked under the railing I began to wade toward the shore as quickly as I could. It's not easy to wade fast and quietly at the same time. I moved several feet, then got behind a piling only two feet from the shore. I stuck out plenty on both sides, but I didn't worry too much. I had had lessons in Korea. I was making a night patrol toward the Chinese lines when a flare went up. And I was standing. You might think the best thing to do in such a situation is to dive flat. Well, that's wrong. The best thing to do is not move. You might think you stand out like the Empire State Building. But you don't. People frequently will not notice the most obvious thing. As long as it doesn't move. So I froze.

He squatted down with an old pie plate. He was three feet in front of me. He began piling the mud onto the plate. Since I hadn't heard the sheriff telling him to get the mud, I thought he was so drunk he had reverted to childhood and was going to make himself some mud pies. And he wasn't too smart to begin with.

That made me hold back. It was almost like attacking an idiot child. I wouldn't have gone for him if he had just gotten his mud, stood up, and left. I mean I wouldn't have gone for him then. Later would be different.

But when he had almost filled the plate, his eyes lifted and saw my knees. His eyebrows shot up and he started to open his mouth.

I clapped a hand over it, and with my other hand clapped to the back of his neck I pulled him forward fast. Since he was squatting, he was easily knocked off balance. I forced his mouth and nose deep into the mud. Since he would make too much noise thrashing around, I got his right arm in a good strong lock and then I lay on top of him. He couldn't move and my thirty pounds weight advantage kept him pressed into the soft mud.

He shuddered and quivered for two minutes. Then it was over.

It was much worse than I ever thought it would be.

I lay on top of Vince for a minute more. To make sure. Then I waded back and got the gun. Then I put it back.

The reason why Old Man Mose had been killed was because of my shoes.

I had walked all around the melon patch in the damp ground. All those footprints. So I went and thought up the camouflage idea.

And here I was all set to walk all around the murder scene with my sneakers. They were a distinctive pattern. They had been made for gripping slippery decks and I used them whenever I went out fishing. They cost nine and a half bucks. Because of four little side holes at the arch they let in cool air, and on especially hot days when I was out taping people I had worn them. I bet no one within a hundred and fifty miles had a similar pair.

"Vince, what the hell's keepin' you?"

I took off the sneakers and put them on the mattress. I

picked up the gun and waded ashore. "Goddammit, what you doin'?"

I grunted out, "Minnit." It was a pretty good imitation.

The door of the shack was half open. I walked through the mud, ducked under the railing, and walked in. They were all sitting together at the table, I was happy to see.

Ray began to talk. He got out, "Vince, you—" before he fell silent.

The others turned.

I brought the gun up and swung the muzzle slowly back and forth. The arc was small but big enough to cover them all in its oscillations. "Freeze," I said.

The sheriff was stretching his arms in a huge yawn. His gun belt was hanging from a nail in the wall three feet in back of him. The gun rack had two shotguns in it. It was four big steps from the nearest club member, who was Ray.

No one said anything. They were staring at the gun. I couldn't blame them. It didn't look like a gun. With that pale plastic stock and the fat round silencer and the round pale-blue drum on top, it looked like a bad piece of modern sculpture or a sloppily designed electric fan.

Then they looked at me. I just wore a pair of swim trunks and my legs from the knees down were black with mud. I was covered with mosquito bites and they were beginning to puff up. I had just killed Vince and that must have given me some sort of an added bonus for my personal appearance which I wasn't aware of, but it all totaled up to something which made the sheriff's next remark, now that I thick back, seem reasonable.

"Now, perfessor," he said, soothing. "You're a little drunk, looks like, an' what you're doin' half naked I'll be goddamned if I can figger out. What you need is to sit down an' have some of our white mule here. So you better sit down. Ray, give your chair to the perfessor."

His right hand was beginning to drop toward the back of the chair. It would also pass by his gun butt. I had to take charge immediately.

I put the lever on single shot, dropped the muzzle, and squeezed off one shot. The gun went *chug!* and the jug blew into splinters. The sheriff's hand went up again and stayed there. I put the gun back on automatic.

They looked at it with respect.

"Well," Ray said agreeably, "I'll be diddle-dog-damned if I ever see a thing like that."

No one looked scared. Joe Sam looked expectantly at the door when he thought I wasn't looking at him.

"Vince isn't coming," I said.

"What you do with Vince?" asked the sheriff.

I saw no reason to get into a debate. Ray was inching toward the shotguns every time he thought my attention was diverted. The sheriff was watching my eyes. In a few seconds I would have to keep both Ray and the sheriff under close observation, and I was sure that within a few seconds one of the others would make a try for my gun or for the shotguns. Then a mess would develop and my chances of coming out of it unhurt would lessen.

I had thought of making some sort of a statement; after all, I was both judge and executioner, and the right to make a brief speech before carrying out sentence was traditionally mine. I wanted them to know exactly why I was there and why they were about to die.

I pulled the trigger instead and swept the gun back and forth across the table as if it were a fire hose. It went *chugchugchugchugchug!*

Although the sheriff had been sitting down, the impact jerked him to his feet. His hands shot out, palms downward, and then jerked up to chest level. His face was contorted.

After a while I realized the drum was empty. Yet I was

still squeezing the trigger so hard that my knuckle was white. No one was moving.

The shack was filled with the sharp, bitter smell of powder. I made sure they were all dead. I bent down and took out the sheriff's .45. I went to each one and took his pulse. I put the muzzle of the .45 in each man's ear. If any one of them had made a move, I would have fired. No pulse beats.

I wiped my prints off the .45 butt with the dirty dish towel. I put the gun back in the holster.

I went underneath the shack and waded out to the mattress. The moon had come up. There was a lot of blood dripping down through the cracks. The towel was pretty well soaked with it. I balled up the towel and was about to toss it in the river when I realized that it might be found downstream. I had bought it yesterday in town. I untied the mike and put it away. I untied the mattress from the pilings and towed it ashore. I wiped the blood from the recorder and my sneakers. I rinsed out the blood from the towel. I couldn't get it out of the sneakers by wiping them, so I rinsed out the sneakers in the river.

I sat in the mud and put the sneakers on. My fingers were trembling. I couldn't even tie the laces. I turned and butted my head against the piling. A little pain would take my mind away from whatever it was contemplating and force it to dwell on mundane things like pain and how to tie shoelaces effectively.

Here is where you make the mistakes, I said to myself. *Slow Down.* Don't try to get away fast. Stick around. Sit and think. *Think.*

I folded my arms on my knees and leaned my forehead against them. I could feel my arteries throb in my upper arms. I must have had a pulse rate higher than a hummingbird's. I took several deep breaths. I thought about diving off the aft deck of my new cruiser into the

Caribbean through the clean, green, translucent water down to the bottom. The wave patterns of the surface would be transmuted into quivering lines that would oscillate across the white sandy bottom. I would spin onto my back and look up at the hull of my boat and the bottom rung of the ladder over the stern.

I sighed and lifted my head. I had shifted down to a lower heartbeat. All right. What am I doing wrong? The answer came: your sneakers.

Of course. Footprints all over again. I took them off and knotted the laces together. I slung them around my neck like a necklace.

What else? Now I was thinking calmly. *What else?*

I didn't move for thirty seconds. Nothing else.

Good. I unscrewed the air valve on the mattress. I rolled it up slowly. The air hissed out under pressure. It sounded like an enormous snake and I didn't care. I wasn't worried about snakes. It was funny, but I didn't give a damn anymore. It was as if I didn't care really about anything anymore.

I put the wet towel inside the mattress. I hung the Kim over one shoulder and slung the machine gun over the other. I wasn't going to throw it in the river so close to the shack. They were bound to drag around it and maybe even send down a skin diver.

I climbed up on the walk. I wasn't sure whether I had touched the railing or not when I came up the first time. I went inside the shack, not looking at the bodies. I took the dish towel and wiped the railing wherever I might have touched it. I put the dish towel back. It was then I realized that everyone knew I had been a guest at the shack—why shouldn't my fingerprints be on the railing?

It was possible to be overcareful. Easy, easy.

I padded along the walk and came out at the parking area. I went past their cars—the cars that wouldn't be driving around at night anymore with mud smeared over the plates.

The thought of that made me feel better.

I turned left at the road and began walking toward Alexandria.

If anyone came along the road, I could get into the bushes and squat out of sight fast enough. As for a possible night-operating snake, I made plenty of noise. Any decent snake would get out of the way, and since no one lived along the road, no one could hear me clumping along. After a mile and a half I put on my sneakers. The ground was packed hard and wouldn't show anything.

Half an hour passed. Kirby should be coming along about now. And three minutes later I saw headlights far down the road. I had told her to alternate the up and down beams every five seconds as soon as she hit the river road. They were going up and down. There was no other car in sight.

I stepped out into the road. She stopped. I had the gun wrapped in the mattress. I put everything in the trunk and got in without a word, I saw that the taillight bulb was still unscrewed. I could drive around at night without anyone spotting my license just as well as they could.

I dressed as she drove. When we got home, I stayed inside.

"Are you all right?"

"Couldn't be better."

"Did you get the information?"

"Yep. I'm just tired." I slid back of the wheel.

"You're not comin' in?"

"I'll be back soon."

"Half an hour?"

I nodded.

"I'll have some coffee on. 'Bye, honey."

All nice and wifely. Our act would have to go on till we

were back in New York, I knew, but I sensed a real concern. Too much concern. And I felt too good when she called me "honey." Honey, I just killed a few people. Keep your distance, if you know what's good for you. But how can you know that? At least tonight you don't have to know. And for tonight I would like to be treated like a nice guy. Maybe for the last time. But that's the way it goes, Dunne. You made your investment capital. Now lie in it.

I drove ten miles north. There was a bridge across the river. No one ever went fishing from the bridge. No farmhouses were near. No kids ever parked nearby at night. I parked and opened the trunk. I set the jack outside and leaned the spare tire against the car in case a curious car might come by. I unwrapped the mattress and with a length of heavy wire I lashed one of the tire irons to the gun very strongly. I left about three feet of the wire sticking out. I whirled it over my head a few times like one of those gaucho bolas they use on the Argentine pampas, and when I had wound up a lot of energy in it, I let go. It sailed in a nice long arc and made a neat splash about seventy-five feet away.

First prize in the Night Olympics, shotputting, to J. Dunne, New York City.

I wired the bloody towel to the other tire iron and sent it sailing after my first contribution.

I was back in Okalusa in fifteen minutes. I went upstairs with the recorder.

She had the air conditioning on. Standing beside my chair was a tall glass of iced coffee and a thick roast beef sandwich. I ate like an animal. When I was finished, she poured out another coffee.

"Put some bourbon in it, will you?"

She seemed surprised. I didn't like to drink when I was working. She poured a jigger.

"More."
"More? But I put in a jigg—"
"Will you put in more?"
I drunk it without stopping.
"Rough recording session?"
"Don't talk."
She got up and filled the glass with straight bourbon.
"Hey!"
"Bottled in bond."
What the hell, why not?

I drank it in ten minutes. She sipped some in her glass. The roast beef kept it from hitting me instantly, but I could feel it beginning to numb the back of my neck. It made me feel sleepy and relaxed. I didn't think I would be able to sleep, but now I knew I could. She was leaning above me.

"You smell muddy. Want a shower?"

I nodded. She went in and adjusted the hot and cold faucets so that when I stepped in, it was just right.

"Hey there, Georgia girl," I yelled, "this is perfect!"
"I'm the puffect executive secretary."
"Executive" was too close to "execute."
I stood there silently in the shower.
"Oh, Christ," I muttered. "Oh, Christ. Oh, Christ."
"Did you say somethin'?"
"No. No. Just wondering where the soap was."
She handed me a fresh bar through the curtains.
I scrubbed my hair.
"Better?"
"Much."

Her hand came through the curtains again, with a tall glass. I took it but I forgot to shut off the shower. I watched it as it filled with water.

It was funny. Very few funny things had been happening that night. I began to laugh. The more I laughed, the more I realized that it wasn't really funny. It was only mildly amusing. But the thought that I was laughing at something that wasn't funny seemed funny, too.

"What's funny?" she demanded.

"It got filled with shower water."

Her arm came through and took the glass. A minute later she was back.

"Put out your hand," she said.

I did. She took it and guided it up to her breast. She was naked. I pulled her into the shower and we kissed. It must have lasted over a minute.

She murmured in my ear, "Why are we vertical?"

"What?"

"Shut off the damn shower," she said. "We're not salmon in the spawning season."

Later she fell asleep with her chin on my shoulder and one arm across my chest. The bed lamp was low and on her side of the bed. It made the tiny golden hairs on her forearm glow like peaches. She was smiling in her sleep.

I was not asleep and not smiling. I couldn't understand why not.

Hadn't I just made love to the woman I had been wanting to make love to for weeks?

And hadn't I just made half a million bucks?

39

Some fishermen found the bodies next day.

I was twenty-three miles west of Okalusa driving out to tape some old dirt farmer's reminiscences when the news flash came over the radio.

I finished the day as if it were any other day. We would

have to hang around Okalusa for a little while before we left. Leaving too soon would not look too good. Someone smart might make a connection. The farmer was named Strickland. He hadn't taken a bath for days and his feet stank.

I drove back. Kirby had left a note saying she was out shopping. It was hot. I stripped and showered. It was hard to believe that last night I had had company there.

When I was still showering, she came home. I came out and dressed in khakis and a cotton shirt.

She was sitting at the kitchen table reading the paper. The banner headline read: SHERIFF AND FOUR MILLIKEN COUNTY MEN MURDERED. I poured myself some iced coffee and sat down. She had unbuttoned the top button of her blouse. From time to time she looked at me and then lowered her eyes.

I had put on the air conditioning. In a few minutes the apartment would be cool enough to make love in. But I wouldn't even go near her. I once talked to the public executioner of New Mexico. He told me that the day of an execution his wife made the children stay home from school. Even if it was a rape-torture murderer that was getting it. And she wouldn't go to bed with him. Not for a few days. "What the hell for?" he wanted to know.

Maybe the executioner was a public scapegoat. Maybe everyone dumped their hatred for the murderer on him. Maybe everyone felt that maybe even a murderer shouldn't be murdered. I should have gone on with the discussion instead of leaving for a date I had with some girl. I might not feel so confused and irritated right now.

She got up and put the groceries away. I picked up the paper. The police were working on a lead. They were convinced it was a black militant action. CORE headquarters in Jackson was suspected of complicity. So was the NAACP in Okalusa. Also suspected was a radical student group in the University of Mississippi, who hated a man who was responsible for law and order in Milliken County, and who had died preserving it.

In other words the cops didn't know a damn thing. I tossed the paper aside. I had caught her looking at me several times when she thought she was unnoticed. It was the kind of look you give to a previously friendly dog who has just given you a vicious bite.

I stood up suddenly. She took an involuntary step backward.

I remembered, years ago, when I was on the force, I had gone up into a slum tenement in Harlem. The neighborhood bully had picked on some smaller man and beaten him up. Later that night there was a knock on the door, and when he opened it, he got an ice pick right in the eye and into the brain. He fell dead on his doorstep. I stepped over him and made sure that nothing was touched until the medical examiner had come.

While I was talking to the dead man's wife, their six-year-old daughter, who had been awakened by the commotion, came into the room rubbing her eyes. There was a big yellow and black bruise on her right cheek and right forearm.

She stood yawning in her pajamas. I didn't want her to see her old man with the ice pick sticking up out of his open eye, so I decided to tell her in a nice way to go back to bed.

I got in front of her, blocking her father. "Look, honey," I began, and I reached out a hand to pat her cheek. She flung up an arm and cowered.

That told me more about her father than any long social worker's report.

I made myself another glass of iced coffee. "You want one?" I asked.

She murmured, "No, thank you."

After she had made a wide detour around my chair, I

got up and followed her into the living room. She looked at me. Her face was tense.

"Kirby, I hired you to help me. You helped. You helped a lot, more than I figured. You were worth every cent I offered, and so I'm going to give you the five thousand bonus. I—"

"I don't want it."

"You what?"

"I don't want it, I said. How much longer do we have to stay here?"

She was going to get that five thousand. I decided to put it in cash to her account at her bank without her knowledge. By the time she received her next bank statement, she would never be able to find out where I was in order to return the money.

"Two, three days."

"Why so long?"

She didn't want to get out as much as I did. What I was worried about was not so much an official arrest. It was a sudden visit by the sheriff's friends at night and the usual drive to some lonely country spot.

"I don't want anyone to connect our sudden departure with anything."

We ate in silence. I went out later for a walk. That night she wouldn't sleep with me. It was no surprise.

In the morning she said, "I'm goin' to have mornin' coffee with Mrs. Garrison. An' I'm goin' to tell her how terrible it is, that nice sheriff 'n' all. 'N' how you were a guest down there at the Club 'n' you feel awful."

"Good. And you can say I'll be finished with my project on Tuesday, and we hate to leave Okalusa."

"A town of happy memories."

"Yes."

"Evvabuddy's been so nice."

"Yes. Push that angle."

"I'll say you tole me you'd like to come back when you

get your Ph.D., 'n' teach down at Jackson, 'n' buy us a nice lil ol' weekend home around heah."

I told her to go ahead. She seemed to brighten up at giving a commedia dell'arte performance. She always did when a scene was sketched out for her and the dialogue was left up to her.

I got into the car. There was nothing to do and I felt restless. I decided to drive to Meridian and see a movie. On the way to the main highway I drove past the sheriff's office. The front door was draped in black.

If he had known what I was down there for, he would have killed me without a second's hesitation. That made me feel a little better.

The black cloth was draped in nice sweeping folds.

Well, as they say nowadays, Tough, baby.

40

We drove north to Memphis three days later. I parked outside the passenger terminal at the airport.

"You and I are going to play rabbit," I said. "We're going to double back and forth over the country. Take a plane for Chicago. Under some name or other. At O'Hare take the airport bus. Taking taxis is too risky; drivers remember unusual passengers. At Chicago take a train for Milwaukee. Go to the airport and fly to San Francisco. Then take the train down to L.A. Fly to Boston. Then take the train to New York. Always use a different name every time you have to make a reservation. Always do your hair differently. Put it under a hat. It's too striking. Say only completely normal, ordinary things to people you have to talk to. Stay out of friendly conversations with people on trains and planes. That ought to bury the scent. You should be back in New York by Friday morning. I'll call you sometime Friday."

"All right. You're not coming with me, then."

"They'll be looking for two people together. I'll hop around by myself as well."

I gave her fifteen hundred dollars.

She looked down at it. I told her it wasn't her pay, it was expense money.

"It's a paper chase."

There was a tone in her voice I didn't like. She didn't like the idea of being hunted. I should have allowed for that and not made that crack about playing rabbit.

She didn't move. I saw she was waiting for me to get out and open the door on her side, as I always used to do. "You better get out yourself."

That made her smile. It was the first time in three days. She got out and I handed her the suitcase through the car window.

She took it and set it down. "The honeymoon is over?"

"Kirby. This is where we begin evasive maneuvers. Because about this time is when a smart cop would begin checking out anyone who'd ever been to the club. And he might very well query Toronto. And when Toronto checks us out and reports that we don't seem to exist, they'll start phoning state police to hold this car for questioning. And they'll start checking airports."

"Why didn't they come over to the house?"

"Because cops trace out the most obvious things first. Because the most obvious things are where the answers usually lie. They're working on the black militants. They'll find nothing. Then they talk to everyone who ever had a cross burned on their lawns. Then they begin on acquaintances of the sheriff. I'm an acquaintance. Then they'll find out that you and I were out late that night. And probably the Garrisons will recall the car coming in late and the shower running. And no one had us over that evening. And we didn't go to the drive-in movie. A little talk with us might be rewarding. They'll be looking for a man and woman together. You go that way. I'll go another. If we go inside here together, someone might remember us. You go in alone and put that hair up under your hat. You're just another Southern girl."

"We're all named Mary Lou."

I wanted to say, no, there's no one like you anywhere, but she said, "I'll be around to collect my money. So long, boss." Then she turned and was gone, in that long-legged stride of hers. Somehow, the further north we came the more her Southern drawl seemed to vanish.

It was as if she wanted to ring down a curtain on those weeks in Okalusa. And it looked as if everything that had happened there would be shoved behind that curtain. Everything.

The electric-eye door opened to let her in. As I started the car, I could see her stop at the information desk. The male clerk leaned over with a smile that looked too friendly. I drove away hating him.

I stopped in town for a canvas bag. I put the Kim in it. A distinctive thing like the Kim would be too easily remembered. On the other side of Memphis I sold the car to a dealer for four hundred bucks. I took a bus back to town and took the next train for Nashville. At Nashville I took a Delta flight to Chicago. At O'Hare I bought *Reader's Digest, Esquire, Pleasure,* and the *Atlantic Monthly.* I took the airport bus, wondering whether I was sitting in Kirby's old seat. I began reading the magazines on the Greyhound bus to Cleveland. Nothing much in any one of them, nothing to distract. The *Pleasure* girls were as plastic as the bags covering the bus-station sandwiches. And with as much flavor.

I dropped the magazines in a trash can and bought several paperback novels on private detectives. At least I would have pleasure picking holes in the heroes.

At Cleveland I took a plane for Buffalo. At Buffalo a plane for Philadelphia. The novels were unintentionally funny. They kept my mind off Kirby and the way she looked at me after she had read the headlines in the Okalusa paper.

At Philadelphia I boarded a train for New York. I had never been so restless in my life.

I started in on the last private eye novel. By then I could have been hired as a consultant to the publishers' private eye author society.

In them the private eye was always handsome. He was in his early thirties. He always had plenty of good Scotch in this apartment. He never drank anything else. He usually shot people in the belly, but in order for you to think it's okay, he usually gets beaten up badly first. So a guy who's been worked over, it's all right for him to shoot someone in the belly.

Now, a good private eye in real life is never handsome. He would attract too much attention. I'm the ideal private eye. Like I once said, I could very easily fill your gas tank at a service station and you would never think, "My, what's this movie star doing here?" I never wear shoulder holsters. Private eyes in novels always wear them, they must have some wildly romantic meaning for most authors. I never could stand the pressure of that back strap going across my shoulder blades. It's simpler and easier to wear the hip holster, and when you're sitting down with your jacket open, it's easy to pull your gun fast.

I know it spoils the drape of one's jacket, but then I'm not a male model.

So the novels amused me for a while. Then I began to get jittery. I threw the unread one away. I did that after I had read three pages and realized I hadn't the faintest idea of what I had been looking at.

At Princeton Junction I stood up. I couldn't walk back and forth in the center aisle without attracting annoyed glances. So I stepped out into the vestibule. As the train pulled out for the run to Newark and then New York, I began to pace back and forth. It was only three steps each way, but it did take some of the steam out of my tension. I had never felt this way before. It puzzled me. I didn't like it.

I smoked and watched the matchstick houses in their neat little rows marching up and down the rolling hills. Last year I had come through here on the train and there had only been woods.

I told myself I wouldn't ever have to look at those stupid houses anymore. They'd never be building housing projects on my coast. Well, maybe they would, but it wouldn't be till 4780 A.D. And by then the Caribbean would have a fifty-foot layer of broken beer bottles and old bedsprings on the bottom. And who would care? I had fifteen good years ahead of me doing just what I wanted to do. To hell with 4780.

Suddenly we were racing across the Jersey meadows. The papers were full of a plan to make a jetport out of them, and there were angry letters to the editors for and against. So long, suckers.

The meadows were used as a vast garbage dump. I watched a huge truck lumber backward to the edge of a sewage-filled creek and dump its load. People lived in horrible little shacks made of scrap lumber with flattened five-gallon cans for roofs. They did the same in the Caribbean, but at least it was warm.

Tremendous signboards advertised Broadway plays and musicals. People went to them for amusement in the evenings after doing things they hated all day. That was not the way to live. The correct way was to do something you liked all day, and to hell with going somewhere at night for fun.

Above the ridge that marked the eastern edge of the meadows, I could see the top forty or so floors of the

Empire State and Chrysler buildings. There you were, my filthy, rotten, unspeakable, misty and magnificent city. Inside you sat Parrish, my ticket away from you.

I bit my lip, trying to control my tension. I couldn't understand what was happening. I was pretty sure it wasn't any delayed reaction about the machine-gunning. Five murderers murdered was simple justice. The hell with them.

So what was it?

I understood as soon as I saw the last billboard, just before the train roared into the tunnel.

The billboard proclaimed the great merits of a musical comedy. It had a famous blonde star, and she was posed against a green background. Her hair had the same spilled-honey color as Kirby's.

As soon as I looked at the hair I knew I had to take Kirby with me. It would be a hell of a job talking her into it, but there would never be anyone else. I was no private eye in his early thirties who only drank the best Scotch.

I was a private detective in his very early forties who knew what he liked. I was going to make a damn good try for that girl. And I only had a few hours to do it.

41

I was the first one off as soon as the train stopped moving. I had been standing in the vestibule with my luggage since Rahway.

I grabbed a phone booth. Parrish was out and would not be back till two. I told his secretary to tell him that Mr. Nelson would arrive a little after two.

I phoned Kirby. My heart was going very fast. I leaned my head against the glass door.

I hadn't felt like that since I asked a girl for a date when I was in high school. I was very shy, very unsure of myself. I finally got up enough nerve to ask her. Her name was Paula Reilly and she had thick ankles and a high-pitched giggle. I asked her if she wanted to go to the movies. She said yes.

When we sat down in the upper balcony, I put my left arm on the rim of her seat. For the next fifteen minutes all I was aware of was my agonizing effort to let it touch her shoulders without her being too aware of it. I finally let it touch. She didn't move away. I was astonished. It was such a precious moment that I didn't want to ruin it, so I let that arm remain there for three hours without shifting it. It fell asleep. When we stood up, it was still paralyzed, and I helped her into her coat with only one arm. She thought I was stupid and clumsy.

Kirby answered after the fourth ring.

"Yes?"

"Mrs. Wilson?"

"You must be the gentleman who keeps callin' himself my husband!"

Her voice was delighted. My heart went up like a skyrocket. "Mrs. Wilson, may I have the honor of taking you to dinner this evening?"

"Suh, it will be a pleasure."

"What time?"

"I'm starvin' for a good meal. Will six be too early?"

"Nothing will ever be too early."

I hadn't meant any note of high seriousness, but it got away from me. She was silent four heartbeats. Then she said, very low, "I have been missin' you, Joe."

"Well, Kirby," I said, "I—I want to—I—"

"Tell me at six, Joe."

She hung up. I felt like yelling and jumping up and down. Instead I went to my bank and emptied my safe-deposit box. I took home Parrish's money and my phony passport. My house smelled stale. I opened the windows and pried loose two ice cubes. I made a drink with cheap Scotch, placed the money in the freezer, and covered it with ice-cube trays and two frozen steaks.

I shaved and went downstairs to the flower shop. I picked out four dozen long-stemmed yellow roses at fifteen dollars a dozen. They would have a hard time matching her hair, but they were welcome to try. I asked the delivery boy if he could take them over right away.

"I got two other rush orders, mister. They gotta go out first."

I gave him a ten-dollar bill.

"Me first?"

"Yessir!"

Money, money. It could do interesting things if properly distributed.

I went out. Seventy bucks. And seldom were seventy smackers spent more happily. I took a cab down to Battery Place.

By now, if money talked, the delivery boy should be ringing Kirby's bell.

I whistled all the way up in Parrish's private elevator. I had forgotten that in my left hand I carried the canvas bag and the Kim with its six-inch reel packed with indictment, verdict, death warrant, and execution. Death and joy riding the elevator together. A subject for one of those old medieval prints.

Parrish came out to meet me. "Mr. Nelson, I'm glad to see you. Are you ready to finalize the deal?"

"Yes."

"Mary," he said, "take the afternoon off."

"But, Mr. Parrish, you said you wanted these three letters typed and—"

"Mary. Afternoon off."

"Yes, Mr. Parrish."

When the elevator doors had closed behind her, he

said, "There's no one within seventy-five feet of here. Come in."

We went into his private office. He reached out and flicked the *off* switch on his private line.

I took the Kim out of the bag and set it up.

"Ready?"

"Yes."

I punched the PLAY key. He listened. He listened the way anyone would listen to something that was costing half a million bucks.

I had forgotten that I had left it on when I slid behind the pilings to try and hide from Vince. The mike had picked up my fast sloshing through the water.

"What's that?"

I told him.

"Wasn't that risky?"

I told him I had no choice.

"Yes. I missed something. Can you play it again?" I reversed it. The shrill, wild, Donald Duck screams of the voices as the tape spun backward didn't make him smile.

I started it again. He turned his back to the tape and stared out across the harbor as it revolved. Then came the *chugchugchugchugchug*. I moved to shut it off. He held up a hand.

"Wait."

There was silence on the tape. Then came a steady *thump thump thump*.

"What's that?"

I didn't know myself. I listened carefully. Then I realized it must have been the blood leaking through the cracks in the flooring and dripping directly onto the mike.

I told him.

"Good. Once more."

I reversed it and played it again.

"I'm satisfied," he said. He let out a deep breath, stood up, and unlocked a wall safe. I thought he was getting the money, but he had turned around and was holding out his hand for the tape.

"No."

"No? I'm paying plenty for it."

"No. You're paying for proof that the contract was carried out. Was it?"

"Yes."

"That reel indicts me for multiple murder. So it's no."

"What are you going to do with it?"

"Erase it right now."

"All right. Once more, please."

He leaned back with his eyes closed. I shoved the Kim a little closer to him, turned up the volume some more, and walked to the far end of the office. I didn't want to look at his face while he was listening to it. It was his memory he was loading. He could have it.

I looked down at the harbor. It was calm and remote. The sky was a deep, clean blue. It was funny. Here was Parrish trying to remember that tape for the rest of his life and here I was trying to forget it. I turned around after a while and watched his face. Then I looked at the slowly spinning reel. When the *thump thump thump* began again, I stopped it, reversed it, and put it on *erase*. In a few minutes I had a clean tape.

I closed the case.

Neither of us spoke for a while. Parrish spoke first. "Wouldn't life be great," he said, "if we could all go back again and erase our mistakes as easy as that?"

"But we'd make them again."

"I suppose so." He sighed. "I don't know where I went wrong," he said. "Should I have knocked my boy unconscious when he wanted to go South? What could I have done with all this knowledge if we were back in June? I couldn't have done a damn thing."

"Mr. Parrish," I said. "I am afraid I have no time for this kind of a discussion."

"Sorry." He lifted his phone, switched it on, and dialed a number. "Bring it," he said, and hung up.

He turned to me. "The money's not here. Not safe. As soon as I read that AP dispatch from Okalusa, I took the money from the bank. I didn't want any red tape while you might be waiting. It should be here at five. It's out at my Connecticut place."

"I'll be here at five."

"Fine."

I went down and sold the Kim to a secondhand dealer for a good price.

Then I thought of picking up Kirby and going somewhere while I tried to talk her into coming down to the Caribbean with me. But I decided it would be better for her to be marinated in all those roses. Let her take a leisurely bath while she inhaled their message and thought kindly of me. It would help make her mellow, and anything that might help me would be appreciated.

I walked around the waterfront again, taking deep breaths of the salt air. I watched a freighter go out toward the Narrows with its signal flags fluttering. I watched the seagulls dipping and screeching in its wake. I leaned on the railing and watched the ship disappear, swinging to the left. The signal *Pilot aboard* made a tiny red dot which remained visible quite a long time. I realized with a smile I had my back turned on Manhattan all this time.

Five to five. I went back to Parrish. It was all on his desk, in neat little stacks. I counted it and put it into my canvas bag. I zipped it up.

"Don't spend it all in one place," he said.

I smiled.

"Well," he said. "Thank you."

"Thank you," I said. We stood waiting for the elevator. There was an awkward silence. We were like two lovers who have ended an affair and for whom there is nothing more to say.

The elevator finally came. I stepped in.

"So long," I said.

I lifted a hand and the elevator started down. The bag's strap was cutting into my shoulder. It was a marvelous sensation.

42

I could hear a drum banging. When I turned the corner, a tuba began going *oompa-pa, oompa-pa*. It was a Salvation Army band, all girls. Under the black bonnets they were smiling. The tuba player wore glasses and was very serious about her instrument. One of the girls was shaking a tambourine.

I went by and rang Kirby's bell. No answer. In the tub, I bet. I waited five minutes and planned what I should say to her as my opening sentence.

I rang again. No answer. She was probably out doing last-minute shopping. I walked back to the corner. I would be able to see her coming and also listen to the band. I went up to the tambourine player and smiled. She blushed.

I pulled out all my loose change and dropped it into the tambourine. What the hell. They helped out in floods and earthquakes. In an emergency they would give me a blanket and a cup of coffee if I needed it. My donation amounted to a little over two bucks. I wondered if anyone ever sent roses to Salvation Army girls. I looked at my watch. They began another tune. They played with enthusiasm and little subtlety. The girl with the tuba kept looking at me out of the corner of her eye. I looked back and grinned. She turned pink and primly turned a quarter of a circle to her left.

The tambourine player lifted her pure, thin soprano and sang, "There is an afterlife, where we shall all meet again."

I didn't believe a word of it. I still don't. But if anyone wants to keep that crutch, they can. I wouldn't ever pull it away from anyone.

I began thinking how to get a passport for Kirby. It would be too risky to try for one in the States. I decided to fly to El Paso with her. We could get tourist cards.

You could pick them up with as much trouble as a bus transfer. In Mexico City I had a contact who would sell us U.S. passports stolen from tourists' luggage. A little expert doctoring and Kirby would have hers. With that we could get into Nicaragua without any problems.

Boy, I had it all figured out.

I went back and rang her bell. She must have gone the other way. No answer. I went down to the corner drugstore and phoned. No answer. I got the chief operator.

"Yes, sir?"

"MU 6–7184. Is there anything wrong with the line?"

"I'll check, sir."

I waited.

She came on again. "No trouble, sir. The line works perfectly."

I thanked her and hung up. I went back and rang again. No answer. I didn't expect one, and I pushed a couple bells on the top floor. When the buzzer sounded, I pushed the door open. I walked up two flights. At the end of the hall was a window opening out onto a fire escape. The catch was open. I pushed the window up and stepped onto the fire escape. I moved five feet to my right. There was her window. The catch was open. A square hole had been cut out of the glass. You can do that with a glass cutter and a powerful little rubber suction cup to pull it out backward. The square of glass was lying on the far end of the fire escape.

I wasn't wearing a gun. For the first time in my life I acted stupidly. Instead of quietly pulling out, running home, getting mine, and coming back, I opened the window as softly as I could. It opened quietly. I picked up a heavy glass ashtray lying on an end table. I could throw it for temporary distraction.

I went into the bedroom. I felt better. There was no disorder. Her dress and shoes and fresh underwear were neatly laid out on the bed. There were two vases in the bedroom, one on the dresser table, and one on the night table. Both were crammed with the yellow roses. They all had opened almost all the way and their fragrance filled the room. A dozen roses lay on the pillow. She had run out of vases.

I walked into the bathroom.

The tub was full. She was lying face down in it.

I pulled her up. She was dead. There were cigarette burns all over her breasts and a wide band of adhesive tape across her mouth. Her hands were tied behind her back with a nylon stocking. There were fingermarks at the back of her neck.

The water was still hot. It must have just happened. It could have taken place while I was listening to the band and giving away money out of happiness. Her pocketbook was on the dresser. There was two hundred and seventy-five bucks in it. It had not been disturbed. The dresser drawers hadn't been ransacked.

Therefore these people were not there for information or for money. They were professionals who had been told to work fast and get out. They were being so well paid that they bypassed any chance money they might pick up. They knew where I lived. They didn't go through her pocketbook or drawers looking for a lead because they already knew.

So this was strictly a punitive expedition.

If Parrish could hire a private eye for some vigilante

work, why couldn't someone down there do the same thing? The technique wasn't patented.

I shoved her money in my pocket. I had very little time. I held her cheek for a second. I let her slip back into the water.

In those private-eye novels I had been reading for the past three days, I knew what the hero would do. He would go home and get a gun. Or if he couldn't go home, he would get one somewhere. He would bust in and have himself a shoot-out. He would kill them with a few well-placed shots. He would suffer a bullet in the shoulder which would miss the bone. Then there would follow an interview with an angry assistant D.A. The D.A. would warn him to watch his step in the future or he would lose his license. The D.A. would walk out of the hospital room and our hero would lie back and drink some twelve-year-old Bell's, smuggled to him against orders by his beautiful nurse. Fade-out.

But life was different. What I wanted was a lot of distance between me and the D.A.

I opened the hall door. No one in sight. I walked down the stairs. I met no one.

Good luck to the son of a bitch who would think of prying up my ice-cube trays. It would probably be the super when they finally cleaned out my apartment. What would happen to my phony passport, I didn't know. Probably the D.A. would keep it as enemy property. Well, the hell with it. I had my contact in Mexico City.

I walked quickly to the street and took a cab to the Port Authority Bus Terminal. I took a bus to Newark. There I phoned Homicide North in New York. I didn't want the super to find her four, five days later. I just told the detective there was a dead body around, and when he began to ask my name, I hung up.

I took the next train to Philadelphia. About nine-thirty we were going by Princeton Junction. Only a few short hours ago I was standing there in the vestibule going the other way, all charged with excitement and romance. I suddenly remembered that my fingerprints were all over the windowsill, the ashtray, her pocketbook, probably the bathtub rim. The police would check out all her contacts, including her last employer of record. Me.

They would have my fingerprints on file as a registered private detective. By then the Okalusa police would be up there wanting to talk to me, and the Rebs and the Yanks would get together and fry me. They would work out that I had probably killed her to keep her from talking and that I had taken whatever money I might have given her. The four dozen roses I had sent would be considered some very clever work on my part to divert any suspicion she might have about my motives.

I got up and went into the men's room. I locked the door, sat down and put my head in my hands. I rocked back and forth. I bit my knuckles to keep my head from exploding. I stayed there until some guy kept banging on the door.

At Philadelphia I took a train for El Paso. I bought some shaving equipment at the airport, cleaned myself up somewhat, and strolled over the border with the canvas bag over my shoulder, just like any tourist might who was going to Juarez to see his Mexican lawyer for a divorce.

I flew to Mexico City. After two days my contact man had my new passport ready. Then I took a ship at Puerto Mexico, down on the Gulf Coast, and made my way south down here.

For the first few weeks after I got here, I tried to figure out where I had gone wrong. Was it in hiring that crummy lawyer up in Toronto?

Shouldn't I have traveled with her after Memphis and spent those three days trying to persuade her to marry me? Then I could have sent her to Mexico City and wound up my affairs down here in New York alone.

Shouldn't I have come over to her place while I was waiting for Parrish to get the money? I wouldn't have had a gun, but maybe I could have scared them off when they came through the window.

What I can't stand is the thought that I didn't go over because I wanted her to be surrounded by those roses for a few more hours.

So maybe it was the roses that killed her.

And then, if I hadn't taken Parrish's offer, I would have just plodded along, a little tail job here, a little industrial spying there, a little pilferage-checking here. And maybe sooner or later I would have noticed what was under my nose and married her.

Well, maybe.

I just discovered something, Father. If you begin drinking pretty early in the morning, you reach a pleasant buzz around ten A.M. So by ten, ten-thirty, you begin sort of drifting through the day. It's like floating out there in the Caribbean, only there's no sharks or barracuda to take a bite out of your ass.

Did you see that little green parrot just now? Twenty, thirty miles down the coast is the Rio Papagayo—the River of Parrots. It's "twenty or thirty" because that's what they say around here when you ask how far. The jungle here—see, I can reach it with a toss of the beer bottle—the jungle is full of those parrots. The full-grown ones are only a bit larger than sparrows. The kids catch them and sell them for about a quarter. The little parrots are affectionate, but I don't want any. I don't want to be responsible for anything living.

When I first came, Narcisco told me that some American mercenary on his way to the monthly revolution up at the capital bought one. He taught it to say "son of a bitch!" and then he let it go. That was eight or nine or ten years ago, Narcisco said. Notice the vague numbers.

Well, thousands of parrots picked it up from him and

in turn taught it to the baby parrots. And so on. At dusk, Narcisco said, enormous flocks of parrots fly overhead, all of them cursing "sunnamabeetch!" This I had to see.

I persuaded Narcisco to sail down the coast one Sunday to the parrot country. But at dusk nothing came out of the jungle except mosquitoes. And when I asked a couple kids where the parrots were, they said it was another town down the coast.

"*Veinte o treinta kilómetros?*"

"*Sí, sí!*"

Well, it's a little after four. I can tell by the sun. I haven't worn a wristwatch since I came down here. You don't need it and besides, the leather band rots off. The metal ones give you a rash.

I'd walk you back, but my legs wouldn't hold me. Don't forget your net and your collection bottle.

If you had one big enough, you could pop me in it. You wouldn't need that cyanide you use. I'm about a hundred and forty proof right now. In a year or so my blood will be straight alcohol. I'll keep.

You could take me back to the States all nicely mounted. With three pins in the traditional places required by our faith. You could explain to customs that you caught a large and stupid butterfly down on the Mosquito Coast.

Bad joke. I apologize.

I remember Parrish saying, "Don't spend it all in one place."

Other funny thing is this. Coming down in the *Santa Rosalia* out of Puerto Mexico, I found a copy of Shakespeare's *Plays* in the toilet. It was in English and was leather-bound. The leather had all rotted away and no one aboard could read English. So they were tearing out the pages one by one.

I began reading it. They had reached *Othello*, Act Four. Somewhere near the end of Act Five I came across three lines. I forget who was supposed to have said them, but I've never forgotten them. They go,

> One whose hand,
> Like the base Indian, threw a pearl away,
> Richer than all his tribe.

Yes, I know you have to go. Be sure to keep your hat on out there. Go with God, *vaya con Díos.* I'll get Narcisco to give you some friction tape. Use it to tape the lids of your collection boxes. It'll keep the ants out.

Watch out for the sun. It's deceptive. It's too much trouble boiling water all the time, so just drink beer. The launch going upriver is supposed to leave at seven tomorrow morning. If you'll get there about eight-thirty, you'll only have to wait twenty minutes or so. They'd never leave without you. They're afraid you'll put the evil eye on them. And if you run across any Americans up the river or in the capital, I'd appreciate it if you'd only discuss the insect situation down on the coast.

Nothing else. Nothing.

By the Edgar Award-Winning Author of
LITTLE GIRL LOST

SONGS of INNOCENCE

by RICHARD ALEAS

Three years ago, detective John Blake solved a mystery that changed his life forever—and left a woman he loved dead. Now Blake is back, to investigate the apparent suicide of Dorothy Louise Burke, a beautiful college student with a double life. The secrets Blake uncovers could blow the lid off New York City's sex trade…if they don't kill him first.

Richard Aleas' first novel, LITTLE GIRL LOST, was among the most celebrated crime novels of the year, nominated for both the Edgar and Shamus Awards. *But nothing in John Blake's first case could prepare you for the shocking conclusion of his second…*

RAVES FOR SONGS OF INNOCENCE:

"An instant classic."
— The Washington Post

"The best thing Hard Case is publishing right now."
— The San Francisco Chronicle

"His powerful conclusion will drop jaws."
— Publishers Weekly

"So sharp [it'll] slice your finger as you flip the pages."
— Playboy

To order, visit www.HardCaseCrime.com or call
1-800-481-9191 (10am to 9pm EST).
Each title just $6.99 ($8.99 in Canada), plus shipping and handling.

Get The Complete First Year of
HARD CASE CRIME
...and Save More Than 30%!

If you missed Hard Case Crime's debut year, this is your chance to get all twelve titles—at a savings of more than 30% off the cover price! A dozen great books including three Edgar Award nominees, two Shamus Award nominees, and oustanding crime classics by some of the most popular mystery writers of all time:

GRIFTER'S GAME *by Lawrence Block*
FADE TO BLONDE *by Max Phillips*
TOP OF THE HEAP *by Erle Stanley Gardner*
LITTLE GIRL LOST *by Richard Aleas*
TWO FOR THE MONEY *by Max Allan Collins*
THE CONFESSION *by Domenic Stansberry*
HOME IS THE SAILOR *by Day Keene*
KISS HER GOODBYE *by Allan Guthrie*
361 *by Donald E. Westlake*
PLUNDER OF THE SUN *by David Dodge*
BRANDED WOMAN *by Wade Miller*
DUTCH UNCLE *by Peter Pavia*

Find out why critics have called Hard Case Crime "the best new American publisher to appear in the last decade" and why *Time, Entertainment Weekly, USA Today, The New York Times,* and the *Sunday Morning* program on CBS have all run raves about our books. All for less than $5 per book (plus just 25 cents per book for shipping)!

To order, call 1-800-481-9191
(10am to 9pm EST) and ask for the
Complete First Year of Hard Case Crime.
All 12 books for just $58 (plus $3 for shipping; US orders only)